the loneliness of hira barua

the loneliness of hira barua

STORIES

Arupa Patangia Kalita

Translated from the Assamese by
RANJITA BISWAS

MACMILLAN

First published in India 2020 by Macmillan
an imprint of Pan Macmillan India
a division of Macmillan Publishers India Private Limited
Pan Macmillan India, 707, Kailash Building
26 K. G. Marg, New Delhi – 110 001
www.panmacmillan.co.in

Pan Macmillan, The Smithson, 6 Briset Street, Farringdon, London EC1M 5NR,
Associated companies throughout the world
www.panmacmillan.com

ISBN 978-93-89109-45-0

First published in Assamese as *Mariam Austin othoba Hira Barua*
by Chandra Prakash, 2014

'The Girl with Long Hair', 'Surabhi Barua and the Rhythm of Hooves', 'Ayengla of the Blue Hills' and 'The Half-burnt Bus at Midnight' first appeared in *Written in Tears*, HarperCollins India, 2015.

Typeset in Sabon LT Std by SÜRYA
Printed and bound in India by Manipal Technologies limited, Manipal

MIX
Paper | Supporting responsible forestry
FSC

Contents

HER STORIES

The Call Girls at the Shelter Home

Japan invaded China. The war snatched from the people the liberty to live as free human beings. The soldiers who arrived in the unfamiliar terrain turned out to be demonic, as if reflecting the brutality of the war. They killed people indiscriminately, culling them like chickens afflicted with disease. The women, whose lives were centred around their home, family and paddy fields so far, now witnessed things they had never seen before. Everything turned topsy-turvy. They whispered among themselves in fear, concluding that these men had lost the compassion that belongs to a human heart. What remained in their bodies were only the parts below the waist. The women were mortally scared. Used as they were to the simple peasant's life, they found the events happening around them absolutely incomprehensible.

Take for example, the case of U-Lien – mother of six, grandmother of fourteen and great-grandmother to three kids. Who could imagine that anybody would lust after her, her body now swollen like a round gourd? Something had happened to her when she was middle-aged. She started gaining weight. And this continued. The older she got, the fatter she became and ultimately, she almost looked like a baby elephant. However, she was quite active, waddling around, doing whatever she could manage. She even visited her neighbours every now and then. People fondly called her 'Ludhumi bai', the fat sister. Her hair, eyelashes and eyebrows had all turned white. People liked her a lot. Her face was always ready to break into a smile. Her nature was like her body – generous and expansive, encircling everybody with a big hug. She accepted that she would not live too long, and lived peacefully in her small world.

That day a few women, along with Ludhumi-bai and Ling Chow, were at Ling-Ten's cottage chatting among themselves. What was there to say really? The same things – the war, the fear, the soldiers' behaviour. Then suddenly, they espied a few Japanese soldiers standing at the gate leading to the cottage. Immediately, Ling-Ten led the women to a door at the back of the house. It was near a well in the backyard and the women managed to escape. But there was a problem with Ludhumi-bai. Her huge frame could not pass through the door. Helpless, Ling-Ten brought some leaves and creepers from the garden and covered her up. He hid himself too the same way and cringed in fear. After a while, from his hiding place he heard a sudden heart-rending cry, as if somebody was slowly butchering a pig with a blunt *dao*, a big knife. Then there was a gurgling sound from the throat and a long bout of moaning, followed by silence.

Ling-Ten was sure that something had happened to Ludhumi-bai. After the soldiers left Ling-Ten, Ling Chow and the women came back. Their blood froze, their eyes shut in horror at what they saw. Near the small door next to the well, U-Lien's fat, naked body lay on the grass, lifeless. It bore numerous signs of physical torture; blood had now coagulated in many places. It was obvious that not one, but many men had invaded the poor old woman's body.

After this incident, Ling Chow and the other women feared living in their own houses. A white woman had opened a shelter home in their area. The women took refuge in this camp. The soldiers did not dare to barge into the camp as it was run by the whites. The women found it safer to stay there.

One day, a group of seven pretty, young girls from the town of Chuchaou, now called Chuzhou, arrived at the shelter. The way they were dressed, the manner in which they talked and moved convinced the peasant women that these girls were different from them. They were incensed. Why were these girls staying in this shelter home? They could get plenty of customers outside. They could make enough money, too. At least this would have ensured that the soldiers stayed away from the housewives of the village. Ling Chow did not hesitate to openly show her hatred for the young girls. 'These characterless girls ... look at their audacity – coming to stay under the same roof with us,' she grumbled.

The girls seemed to understand the hostility of the women. They kept to themselves, in one corner of the shelter. They did not go out of their way to communicate, or try to make any overtures towards the others.

But one day Ling-Chow couldn't help asking one of them, 'Why are you here? You don't look as if you fear the men.'

One of the prettiest girls in the group replied, 'We heard that a white woman has opened a shelter here and that the soldiers didn't trouble the inmates. That's why we are here.'

Another said, 'Yes, granny, you are right. We know men. But we are unable to recognize *these* men. These soldiers who have arrived from a foreign land, they are not the kind of men we have known.'

'We too hate the enemy; we hate those who invade our land,' chimed another.

That night, the women in the shelter were in for a shock. There was a huge ruckus in front of the shelter home around midnight. The women woke up, startled. They heard sounds of the gate rattling and then, a burst of bullets. The foreigner woman decided to investigate, approaching the gate with a lamp in her hand. The women huddled together, trembling in fear. Outside stood around a hundred armed soldiers. They had come here sniffing the flesh of women. The white woman who managed the shelter returned after meeting the soldiers and stood with her head bowed, facing the women. She told them that the soldiers wanted five to six women, otherwise they would enter the home. Everyone went silent. The sound of rattling and kicking at the gate kept getting louder. They would enter the shelter any time.

The women saw the lamp in the white woman's hand was swinging from side to side like a pendulum, and she was shaking uncontrollably. 'How can I tell any of you to go out there, and that too for something like this? But still, I have to ask – is there anyone at all who can save these housewives?' she whispered, her voice croaking with unshed tears. The ruckus outside was almost unbearable.

Suddenly, the young girls from Chuchaou stood up. Their leader gave instructions, 'Get ready, comb your hair, try to smile. We have to go to work.'

The girls got ready to walk out to the gate. The white woman drew a cross on her chest and bowed her head, saying, 'God will bless you for this deed.'

'Your God doesn't know us,' one girl grimaced and spat. Then they went out to the courtyard.

The racket outside, the firing of the rifles, stopped. The women inside made their beds. A few of them fell asleep.

But Ling Chow couldn't sleep, her head hidden between her knees. The space next to her was empty now. This was where the pretty girls used to sleep. Her eyes brimmed with tears. She tried to wipe them away, but in vain. She could feel her heart contract with sorrow. She had been cruel to the girls. She could still hear the young girl's voice, 'We know men … But these men, these soldiers who have arrived from a foreign land, they are not the kind of men we know.'

As the words reverberated in her ears, Ling Chow could feel her tears flow endlessly.

The Girl with Long Hair

Mainao stands on her toes, on the threshold of youth. She is a cheerful, attractive girl with small twinkling eyes and rounded limbs taut with the touch of the sun and rain. Her complexion is a sunburnt brown, with tints of copper-red. When Mainao laughs, her small eyes crinkle and look even smaller.

The firstborn in her family, Mainao has three younger siblings. Her father teaches in a primary school about three kilometres away; her mother takes care of the household. They are not too badly off. There is enough rice in the granary, cattle in the shed and plenty of areca nut trees and betel leaf creepers in the kitchen garden.

This is the year of Mainao's all-important matriculation exam. She works hard on her lessons morning and evening, although she is not that good at studies and would much rather do the household chores. And how well she does the chores! When she sweeps the courtyard, it looks so neat that you could eat off the floor. When she cuts loose the warm shawl with a *farou-megan* motif from the loom, even the pigeons on the roof coo their approval: 'Why Mainao, you've worked our eyes and feathers into the loom so deftly!' When she weaves an *arnai sador* in the *dhekia* pattern, the ferns underneath the betel nut tree bow shyly, wondering, 'Are we that pretty? O Mainao, you've made us look so good with your weaving!'

Mainao has long, lovely hair reaching down to her hips, black, silky and well-oiled. When she gathers it all up into a bun at the nape of her neck, it looks only a little smaller than her head. She is rather proud of her hair. She would beg her mother for money to get it trimmed at the beauty parlour in town, about a kilometre away.

Her parents scold her sometimes because of her preoccupation with her hair. But who could be angry with Mainao for long? She will be crestfallen for some time, and then grin. Nowadays, she likes to imitate a Hindi film heroine with long hair. Like her, she embellishes her hair with colourful clips. However, her mother and others who see her busy with the household chores – swabbing, weaving, cooking – are not aware what goes on in the girl's mind. When she returns from the parlour in town, she washes her hair with hibiscus petals or *jetuka* leaves. Then, with the colourful clips adorning her hair, she stands near the gate in front of the house.

At these moments can anyone peep into her mind? No. Secretly, she plays and laughs with a young man. In her mind, the image of the young man is vague. He is somewhat similar to the handsome young actor who courts the heroine Mainao adores, with his songs full of yearning while running on the beach. Sometimes, he looks like the son of the headmaster of her father's school, who is now studying somewhere in a distant city outside Assam. When she thinks of the headmaster's son, she is assailed by the citrous scent of a lemon flower.

He had visited their house once. His father, the headmaster, had sent some papers for her father. He was home on summer holiday. Mainao had served him tea with steamed *tekeli pitha* filled with ground sesame seed and jaggery. After he finished off three in one go, her mother asked if he would like to have some more. He asked for two more. Mainao's parents had praised him a lot. After he left, the house was filled with an aroma like that of lemon flowers. Perhaps he had bought a bottle of perfume in the city where he was studying, she thought. She wanted to ask him if he could bring a bottle for her too, the next time he came home. She would pay, of course. She had some money stashed away from selling three pigs, some chickens and pigeons.

One day as she went into town with her friends, she tried to sniff the perfume bottles in the cosmetics shop. She was disappointed; not a single bottle had that lemony aroma. So she bought another, which was quite nice too, and came in a beautiful bottle. They had reached home late that day. Her mother was waiting anxiously at the front gate; her father had cycled to the four-lane junction nearby searching for her. At home, she faced a barrage of admonishment from her parents. Wasn't she aware of what was happening all around? The *andolon* was at its zenith.

How many boys like the headmaster's son were left, anyway? Most of the young men had left studying and work behind and joined the agitation. The boys had learned lots of new things, even how to use guns and ammunition. They had a lot of power now. Even the elderly folk in society were scared of them. The demand for their own state had changed a lot of things. Wasn't Mainao aware of all this?

Mainao does not bother much about these things. Sometimes people come out in processions, sometimes there is a call for a bandh, sometimes the boys get into skirmishes with the police and the army personnel. But these things had been happening elsewhere – not in her village. She has heard from others that sometimes there are even shootings between the different parties. But these meetings, processions, people piling into buses and trucks to hold public demonstrations, or shutting down roads and train lines, have been happening all the time. What's the big deal? She has grown up seeing it all.

Her ears are tired of hearing the same old instructions from her parents – don't go there, don't do this, and so on. These things have happened, and will continue happening. This is her philosophy. For such mundane events, why should she stop going to the bazaar if she needs threads for the loom, or when she wants to buy a pair of earrings or clips for her hair, or a necklace? So, she gets very angry when her parents go on and on with these warnings. Isn't there anything else to talk about?

Mainao is basically a happy-go-lucky girl. She hardly finds anything to be unhappy about. How can she stay morose, especially at this time of the season? After all, Durga Puja is round the corner. There is a small shrine dedicated to God Bathow in a corner of the courtyard, which she swabs to a perfect red. Next to it is a *sewali* tree. She can see its base covered with the white flowers in the morning, giving out a heady fragrance heralding the autumn festival. The shops are full of colourful balloons and garlands. Like every year, in a corrugated tin shade in front of the house on the railway line they have started making the idol of the devi. By now, Mainao has finished weaving the red *dokhana*. It is of the brightest red, and on it she has woven designs like those on the Assamese mekhela sador. The flowers in the pattern are yellow; spattered between the lines are *butas* in black and white. She had already gone with Binuma, Champa and Reema to the town to thread her eyebrows and trim her hair. They are her friends studying in the same class in high school. Their group of ten to twelve girls have all grown up together, and are inseparable. Binuma has bought a beautiful paat silk mekhela sador for the festival. Mainao has copied its design in her dokhana. When her friends saw it they praised Mainao to high heavens for her artistry. Champa has bought a blue churidar kameez with white flowers. Reema has bought a saree with bright *chumki* work. Then there is Biju … and Konika … and Nilima. All of them have bought new clothes for the festival. Each new outfit bought by any one of the group called for a celebration. Mainao had wanted to buy a churidar set too. But the boys involved in the agitation had given strict instructions that girls of their community could only wear dokhanas.

A *pehi* of Mainao, her father's sister, who was a college student, had to use a bicycle to reach the college in town.

Finding the dokhana cumbersome, she had stitched a salwar-kameez set to wear to college. The salwar suit had by now almost become a uniform for the girls. But those boys had only warned the girls of their community about wearing it. One day, a few boys took a pair of scissors and cut her aunt's clothes into shreds. She wept all the way home. Her friends had used a copious number of safety pins to hold up the outfit somehow.

That day, her aunt ran a high temperature. It took three days for her to recover from the fever. Mainao sat next to her, regularly changing the wet handkerchief on her forehead to help keep the temperature down. Her heart went out to her aunt. Such a bright student, and now lying like this, she thought. Her pehi was mortally insulted at the treatment meted out to her in broad daylight and in front of so many people. She was mortified at having to walk in public in her tattered clothes. These days when Mainao thinks of wearing something else other than her usual traditional dress, she instantly remembers the face of her aunt, burning with fever.

There were only three days left for the puja. Mainao has finished her puja shopping. She had gone with her friends to the town to buy a pair of earrings with red stones. The parlour was getting crowded, so she had gone early to finish her beauty regimen. Then suddenly, they heard that the people of their community were not allowed to participate in the Hindu puja celebration. The boys engaged in the andolon announced the ban and warned that those who defied it would be punished. Their word was law. People these days bowed to their diktat, and not unwillingly either. They reasoned that the boys were trying to offer something to the people – a dream. It would come true, wouldn't it?

So, what Mainao regarded as something distant, and not affecting her, became a reality. She would not be able to visit the pandal of the puja. Binuma, Reema and her other friends would go and she would have to stay back – washing, sweeping, cleaning the cattle shed. She would not be able to wear the new outfit she has just woven.

How could it be possible? What could she do? The devi's idol has been put on the pedestal, the *dhak* has been making a pulsating sound, the air smelt of *jilepis* and savoury bhujia, the colour of the balloons dazzled the eyes.

Her friends Binuma, Reema, Champa and the gang had gone in a group to visit the puja venue. On their way they called her asking if she would come. While coming back they brought little mementoes for her. As she took them from her friends her chest seemed to contract with sorrow. Seeing her like this, the eyes of her friends too filled with tears. They gave her an idea. After the next day, the puja would be almost over and the idol would be immersed in the river. So she could go to the pandal that day with them. Who would notice her among so many girls? They would put her in the middle, hiding her and take her back home. It was going to be their secret. Even Mainao's parents did not get a whiff of this plan.

In the afternoon, Mainao was ready to go to Binuma's place. When she found her mother looking at her suspiciously, she said in defence, 'What are you looking at? I couldn't wear this for the puja, I might as well wear it to Binuma's. Her mother has just got the loom ready for a new set of clothes. She has asked me to come over to see it.' By the time she finished with her explanation, she had already reached the gate. As a precaution, she told her mother not to worry in case she got late.

The girls did not wait for sunset. As soon as Mainao arrived they took her under their wing and set off for the pandal. A few of her friends told her to change out of her prominent dokhana. But Mainao remembered her aunt's feverish face and refused. Someone, probably Champa, said, 'Oh, from a distance it looks like a mekhela sador. Nobody will notice.'

Mainao was entranced at the sight and sound of the balloons, the *jilepis*, the beating of the dhak and the lights.

Her apprehensions vanished. She dressed her beautiful hair with a new hairband. Her hair caught the breeze and swayed like waves; she looked like a dragonfly fluttering about.

When she returned home it never occurred to anyone that she had already been branded a criminal. Within the span of a day, Mainao became an enemy of her people; she was like a hillock in front of a river of revolution. That night itself, a meeting was called by the protesters. They congregated in the courtyard of Mainao's house; a few leaders of the movement came too. The accused Mainao was yet to change out of her red and yellow clothes, the new hairband was still adorning her hair and the generous splash of perfume stuck to her outfit. She was crying with her head between her knees and, for the first time, she felt the events around her were consuming her skin like burning charcoal.

One of the movement leaders declared their verdict: her hair should be snipped off. A girl who defied the diktat should be taught a lesson. Somebody brought a pair of scissors and Mainao's weeping increased. No, she would not allow it ... she would not cut her precious hair. The arrogant boy who had brought the scissors was ordered to start snipping all the same. The stocky boy, perhaps about five years older to her, dragged Mainao to the centre of the courtyard. Her soft wrist showed the marks of his rough fingers.

Mainao was not a weak girl; she tried to push the young man away. But he was stronger and held her firmly. It was not very easy to trim Mainao's hair. The woman in the beauty parlour always brought a special pair of scissors when she visited. First, she would spray water from a bottle and then carefully trim Mainao's silky hair. The boy's scissors was not very sharp and he had to use all his force to cut her hair. She cried as if her heart was breaking. Binuma and her friends were watching the event unfold from a distance. Now they too started weeping. Look what had come of their innocent fun!

Mainao's parents watched without protest. Their daughter was in the wrong. There were so many girls in the community, but she was the only one to go against the diktat of the leaders – that too without informing anyone. They prayed that the matter would end with the snipping of their daughter's hair, and not go beyond to guns and shootings. People watched the man and Mainao. From a distance the pair looked as if they were lovers entangled with each other. The man could only cut her hair by grabbing her close to his chest. And Mainao was jumping like a *kawoi* fish rubbed with salt to smother it. With each snip of her hair, Mainao would curl up, as if in death throes. Her heart-rending cries filled the air. In the tug of war between the two, the red dokhana slipped off, the beads of her red and yellow necklace tumbled down on the courtyard.

Now she was just in her blouse and petticoat even the lower hooks of her red blouse had come off in the struggle. Her breasts, in the new bloom of youth, showed from beneath the torn blouse. Her lovingly woven red and yellow dokhana lay crumpled on the ground, and on it were unevenly cut tufts of hair. Then an elderly man from the audience put up his hand and ordered that it was enough. He was the priest. Even the young men could not defy the sternness of his voice. Mainao somehow held on to her blouse, its remaining hooks almost coming off, and ran into the house.

Now another crime had been added to Mainao's original sin. Her virgin body was touched by a man in full public view. Nobody could deny it, all of them had seen it. The young man could hold on to her only by grabbing her close to him. She had lost some of her clothes. She was seen touching his body. So another meeting was called at the temple courtyard. Mainao was summoned to it along with her parents. A trial was held and the verdict given: Mainao must marry the man who had cut her hair. Why? Because of the age-old story of Asagi and Baisagi that had been told for generations.

Legend has it that the sisters Asagi and Baisagi often stole from the fruit garden of the handsome Chandrabao. One day he set a trap and caught them both. Then he held their soft hands and freed them. But the matter did not end there. The next day darkness descended at daytime, crows cawed unnaturally. In fact, everything looked abnormal. People understood that somewhere a young man and woman had committed a sin. At a public gathering Chandrabao and Asagi-Baisagi confessed to their sin. What was the sin? When Chandrabao freed the young women he must have had to touch their bodies. So the verdict was given. Chandrabao must marry both the sisters. Otherwise who would marry young women who had been defiled by the touch of a stranger?

The precedent of this judgment was followed by the people of Mainao's community. Like Chandrabao, that man who had cut Mainao's hair had to bow to the rule too. Who dared to defy a social diktat in force for hundreds of years? After all, oral narratives held their people together

And what about Mainao? What was she thinking through all of this? Her mind was absolutely blank. All she was searching for was the smell of a lemon flower. When she tried to breathe in that refreshing smell, something else, a stinking odour of sweat mixed with the mouldy smell of an unwashed pair of jeans assailed her nostrils. And slowly, that awful smell travelled from her nose to her breasts.

The man was asked to stand up. Someone with a deep voice asked Mainao to kneel down and ask for the blessings of the people. But she kept standing as if she had turned into stone. The ability to speak, walk or move her limbs seemed to abandon her.

Streams of tears flowed down Mainao's cheeks. She wiped them, but they flowed again; she wiped them again, but they flowed nonetheless.

The House of Nibha-bou

It is easy to find Nibha-bou's house. You just have to mention the two aromatic *bakul* trees that guard the gate leading to it and people will direct you. Though she is no relative, we still call her 'bou', since she is quite like the respected wife of an elder brother. It was her mother-in-law who had planted the bakul trees. She had, in fact, brought the saplings from her maiden home. She was very fond of gardening. When Nibha-bou entered the house as a new bride, she found it neat, well-kept, and surrounded by flowers and a tamarind tree. Her father-in-law was a teacher at the local high school. Her husband was the eldest among his siblings and worked in a bank. There was another son and a daughter.

When her sister-in-law got married, Nibha-bou took pains to make all the arrangements without flinching at the costs. Life was going well – until the matter with Bijit, her younger brother-in-law, transpired. He had gone to the university to study but disappeared from the hostel after just six months. He had gone chasing the fire in the hills.

In the beginning, he visited the house from time to time, under the darkness of night. The people in the household could not recognize the boy they had known, now dressed in fatigues and carrying a haversack with a heavy gun. They were scared of this new person whose hands were obviously stained with blood. Then his visits became less frequent and eventually they stopped altogether. The family did not see him for the next couple of years. They heard rumours that he had by now become a high-ranked leader of the extremist group he had joined. He was also said to have had a hand in quite a few killings. The once-handsome young man everybody in the house loved had now become a dreadful name, on whose head the government had put a huge price.

By then, the people in the house had lost all contact with him, except for seeing his name in the newspapers from time to time. The years rolled by. Nibha-bou's mother-in-law was mostly confined to the bed. Nibha-bou herself had become a mother of two, a boy and a girl. She took over all the responsibilities of running the house. Slowly, the image of the boy who had run away to the hills faded into memory. Time does not wait for anyone. So too Nibha-bou's house took on the usual pace of an ordinary life.

~

Nibha-bou was known for her meticulous housekeeping. Even at a young age, people noticed her acumen. As a child she liked to play with pebbles, leaves and flowers instead of the usual dolls girls of her age liked. When her father brought dolls for her she put them neatly in a row in her mother's glass-fronted almirah. When she was a little girl, after giving her a bath, her mother made her sit on a reed mat on the floor, placed a small basket with stones next to her and carried on with her household work. The little girl did not bother her. She played with the stones happily. Sometimes she arranged them in circles, sometimes in rows and sometimes in squares. Whenever her family members found some unusual pebble, they brought it along for her. Thus, the basket had stones of different hues – black, white, grey, brown with a black streak in the middle, and in many shapes – flat, round, elongated. When she was a little older, Nibha added flowers and leaves to the basket to play with. When she finished playing, she would not put all the pebbles together in the basket haphazardly. She would arrange them according to the shapes – the flat ones on one side, the round ones on another, and the long ones separately. Sometimes she arranged them by colour. The white ones on the edge of the basket, the black ones in the middle and the brown ones between the two.

Nibha was a quiet child, but if anyone disturbed her pebble arrangement she lost her temper. She wept inconsolably on such occasions. She was the youngest of the lot, and had two elder brothers. They were fond of her but they teased her too. So, sometimes they mixed up the pebbles just for the fun of seeing their otherwise docile little sister getting angry. When such pranks were played on her, Nibha cried copiously and chased her brothers, which further amused the boys. If their parents discovered their mischievous prank they were reprimanded severely. When their mother scolded them, they did not bother much. But their father would get really angry if Nibha cried due to their mischief, and he would give them a piece of his mind. He could not bear the sight of tears on his beloved daughter's cheeks. If she liked playing with the pebbles, what was their problem, he asked. So the brothers took care not to mess with her when their father was around, leaving Nibha at peace with her precious stones.

As Nibha grew up, the brothers did not stop their teasing, but changed only the objects of their pranks. Now the desk replaced the colourful stones. Her father had ordered a separate table for Nibha. It was rather big, with a blue laminated top. Nibha loved it. She arranged her dictionaries on the right side, pens and pencils on the left. In the middle, she kept her exercise books – the English ones on one side, the geography books next to them. Her brothers would mix up the books, playing the same old game. Of course, she lost her temper, but her father scolded the boys and she won.

Nibha's school uniform, a pink skirt and white blouse, was another target of their mischief. She took extreme care to make it look perfect. She boiled *sagudana* and strained it to prepare the starch for ironing. Even when drying it in the sun she followed her own method. She did not hang it from the clothesline like the other members of the family did with their clothes. First she would spread a reed mat on the floor and then place a *murha* on top of it. Next she would arrange the skirt round the murha. Then she sat nearby with a stick in hand to shoo away the crows, fearing they would sit on it. Observing her meticulous way of drying her skirt, her father ordered a special-sized murha for her. Nibha would then collect the half-dried skirt and iron it. When she set off for school in her freshly pressed uniform, not only her parents, but even her naughty brothers broke into a smile.

So the brothers' next target became the special murha. One of them would sometimes take it out to the verandah to sit on it and read the newspaper. The other would sometimes make it a point to sit on it while putting on his shoes. Seeing this Nibha lost her temper as usual; her face turned crimson with anger. She was a big girl now; she couldn't cry like a child now. Even then she screamed, complaining to her parents. If her father heard any of this, he left whatever he was doing to attend to her and magically the murha would be back in its designated place. But to give them their due, the brothers took care to dust the stool before putting it back.

~

Nibha grew up like this. When she became a college girl, she outgrew the stones and starched skirts and began looking after the knick-knacks around the house. When her mother suffered from a tennis elbow, Nibha took over most of the work at home. Studies, household work, looking after her father and two brothers – there was so much to do! She was on her toes throughout the day, moving like a spindle. Sure, she took longer than others to finish her chores and had to work harder. It was her nature. When the examiners checked her papers they automatically added two extra marks. 'Look at her writing, the way she has stayed within the margins, and the paragraph breaks – everything so neat, such a pleasure,' they would say to one another in the staff room. At home too, everything she touched bore the stamp of her immaculate habits.

~

This was the Nibha welcomed lovingly by the woman who had planted the two bakul trees at the entrance to her house. Before her marriage, her then prospective mother-in-law had gone to visit Nibha's house with a relative. She noticed a garden in the front, not too big, something that a woman could look after. In the drawing room, she saw a painted earthen pot filled with coloured sticks which had actually been collected from a broom. On the dining table she discovered a table mat set in black with embroidered flowers in red and yellow. The guests were served perfectly round, fried luchis arranged on white plates with red borders and accompanied by home-made radish pickle with ground mustard. She admired the tea-cosy embroidered with a peacock whose fans were spread out, looked fondly at the girl who was running around and immediately took a liking to her.

~

So, under the canopy of the bakul trees Nibha entered the house, led by her appreciative mother-in-law, as the daughter-in-law of Romen 'Sir', wife of Arnab Deka, and 'bou' to Reema and Bijit. Her mother-in-law had already kept the house well-organized; Nibha just had to add the finishing touches. Like stitching a bead border, or a lace, to enhance the beauty of an already embroidered tablecloth. Nibha-bou found that everyone in the family was very orderly by nature. Of course, this was all due to her mother-in-law. There was no one who would take away her murha or crinkle the bedspread. If anyone in the family saw a corner of a bedcover slightly askew, they would immediately straighten it.

And then, if there was some problem, everybody started discussing together how it could be fixed. For instance, the matter of the window in the kitchen near the gas burner. It looked rather bare. The other windows in the house had pretty curtains with animal motifs. So something had to be done about the kitchen window. They put their heads together to design a curtain which would not get burnt by the flame. It was decided that the curtain would be fixed to the window frame and, for the air to pass through, there would be holes cut into the material which would be covered with mesh. Nibha-bou brought out the sewing machine. On the way back from office her husband bought the green curtain material and along with it some yellow mesh. The curtain even got a name: *hengul-haital*, like the vegetable-dyed coloured paintings of old times. The curtain was installed; it would not fly about in the breeze to be burnt by the flame but air would filter in through the holes. Nibha-bou's mother-in-law fried sweet *malpua* and made coffee to celebrate the occasion; everybody enjoyed the afternoon heartily. This way, the people in the house tried to forget the fearful news about the young boy, though it was not easy to drive away the thought of him living somewhere in the unknown hills.

Anyone who visited Nibha-bou's house could not help noticing how well kept it was. It was not that it was full of expensive things. But even the ordinary knick-knacks were arranged tastefully around the house. For their honeymoon, Nibha-bou and her husband had gone to Goa. From there she had brought a table lamp made of shells. She had bought the chandelier hanging from the ceiling in the drawing room from a local woman selling her wares on the street. When her in-laws went to Puri on a pilgrimage they brought back a colourful wall-hanging in red and blue, with a mirror work design of a horse-drawn *rathyatra*. It was framed with good quality *bijuli* bamboo. When the light from the window entered the drawing room and filtered through the shell chandelier to fall on the wall-hanging, it created an ethereal effect. Nibha-bou had placed a small pot she had painted near the basin adjoining the kitchen. It housed an aloe vera plant. She had read, or her father-in-law had told her, that this plant sucked in the smoke that spewed as food was prepared in the kitchen. Next to the dining table were two pots with areca palms. Just below Nibha-bou's bedroom was a jasmine plant which enjoyed abundant sun and fresh air. The most beautiful of the lot was to be found in the passage that was flanked by the living quarters – a huge pot which held the queen of the night. At night, they switched off the light and looked on silently as the white petals of the flower opened one by one, looking like white lotuses. A heady perfume would fill the air.

Whenever people in the house found time, they would check to see that everything was running properly and the flowering plants were in good condition. The furniture that her mother-in-law had brought from her home, as part of the trousseau, still looked new and perfectly polished. The woollen wall-hanging from Arunachal Pradesh, the replica of a painting from the National Museum in Delhi, the pair of clay *saliki* birds bought at the town fair during Durga Puja, the bunch of dried *makhioti* creepers in a curd pot – everything looked spic and span and enhanced the ambience of the house. The children, Nibha-bou's own and her sister-in-law's son, played amidst all these beautiful decorations, but were careful not to touch or break anything, unlike many children of their age.

Like these alert children, the people in the house also tried to live their life cautiously despite the incidents happening around them. But how long could you avoid reality? One day you have to confront it. So Nibha-bou's household too had to come face to face with it. They did not have a choice. The events cruelly sucked them into a vortex. True, the household had faced policemen and army personnel looking for the son before, the one who had disappeared into the hills. But that day they were totally unprepared for the way things turned out. Frankly, compared to the earlier days, things were getting a little better. A branch of the insurgents had come out in the open – from the hills, from the forests, even from abroad. There was even an offer by the government to engage in talks with them. Under such circumstances, the family was surprised to see a group of men getting down from two vehicles in front of their house one night. Some of them were in regular clothes while the rest wore army fatigues. The men in uniform followed those in ordinary clothes. They did not talk much but embarked on their mission right away. The men in civil clothing asked how much money their absconding son had hidden in the house and instructed them to hand it over immediately.

The people in the family were dumbstruck. The son had left long ago and had not kept in touch with them for years. Where would they get the lakhs of rupees demanded by the intruders? The men insisted that they had fought together against the government, so now just because they had 'surrendered' didn't mean they did not know about the money. They had inside information that their son had crores of rupees at his disposal. If they did not give up the hidden cash they would search the house.

Then they did just that, systematically dismantling everything after making the family members sit in the passage, mutely watching. Nothing was left intact. Their beautifully kept house looked like a forest devastated by a fierce storm. The people in the house felt like birds in a broken nest. Around them were lying egg shells, yolks, dead chicks whose eyes were yet to open.

The men left before dawn broke. But not before pulling out the queen of the night from the pot; a few of them used their shoes to check the earth to see if there was anything hidden there. The plant was until then showing off seven blooming flowers, but now they were lying forlornly on the floor. One could see life ebbing away from them.

It was also ebbing away from the people in the house, who had been up through the night, witnessing the terrible events. Nibha-bou's two children had taken shelter in the lap of their grandparents. Her mother-in-law somehow fell into a light slumber towards morning, still sitting on the chair. Nibha-bou's husband had paced protectively around his family throughout, grinding his teeth in frustration, but then one of the intruders ordered him to sit down. As soon as they left, he took the motorcycle out and went looking for a doctor. His father was having problems breathing. Towards early morning, as he sat on his chair, a *ghrr-ghrr* sound escaped from his chest.

Nibha-bou's mother-in-law tried to get up, though she was still groggy. Both women had lots to do. The father-in-law, who was lying on the armchair with his chest going up and down, making an ominous sound from time to time, had to be given a glass of hot water to drink; the sleeping children had to be shifted to the bed and covered with a blanket; something had to be cooked for breakfast, at least for the children, and a cup of tea for themselves. They also had to check the ducks and chickens in the cage, as well as the two cows and goats, and set out a change of clothes for Nibha-bou's husband who had gone out to look for a doctor.

But it was difficult. The beds were in a shambles; the kitchen was witness to ruthless searching; the chairs and tables were upturned on the dining room floor; clothes that had been removed from the almirah were also on the ground. Everything was dumped on the floor, making it difficult to walk; the earth from the flower pots was scattered all around; the beautiful wall-hanging depicting a *rathyatra* scene was lying in a dirty heap in a corner; the cowrie shells from the chandelier were scattered everywhere; the pretty curtain in the kitchen, so meticulously planned and stitched, was hanging in two strips – they must have taken the other parts to make a bundle to pack something they wanted to take away.

Nibha stood stunned amidst the mess, unable to move. What should she do now, whom should she call for help? When she was young and her brothers teased her by mixing up the stones in the basket, she just had to weep and her father would be by her side. But whom could she call now? She was trembling all over; extreme tiredness seemed to take over her body. She felt as if she would not be able to carry on. Is this how things would end for her, lying dead, amidst all this destruction? There was nothing she could see beyond it. Nobody could do anything about it. Her knees shook uncontrollably. In front of her eyes a dusky mist was spreading just as her ears were deafened by a tremendous clap of thunder.

Unable to stand any longer, Nibha-bou sat down heavily. The pair of clay saliki birds she had bought at the fair lay broken into pieces at her feet. Her husband had brought home an abandoned weaver bird's nest which hangs upside down from trees. She had carefully put the birds there and hung it from a dry branch in the corner of the room. The clay head of the broken bird had many fissures. As soon as she took it in her hand, it crumbled into smithereens.

Something happened then to Nibha-bou. It was not a live bird with a flimsy heart she was holding, but a broken earthen toy. But as she held the earth that had once formed the head of the bird, she started weeping. She cried silently. On and on the tears flowed from Nibha-bou's terrified eyes that had not once shut that night.

Ayengla of the Blue Hills

Ayengla lives amidst the blue hills. She is a happy woman. And why shouldn't she be? She has a loving husband, two children, paddy fields, and a *chang ghar* with pigs and chickens. Her husband works as a security guard at a bank, some distance from the village. He goes out early in the morning and returns late in the afternoon. How proud she is when she sees him at the doorstep in his uniform!

Ayengla works hard, running the household single-handedly – doing all the chores, tending the fields and caring for her daughter and son. She loves the blue hills that rise behind her house. On most days, they are covered with cottonwool clouds, which at places hang like soft balls from the sky and sometimes they cover the blue hills with veils of mist. On sunny days, the hills shine like jewels under the sun. Her heart aches with yearning if she cannot see them, even for a day. No wonder she felt so lonely when she visited the town in the valley a couple of times with her husband. She was homesick for the hills.

These hills have also given them a lovely little brook. Every day, when she leaves for the fields she can hear it gurgling from afar. The brook itself isn't visible; one has to go deeper inside the forest, to a quiet bowl-shaped clearing surrounded by the hills to see it. Here, it tapers off to a spot flanked by two big stones. Perhaps there was just one big rock long ago, which was then worn down the middle by the water.

Not too many people come here; sometimes animals visit at night to drink water. Ayengla often wonders about the source of the brook.

They say it begins in that steep hill over there, beyond the dense jungle where nobody lives. She tells herself that she'll go there some day with her husband; surely they can hack their way through the wilderness with his curved dao. Alas, for years her plan has remained just that – a plan.

The brook has made a little pond between the stone slabs. The village women come here to wash clothes and have a bath. On the bank stands a tree as ancient as the brook, a wild orchid blooming among its boughs in vibrant yellow bunches.

Yes, this is Ayengla's own private nook. When she sits by its bank, she feels a great sense of calm. While going about her chores, she often hums a few lines from a song that her grandmother had taught her, a song she had been named after. A song about a cheerful young woman named Ayengla, who charmed the sun god and brought him down to earth.

She is quite content with her lot. From time to time though, she muses: What do people want? Why do they create problems and conflicts? Recalling the incidents of the recent past, she trembles at the memory of the gun-toters who emerged from the jungle at midnight and knocked at her door during the first week of every month. She is loath to part with her husband's hard-earned money and the share of rice that they demand, but does she have a choice in the matter?

Poor Ayengla cannot make sense of all this. What do they want? If they did succeed in getting their own state, who would rule it and who would have to leave? What had happened to her beloved hills? Last month, an army truck had just turned around a bend in the hills when a landmine planted by those in the jungle had blown it to smithereens. Every single jawan in the vehicle was killed. The villagers' description of the scene of the accident was enough to make Ayengla lose sleep for several nights – haunted as she was by the spectre of bloodied, dismembered arms and legs. Sometimes she pulled her sleeping children so close to her that they cried out in pain. If only she could, she would have clung to her husband like this too. Fear and apprehension had taken root, making endless little ripples in her pool of contentment.

After the bomb blast, the villagers barely stepped out of their houses. A funereal silence now shrouded the entire village. The weather, too, had been dark and overcast of late, with thick curtains of mist all over. Most men were already in hiding; most women had long since borne the brunt of running the households and working the fields anyway. The place was now overrun by armymen who would barge into houses at will, demanding 'Where's *deshlaga dushman*, the enemy?' and warn the villagers of dire consequences, if they were to ever give rice or money to 'those men'. The jawans did not allow anyone to harvest their crop and even burnt whole paddy fields to prevent those in the jungle from getting their share.

But those men continued to come out of the jungle at midnight all the same. They did not demand chickens or pigs like in the past. Just a bit of salt, if possible. Caught between the deshlaga dushman and *basti laga,* their own people, the villagers became the proverbial blade of grass between two warring buffaloes.

On that fateful day, when the sun broke through the fog at last, Ayengla had gone along with a few other women to the brook to wash clothes. That morning Ayengla gathered all the dirty clothes in a bundle. Many of the village women were already at the brook washing their clothes. She went to sit by it. Whenever she came here, Ayengla felt a calmness descending over her. Often she hummed a few lines of the song her grandmother used to sing. The lyrics were actually from a folk tale which her grandmother had learnt from her own granny. Even today, as she soaped the clothes she started crooning softly. The song was about a girl who was pretty like the stream, and always laughing happily. Her name was Ayengla. Her grandmother had named her after this character. When she was young she often listened to her grandmother tell her this story and came to love it, so her grandmother gave her this name.

Ayengla of the story had fallen in love with the sun god. One day when she was busy in the field she saw a handsome ethereal figure standing in front of her. It was her beauty and the sweetness of her voice that had brought him down to the earth. The godlike figure told Ayengla at the outset that he would not be able to stay with her all the time, and that it was not possible for him to be tied down with family life, children and so on. But he promised that he would come to her as soon as people saw the sun set every day. Ayengla built a cottage in the hills where the sun was seen last after the day's end. She took leave of all her relatives and went to live there. As soon as the evening set in beyond the hills, Ayengla's little cottage became bright with the sun's presence. She spent the whole night in the company of her lover. Then as dawn broke, Ayengla's house became dark. But soon she found herself very restless. For the sake of the sun god she had left all her near and dear ones behind, and begun living on this peak. Her days, without speaking or hearing anybody's voice, became unbearable. She also wanted a family, and to have children. Her lover did not want to be a part of it. He was a god and did not like any kind of restrictions.

A year passed by like this. She saw that every day when he came to meet her, the sun god took off his bright, shining crown, and appeared to be like any other common man. He ate the dinner Ayengla cooked, slept on the bamboo cot with her. One day when he was asleep, she took the crown and threw it down the slopes of the hill. The sun god woke up in excruciating pain, and in front of Ayengla he transformed into a bird. The bright yellow bird started flying after the crown rolling down the hill. Ayengla wept copiously as she followed the bird. What had she done? She had lost something so precious to her. Wherever she ran, her tears created a stream. The crown rolled down and stopped at a place looking like the bottom of a bowl. The sun god, in the form of the bird, snatched the crown and flew away carrying it in its beak. Ayengla cried so much sitting on the stone slab that it broke into two. Her tears made a puddle and the stream carrying her tears joined it to make a pond. Ayengla cried day and night, and one day she too disappeared into the little pond.

Ayengla often mused about her namesake from the story. Even today as she washed clothes, she was thinking of her. She was tired of all this talk, repeated again and again – about the army, bombs, dead soldiers, the anger unleashed by the soldiers on the village people, the fear of revenge. All this gathered into a feeling of fear that spread like a sheet of apprehension on the people's heads. At these moments, Ayengla felt like crying her heart out like the folk tale's Ayengla, and sweeping everything away at one go. The women were chatting, discussing, and leaving with their half-dried clothes already. On the way, they came across some groups of soldiers. When they saw the women, the soldiers stood aside to let them pass.

The women were exchanging news about their children. Ayengla's daughter had an upset stomach; God knows what she ate and where, and now she was sick. But she was getting better after taking the medicine her father had brought, so Ayengla was able to come out today to wash the bedsheets the girl had soiled in her sickness. Ayengla was washing these sheets, vigorously slapping them on the stone. As usual, she softly sang the song of the brook's origin. She was almost finished when somebody came from behind and grabbed her. Four to five army jawans lifted her up and took her to the jungle near the brook. Ayengla turned to stone. When she regained consciousness it was evening. She did not bother to look for her clothes. Walking unsteadily like a drunk man, she reached her home and lost consciousness again. For one day and one night, she lay like this in the hospital. After a week when she returned home, the happy, ever-laughing Ayengla had disappeared, she was now a stone-like person devoid of emotion. Wherever she was told to sit or lie down she would, without any protest, without any response.

But how long could people spend time with this woman who had turned into a stone-like being? Yet, people tried. They offered puja to the gods; her aunts on both her parents' sides brought her home so she could have a change of scene. Her husband, too, tried his best. But it was of no use. Some suggested that she would be better if she had a baby. A baby needs care and she would compel her to come out of her stupor. But it was painful to watch the pregnant Ayengla. From the stone-like woman came out a still-born baby, a girl ahead of her time. People thought Ayengla would die. But she was a young, healthy woman; it was not easy for death to take her away so soon. After some months, she sat up. By this time her husband had brought home a new wife. Ayengla dragged her cot out from the house into the open space in front. She sat there day and night.

She still does. The new wife has given birth to three children. Her own children are busy with their own work and lives. But Ayengla carries on in her stone-like stupor. Her hair reaching to her hips now has more white than black. Wrinkles have invaded her face. She never talks to anyone; no one tries to talk to her either. People come and give her something to eat; a woman comes and changes her clothes. For a while the women used to take her to the brook to give her a bath or wash her hair. But Ayengla, who sat like a quiet child always, changed into somebody else as soon as she reached the spot. She ran helter-skelter, tears streaming down her cheeks. Her endless tears seemed to make puddles, and break down even the stones. The women were scared of this Ayengla.

One day, her husband's second wife took Ayengla to the brook to give her a bath. There the ghost of Ayengla, the wife of the sun god, took possession of her. She trembled furiously as she sat on the stone slab and started crying silently, her body shaking from head to toe. The second wife got scared and ran away. She had never seen the numb, stone-like woman behave in this way. She fetched other women from the village and found Ayengla sitting between the two slabs where the brook had disappeared. She was trembling like a banana leaf against the wind. From time to time she gnashed her teeth.

Suagmoni's Mother, the Storyteller

Meet pretty little Suagmoni, named after the aromatic fine rice. Her mother's days and nights were woven around her. Not only her, but everybody in the house was under Suagmoni's spell, though she was not a little girl anymore. Last year, she had started going to the local school. Suagmoni was her mother's first child, and the first grandchild in the family on both her mother and father's side. Understandably, she was the star of the family. Her mother called her Hiya, or heart, and sometimes Hiyamoni. There were other names too, depending on the occasion – Maajoni, Sunjoni, Dehajoni and so on – all bestowed on the special girl of the family.

Suagmoni rustled about busily throughout the day with this and that; sometimes she seemed to not even miss her mother. But at night, she had to sleep next to her. Unless she put her hands around her mother's neck possessively and listened to a story she would not be able to sleep. Her mother too waited for this moment; this was her exclusive time with her daughter. Every night, Suagmoni would beg her, 'Ma, tell me a story.'

'Which one?' her mother would ask. By now she had finished her bagful of stories and would have to repeat an old one.

Tonight, Suagmoni thought for some time and decided, 'You tell me the story of the ogress who liked pitha. Of course, you can also consider the story of Paanesoi, Tejimala, Tikhor, the flower girl ...'

All these stories were traditional Assamese folk tales and she had become familiar with each after hearing them from her mother. Today, too, she was clinging to her mother's neck. Her eyes were getting heavy with sleep but she forced herself to keep them open. How could she sleep without listening to a story? Though she was already a schoolgirl, this childhood habit of hers had remained. She always put her hands inside her mother's sador which covered the breasts. She would not listen even if scolded. This was her comfort zone during storytime. While listening to a familiar story, she asked many questions. Her mother had to answer each of them, she could not cheat her way out of it.

Today Suagmoni had picked the story of the ogress. Her mother wanted to tell an easier story – of the old man who planted the yams. But Suagmoni was not interested. It was boring – the old man planted the yams, the jackal saw it and ate them all. So the next day, after planting another lot, the old man lay there as if dead and then when the jackal came, he got the beating of his life. 'What is so interesting about this story – tell me?' she complained. Her mother had no choice. She had to tell the story of the ogress who was greedy for the delicious pitha.

'There was a cowherd in the village. Every day he took the herd of cows out to the field for grazing,' Suagmoni's mother began.

'How come there was only one cowherd? Why didn't you mention his other friends?'

There, Suagmoni's volley of questions had been unleashed.

'Oh, yes, I forgot. Now all of them reached the grazing field,' her mother conceded.

'Did the boys go to school like us?' This was the cue for Suagmoni to talk about her friends in school. The next day Upasana would sing, Nitul would recite a poem, Rimjhim would narrate a story.

'What will you do?' her mother asked.

'I will sing a song as part of the chorus. Julie miss has taught us.' Then Suagmoni started describing her teacher and sang a few lines of the song she had learnt. Her mother was happy to let her go on. She was rather tired after working the whole day, taking care of household chores and frankly, she was in no mood to narrate a lengthy story.

'Now go to sleep. You'll have to leave for school early tomorrow,' she coaxed her daughter.

'So you are not going to tell me the story, right?' Suagmoni's face clouded. Who in the family could bear to see her dark face?

'Okay, listen then. The cowherds let the cows graze in the field. Then they climbed up the tree where lots of pitha were hanging; they had ripened during the night and were now ready for the cowherds to devour.'

'What kind of pitha were they? If they were the white *tilpitha* stuffed with black sesame and jaggery they were sure to break down into pieces. Were they the harder variety of *ghilapitha*?'

'Oh, maybe they were *borpitha*.'

'Hunh, they must have been borpitha. I haven't had borpitha in a long time. Would you make some tomorrow? Make a few extra ones. I'll ask my friends Manu, Kuku and all, to drop in after school. Tell me, will you make them or not?' Suagmoni hugged her mother tightly; she was smiling.

'Okay, I promise. Now tell me, do you want to listen to the story or not? If you don't, I'll go and start cleaning the *komal saol* for the borpitha tomorrow.'

'I'll do both. I'll listen to the story and also eat the borpitha. Now tell me: what will you do for the stuffing? Sesame seeds or scraped coconut?'

'Let's see. The pitha the cowherds ate had a filling of sesame and jaggery. When the breeze blew, its aroma was carried by the air far into the land.'

'So that's how the ogress could smell it? It must have been very windy that day.'

'Yes, you are right. The wind that day was rather strong. The air was filled with the tempting smell of the pitha. Presently, a hunchbacked old woman reached the place. She stood under the tree and started begging, "O my dear boys! Please give me a pitha!" One of the boys shook the branches and four to five pithas fell down on the ground. But the old woman did not make any move to collect them.

'She begged again, "All these pithas have fallen on a cowdung heap. Why don't you climb down from the tree a bit and hand them over to me?" So one cowherd climbed down a little and shook the branches and a few ripe pithas fell down.

'"Oh, these have fallen on dog poop. Please come down and give them to me yourself, my son!" the old woman coaxed.'

'And so he came down, right? Now the old woman would show her true self – an ogress!' Suagmoni intervened at this point but she was also scared, and held her mother's neck tightly. 'And then what happened?'

'What happened? You know already. Do you remember his name?'

Suagmoni's voice now cracked with dread. 'What will happen to Bharat now, Ma? How much will his mother cry?'

'Of course, she will cry and cry. But it was not that easy to trap Bharat. The ogress put him in a sack and then placing it on top of her head walked away quickly. However, on the way, she had to attend to nature's call. As soon as she went to the jungle, Bharat got out of the sack and ran away.'

'Why, before he left, didn't he put pebbles, stones and chunks of earth in the sack?' Suagmoni was not going to let her mother continue unless she provided all the details.

'Oh, yes, yes. I had forgotten. Bharat even put some thorny *kotkora* branches in the sack.'

'And then the ogress lifted the sack on her head.' From this point Suagmoni started to tell the story herself. She was not afraid any more. She was in a merry mood now. 'Ha, ha, ha, the ogress went on unsuspectingly with the sack on her head.'

Her mother continued, '"Oh, you are kicking me," she uttered as the pebbles hit her head.

'The thorns pierced her head. She screamed, "You are scratching my head with your nails, are you? Wait, you'll see what I will do to you; I'll fry you alive in hot oil." The hard chunks of earth hurt her head and she got a headache. She screamed again, "So you are hurting me with your knuckles? Wait, my daughter is going to cut you into pieces."

'Reaching home, she was furious when she found how she had been taken for a ride by Bharat. The next day, she reached the tree of pitha again and started whining, "Please give me a pitha! Oh, I am so hungry, I can't stand it anymore."

'But didn't the boys know that she was actually the ogress?' Suagmoni wondered. Her eyes were shadowed with fear.

'How will they know? The ogress doesn't appear as herself; she takes on different looks. So Bharat came down from the tree again. He was very soft-hearted. He felt sorry for the woman who was his grandmother's age and was now begging for a pitha. The ogress repeated her complaint, "Look that pitha has landed on a cowdung heap, the other one has fallen on a heap of dog poop. Why can't you climb down a little to hand over the pitha? Is it too much trouble for an old woman?"

'And so Bharat again came down from the tree, isn't it?' Suagmoni's voice was heavy with unshed tears.

'Yes, he did. This time the ogress didn't wait a second; she pushed him into a sack and walked fast towards her house.'

'Didn't his friends come to help him? They just looked on?' Suagmoni's eyes were half-closed now with sleep.

'Everybody loves their own life. Who would risk it to challenge the ogress? This time she didn't make the mistake of stopping anywhere. Reaching home she called out to her daughter, "Malati, come, come, look what I have brought for you! A whole man! Hurry, fry him and we'll have a feast." She threw the sack on the floor and went out to have a bath.'

Suagmoni's face became even sadder. She hugged her mother tighter. And then she fell asleep. Her mother covered her with a soft sheet and tucked in the mosquito net. There were some chores still to be finished. On top of it all was her daughter's request for borpitha. She would have to soak the sesame seeds, then she would have to dry it under the sun next day. The komal saol too had to be soaked and then when it became soft, she would have to grind it. All these steps had to be completed to make the borpitha.

The next day Suagmoni had to sing with the chorus in the school to celebrate Independence Day. She was to wear a green dress. Her mother had already stitched a new one; she only had to sew on the buttons. She kissed her lovely daughter's forehead and stepped down from the bed. Before leaving the room she looked at her daughter again through the mosquito net. When she was asleep, she looked so different. She was not the naughty girl who sometimes got a scolding for running around during the day. Now, she looked like a princess from a fairy tale, a beautiful fairy from heaven, a mermaid of the seas. Her mother got absorbed admiring her pretty daughter. At these moments she felt that the world was beautiful, life was beautiful, that to live itself was a beautiful experience. She lifted the net to kiss her daughter again. Half awake, Suagmoni encircled her arms around her neck again. She waited a bit and then finding her daughter deep in sleep, slowly got down from the bed.

In the morning, Suagmoni's father took her to the school on his scooter. Her friends, Kuku, Munu, Upasana, Nitul, Rimjhim, reached around the same time. First there was to be a flag-hoisting, then a musical programme to be followed by snacks and sweets. Once she left for school, Suagmoni's mother got busy preparing the ingredients for making the borpitha. Today the usual classes in the morning would not be held and so school would be over by noon. Her daughter should arrive home by one o'clock. Her friends would come to enjoy the delicacy too. Suagmoni's mother tucked the ends of the sador tightly around her waist and continued with the preparation.

But that morning, the ogress arrived in Suagmoni's village, hiding in the shadows. Nobody knew how or when she came and then disappeared. There was a huge ear-shattering sound and then she put the soft limbs of the children in her sack. Her aim was faultless; it was a 'completely successful mission'. A few children had just joined their hands in a namaskar after the flag-hoisting for the Independence Day commemoration when the ogress screamed loudly; everything around them trembled at the impact. And in a moment the tender limbs, soft like flowers, were pushed into the ogress' sack. Then they were emptied into a wok of boiling oil; *srrr-srrr* ... the sound of something freshly fried escaped from it. The ogress finished her bath and sat down to enjoy the meal of tender meat.

On the other end, a great hullabaloo took over the village. Suagmoni's mother abandoned the frying pan in which she was preparing the borpitha, and sprinted towards the school like a madwoman, but she fainted midway. At home Suagmoni's grandmother fainted too; from time to time, she opened her eyes and then became unconscious again. Her grandfather locked himself in the prayer room and refused to come out. Her two aunts ran through the paddy field and found their sister-in-law lying unconscious near the big pond. Who was going to look after whom in the melee? Suagmoni's father was crying his heart out sitting under the bakul tree near the school. At times bursts of anger intercepted his weeping. Everybody was in shock, unable to fathom what had happened. They could not keep their eyes open, their ears were deafened as if with thunderclaps, their hearts felt they had broken into many parts, their limbs refused to move, they could not utter any sound. Their bodies turned lifeless like stones. There was no blood in their veins, there was no flesh, their hearts did not beat, their body temperature was no longer normal. They were frozen into chunks of ice.

The people turned stone-cold, but time did not wait. The sun rose in the morning which turned into noon and in the evening the moon and the stars brightened the sky. Time also pushed the people to go on. For the first few days after the incident, Suagmoni's mother did not drink even a drop of water, a few days later maybe a few drops, and then slowly, she started having tea and biscuits. One could not live on saline drops for days after all. Suagmoni's grandmother too recovered a bit; though she had to put water and oil on her head every day to cool it, she did not faint at regular intervals. Her grandfather too did not spend the whole day in the prayer room, but only the morning hours. Of late, he had even started going to the kitchen garden with the spade. The aunts had resumed college.

But Suagmoni was not there. The girl who used to run from one room to another like a butterfly was no more. She had become a framed picture on the wall. Somebody had collected her pictures in many moods and framed them to hang on one side of the wall. In front of her house was built a memorial. Her name was inscribed there along with the others who were destroyed that day. But nothing was left of the little girl Suagmoni. Her mother's hands often reached out to the place where she slept at night. She was becoming so thin that the sleeves of her blouse looked like loose shirt sleeves. Her father's hair had started going grey prematurely, his once-healthy skin was now drained of colour. Suagmoni was not there to sleep between her parents. The girl who held her mother tight and rested her hand on her breast and begged for stories was gone. The couple became like an arid field starved of water. Everything around was silent and without succour. In that field not a blade of grass could grow.

At night when Suagmoni's mother retired to bed, her daughter's soft touch, her demand for a story – *Ma, please tell me a story. Please!* – invaded her thoughts. She remembered how she had left the story of the ogress halfway. She felt like telling the whole story now. Suagmoni hated the evil ogress who had carried off her favourite hero, Bharat. When her mother came to the point in the story where Bharat filled the sack with stones, earthen mounds and thorns, Suagmoni was so happy that from then on, she took over.

You are scratching my head with your nails, are you?

You are kicking me, are you? Wait till I reach home. I'll fry you alive and enjoy your meat.

Suagmoni enjoyed imitating the voice of the ogress, and the way she was cheated by Bharat. She widened her eyes until her pupils turned into big balls so she could imitate the evil demoness.

Now, when she tried to sleep, Suagmoni's mother always hugged the pillow her daughter used sleep on. Her tears had soaked through the pillow stuffed with soft *simolu* cottonwool and turned them into uneven lumps, like the sack of the ogress filled with earthen clods. When she hugged the pillow close to her chest, *kotkora* thorns seemed to pierce her body, the sharp stones stabbed her heart, leaving it bleeding. Her ears seemed to be always humming with that thundering sound. At this point she felt like telling her daughter the complete story.

Suagmoni despised the ogress for trying to kill Bharat. She clapped, elated, 'What fun, what fun! He killed the wicked ogress!' when her mother came to the part where Bharat hoodwinked and killed her. She always told the last portion of the story to Suagmoni, who was no more, before she fell asleep. She picked up hard clods of earth from the dry field and threw them to the sky. When the ogress died she felt relieved. Suagmoni too felt happy and would clap her hands in glee.

After Suagmoni was no more, she ran her fingers lovingly over the pillow every night. 'Listen to what happened next,' she would say to herself, silently. The story kept running in her mind like a churning wheel. She told her daughter the story, every night, even though she was not there.

'Listen, my dear, the ogress reached her house. She instructed her daughter Malati to cut up the victim, fry him in hot oil and then went to the river to have a bath. By now Malati had ground the spices, heated the wok with oil and was sharpening the machete. Malati asked Bharat to lie down. It was now that Bharat dipped into his sack of tricks.

'"Bai, my elder sister, you are going to eat me anyway. But please fulfil my last wish before I die," he said. He was granted his wish and he put on the the daughter's *riha-mekhela*.

"Now you lie down," Malati ordered. The machete in her hand was ready to strike.

'"How will I lie down? Please show me."

And then Bharat cut her up, Suagmoni chimed in. *Now Bharat will go back to his mother.*

'He killed the daughter.'

He now put her body parts in the hot oil.

'He tied a broom to the cat's tail.'

He tied Malati's head in a rope and hung it on top of the wok.

'The blood from the head streamed into the hot oil and it seemed that something was really frying in the pan.'

Mother and daughter took turns to take the story forward.

What happened next?

'The ogress was about to return home from the river. Bharat, dressed in Malati's riha-mekhela, ran away through the jungle behind the house.'

Would Bharat's mother recognize her son dressed in Malati's clothes? Suagmoni would giggle.

'Why not? How can a mother not recognize her own son?'

What did the ogress do after she returned?

'She was getting ready to enjoy a good meal but found the door shut. She heard the sound of somebody sweeping the floor and shouted, "Oi Malati! Are you still sweeping the floor?"

The cat, with its tail tied to the broom went round and round the floor of the room. The ogress was getting impatient, "Are you going to open the door, Malati, or go on sweeping the floor?"

Meanwhile, the blood dripping from Malati's severed head dripped into the hot oil and made the *serr-srrr* sound, as if something was being fried.

'"Hei Malati, how long will you take to fry the meat? Open the door!"'

Did Bharat reach home by now? Suagmoni asked; she was biting her nails nervously.

'By the time Bharat reached home it was evening. People from the whole village were gathered in the courtyard already, since the boy had not returned by then. They were getting ready to go searching for him with fire-lit bamboo poles in hand. Just then Bharat arrived.

He was wearing a riha-mekhela like a woman? Suagmoni found it difficult to imagine Bharat in clothes like her own mother.

'Oh, by now the clothes were torn into shreds. When he was running through thorny bushes, barefoot over jungle paths strewn with sharp stones, who cared for clothes? His soles were bleeding, and so were his hands. The villagers felt sorry for him. "Who did this to him? He was such a nice, quiet boy, he didn't even step over a dead snake, and preferred to go around it to cross the road, and now look at how his body is in great pain," they said amongst one another.

'Bharat drank a whole pail of water and then divulged his story. The people were terrified. By now the ogress must have broken the door to enter the house. And then she would find what Bharat had done.

'They got ready. Whatever was to happen would happen; they would put up a fight. They knew very well that not only Bharat but the whole village would be ravaged by the ogress.'

Ma, the ogress had sharp teeth, her nails were razor-sharp; you told me she could even slice through an elephant's stomach. Suagmoni's eyes were round with fear.

'Yes, the ogress had lots of power.'

But the villagers didn't have sharp nails, they didn't have sharp teeth like her. What will happen now? She could arrive in the village anytime. Suagmoni's heavy sleep-laden eyes were now wide open.

'The ogress broke open the door and on seeing the cat with the broom tied to its tail, scolded her daughter, "You are such a big girl now, but you haven't outgrown your childish pranks yet." Then she entered the kitchen and saw her daughter's severed head, yelled in agony and set off for the village.'

And then what happened, Ma?

'What was to happen, happened. A fight between the ogress and the villagers ensued. It went on for seven days and seven nights. The trees fell one by one, the hill was flattened, but the fight continued.'

Who would win, Ma?

'The ogress looked frightening, yes, but her life energy was hidden in a saliki bird's heart, which stayed hidden in the hollow of a gourd.'

Where was that saliki bird? Could Bharat find it?

'Of course, he could. He brought out the gourd. When he broke one of the bird's legs, the ogress also found her leg broken; when he twisted the wing, her arm broke. Ultimately the villagers killed the bird.'

Oh, great, what fun! So the wicked ogress was killed, after all.

'Yes, she was killed.'

What happened to the tree with the pitha?

'People brought its roots and planted portions in their houses, so everybody could have their heart's fill of the pitha.'

After finishing this quietly told story, Suagmoni's mother stopped. Then she spoke to herself, 'The children who waited to enjoy the borpitha did not have to fear the ogress anymore. How could she take them away? She was killed after all.'

Had Suagmoni been alive, she would have jumped up in glee when the story ended like this.

Suagmoni's mother hugged her late daughter's pillow tighter. Her tears moistened the pillow stuffed with cottonwool. But they did not stop.

Author's note: In 2004, on 15 August, India's Independence Day, the militant group, the United Liberation Front of Assam (ULFA), detonated a bomb at Dhemaji parade ground. Thirteen people, including ten school children, died in the blast.

Surabhi Barua and the Rhythm of Hooves

'Once upon a time,' began Grandfather, 'there was an old woman who slept inside her *pera*.'

'A wooden box? Why did she sleep in a box?' the little girl wanted to know. 'Wasn't there a cot?'

'Yes, there was a bamboo cot.'

'Didn't she have a bed like ours?'

'Those days, they didn't have beds like ours.'

'But why did she sleep inside a box?'

Grandfather's voice dropped to a whisper. 'The old woman had a basket of silver coins, three seven-strand necklaces, one *jonbiri* necklace with a crescent moon locket, two heavy *gamkharu* bangles ...'

'Ah! So she was scared that a thief would steal them all?'

'Right! So one night a gang of thieves raided her house. They carried off the box after breaking into the house.'

'So the old woman was inside the box?'

'Yes, the thieves carried her along unknowingly. On the way, they had to cross a small stream. The thieves folded their clothes to cross the stream but water entered the box. The old woman shouted, "Lift up, lift me up, thief! My hip is wet."'

The little girl listened. Then she asked, 'Kaka, would you allow me to enter your box?'

'What will you do inside the box?' The old man did not seem to like the idea.

'No, I want to see how the old woman crossed the stream while still inside the box.'

The old man was very fond of his granddaughter. He allowed her to sit inside his old wooden box and the girl sang with gusto, 'Lift up, lift me up, thief! My hip is wet.'

That little girl, Surabhi Barua, was now twenty-six years old and a professor in a college. She liked to go deep into things using her own judgement and experience everything before making up her mind. And now, even before the sun was up and the mist was thick, she was ready to leave home to go somewhere. Over her sweater, she wrapped a red Naga shawl with which she also covered her ears and head. If one did not look intently, it was difficult to recognize her face. Why had Professor Barua covered herself like this? After all it was not that cold yet. Was she trying to hide herself from public gaze? Perhaps.

Surabhi Barua organized her luggage in the cycle rickshaw. Before climbing into the rickshaw, she looked back at her house. Her mother was standing at the gate leading to the compound. She was wiping her eyes with the end of her sador. She opened the gate, approached her daughter and said, 'You didn't eat anything.' She was wiping her eyes again. Surabhi did not say anything. She touched her mother's feet and got up on the rickshaw. Then she told the rickshaw-walla, 'Please hurry up! I have to catch the first bus.'

The first bus from this small town left for the city of Guwahati at five o'clock in the morning; today it was leaving a bit late because of the mist. Surabhi closed her eyes and tried to calculate the time. The bus would reach Guwahati around three o'clock in the afternoon. She would have to spend one night there. The next day at six in the morning the train would leave for Delhi; from Delhi she would have to take a connecting train to the small hilly town. She would reach the town the next morning. Everything was arranged; someone was going to receive her at the station. Her room at the hostel was also ready. She had gone there once before to appear for her interview at the study centre. Surabhi Barua's curriculum vitae was exceptional. The interview had gone very well. It had been easy to obtain the research scholarship for the span of three years.

As the rickshaw progressed through the screen of mist, suddenly Surabhi Barua felt very restless. She felt like flying to the peaceful institute in the hill station and immersing herself in the books. Then she would forget everything. It was too early for the shops to open. The orange-coloured sun was trying to peep through the mist, which was lifting a little now. The road was becoming more visible. Torn sandals, strips of clothes were scattered all over. A few street dogs were eating something by the roadside. Surabhi Barua felt her skin prick. Last night, this place had witnessed a huge incident. All these days the andolon for self-assertion was on, but there had never been any confrontation with the police and military. They had taken out processions with flaming torches, organized meetings, sat in protest in front of the oil refinery; sometimes they beat drums and cymbals to express their protest. The young men also shouted slogans of self-sufficiency and sold vegetables from carts on the street. Surabhi Barua observed that when these young men came along with their carts and announced their arrival by blowing a horn, the women from the houses emerged and bought their wares with great respect. They did not protest if the vegetables cost more, or were not fresh, but took them to the kitchen as if they were *nirmali*, flowers blessed at the temple.

Surabhi Barua's first clash with the protestors had been with the boys who talked glibly about self-sufficiency. By this time everyone knew about her opposition to the agitation. She was a woman who liked to judge things coolly, and so she could not flow with the tide of sentiment. She became one of the few who stood against the Assam agitation. She wrote a few articles stating again and again that this overwhelming sentimental outlook would stand in the way of constructing a strong Assamese identity. These articles came out in a Leftist magazine. Though the magazine had a small circulation, people came to know about the articles and whenever they appeared, there was some trouble in the town. Once the young men got together at the main tri-junction of the town and burnt the magazine in full public view along with her effigy. She was almost excommunicated. Now these things had stopped. Surabhi Barua had now been relegated to the fringes of society.

Perhaps it was the sight of the dogs trying to slurp at the dried blood, the torn sandals and torn clothes on the road, or maybe thinking of these things Surabhi Barua could feel her heart pounding fast. She felt as if she might faint. The back of her head felt unusually hot. She started sweating. It had been like this for the past one year, ever since she started opposing the movement. She realized that she would feel this way for some time now. She opened the water bottle and took a gulp. Thankfully, the bus stop was not very far away. A white car passed by. Did it bear a Red Cross sign? Who was driving the car? Surabhi Barua looked on until the car disappeared into the mist. Into her mind floated the image of a man she had met six months ago. He was quite handsome but that was not why she found him attractive. Somehow when she first saw him she felt that he was uncomplicated and open. Dr Alok Kalita had come straight to the point after meeting her and proposed. Even without knowing him, she had become excited by the prospect of spending her life with him. There was a secret fountain bubbling inside her heart. She took some time to think before accepting the proposal.

Both things happened on the same day. That day she had entered the classroom as usual. Which class was it? Oh yes, the first year of the higher secondary class. She always felt excited about this batch. As she looked at the young, fresh faces of the students who had just graduated from school, she immediately became fond of them. Soon these young faces, ready to burst into laughter at the slightest opportunity, would mature into faces of students of the degree class, quieter and more experienced. She waited eagerly for the young new batch every academic year. Since she joined the college, she has taught three such batches.

That day she was supposed to discuss a poem. It told a gentle love story between a dacoit and a pretty girl. The previous day she had only read out the lines to her students. The poet had composed the poem with great skill, in a rhythm echoing the sound of horses' hooves. Surabhi Barua was explaining to the students how sound could transform into notes of music through lyrics. A student who performed well and looked younger than his years had commented, 'Madam, it seems as if the poem has the pace of a galloping horse.' When they heard the story in the poem, the young faces seemed to fill with sadness. When his lady love died, the dacoit did not care for his safety any more and came out from his hideout with a sword in broad daylight. He was shot dead like a street dog. Surabhi Barua was yet to elaborate on the story of the lovers' transformation into ghosts and the scene where the dacoit's body lay on the street. In fact, today she planned to elucidate those parts of the poem. But as soon as she opened the attendance register, the students left the classroom en masse. A few shouted loudly while going out, 'Get rid of the Badans of the land,' probably referring to the historical figure of Badan Borphukan, who had betrayed the country during the Ahom rule. A few shouted, 'Jai Ai Asom!' *Glory to the Motherland of Assam!* The register remained open in her hands. She was stunned. She met the eyes of the young student who had done so well in the exams. He also walked out slowly. When she came out of the classroom she saw that even Professor Bijoy Bordoloi's class of the degree students was emptying out. He was a veteran at the institute and had only three years left before retirement, but they were openly criticizing his Leftist ideology and shouting in unison, 'We won't allow, we won't allow this CPM-*giri*.'

Bordoloi did not belong to any party; he was a well-known intellectual and historian on Leftist ideology. Surabhi Barua had heard that these days he was hounded by shouts of 'The Badans of this land, be warned!' The college premises seemed like a crow's nest on fire. The teachers in the staff room sat silently. The principal advised Surabhi Barua, 'You better take a few days' leave.'

Two of her students came towards her and requested, 'Baidew, please go home. We'll accompany you.' A young girl whispered, 'Lots of these boys are outsiders; they're not from here.' The principal had offered a police escort to Bordoloi and Surabhi. She had refused. Even the rickshaw-puller had turned his face away from her. As she stepped out on the road to go home, a few students quietly walked on with her, keeping a little distance, as if spreading an invisible protective net around her. That boy who had found the rhythm of a galloping horse in the poem was one of them.

The rickshaw-puller was taking a shortcut now. The main road was much longer. There were no torn sandals, tattered clothes or stray dogs on this pebbled road. The neat little houses with small gardens in front were still asleep. Who could tell from this peaceful scene that there was a fire of conflict burning all around?

That day too Surabhi Barua had taken the dirt road from the college rather than the main road. She had been asked to avoid it by her few loyal students. There was some incident on the four-road junction, she was told. It was only yesterday, or was it long ago? How much time ago? Twelve hours? Ten hours? Maybe even less, but within that time so many things had happened.

She had just changed her clothes after coming back from the college when she found that Alok's mother was visiting.

To tell them that she was unable to welcome Surabhi as a daughter-in-law of her house. The people were on one side and Surabhi was on another, she had said. They did not have any problem with her as a bride-to-be, but now she had become a dangerous association. That afternoon some people had thrown stones in the direction of Alok's clinic. He was a doctor after all; he had to deal with the people every day. How could he go against them?

Surabhi Barua understood that this excuse had come from the doctor himself. His mother did not even accept a glass of water at their place. Neither did she did show the courtesy of meeting her at least once. She hurried out as soon as possible. That evening she heard someone, perhaps her elder brother on his way back from college had mentioned, that some boys had severely beaten up Professor Bordoloi and the cornea in one of his eyes was damaged. He had been taken to the city for treatment.

The day had arrived like a devastating storm. Like people who try to assess the losses after a storm, Surabhi Barua looked back on that terrible day. She knew that more days like this, or even worse, were waiting to unfold in the future. That day itself she had sent off her application to the study centre. She had previously done a three-week course there; her work had impressed the director and he had informed her that the institute was eager to support scholars from the Northeast to do research work. When she had gone to the hills where the institute was located, she had taken along with her a secret fountain of hope. As she reminisced about that horrible day and its aftermath, she made up her mind. At midnight she took out the page that contained 'The Highwayman', the poem by Alfred Noyes she had intended to teach in class. She read it out to the rhythm of horses' hooves:

> The wind was a torrent of darkness among the gusty tree.
> The moon was a ghostly galleon tossed upon cloudy seas.

The road was a ribbon of moonlight over the purple moor.
And the Highwayman came riding—
Riding—riding—'

The wind was a stream of darkness among the trees caught in the madness of the storm. The overcast sky looked like a sea. In that sea the moon was a ghostly galleon boat. The water took on a purplish tone. The road was like a ribbon of moonlight. On that ribbon came riding the dacoit to meet his lover. The girl with pearly lips tortured to death by the king's soldiers – her body and her lover's lying on the road – their ghosts floating in the air on moonlit nights. The story in the poem brought tears to Surabhi Barua's eyes. She felt as if the atmosphere around her was the same as where that young horseman lay in a pool of blood on the street, the girl tied to the pole, her mouth gagged by the soldiers, their ghosts trembling in the air.

The rickshaw arrived at the bus stop at last. She bought a few newspapers and magazines. She was impatient to get into the bus. Bus, train, another train, and then into the bosom of the hills surrounded by cedar, pine and fir trees and that beautiful house filled with shelves full of books. Nothing else. She remembered her mother's face and how she wiped her tears. Well, her brother and sister-in-law might have regarded her as a liability, her relatives might have likened her to a sickly street dog, but why did her mother behave in that way? Why didn't she utter the words that Surabhi should not leave home, that whatever further studies she wanted to do she could just as well do from her own place? She would have stayed on. And what about that handsome man? Why couldn't he come personally to collect the engagement ring given to her? Wasn't he the one who had proposed to her? She remembered her colleagues, their faces sullen and eyes downcast so they could avoid looking her in the eye. She remembered her father. Had he been alive, would things have taken this turn?

Surabhi Barua was in college at that time. It was when she learnt to think deeply about the world, and about herself too in a new way. She devoured books hungrily, joined the existing Study Circle in the college, took part in plays, and wrote articles. One day, the principal of the college had sent for her father. He spoke to him about her. He talked about her thoughts, her work, her friend circle and also cautioned him to keep an eye on her. The college expected good results from her; she should not waste time on unnecessary diversions. The principal was especially opposed to her philosophy, her idealism. And what did her father say in reply? Standing in the queue in front of the ticket counter at the bus stop, she remembered that her father had told the principal that he had full faith in his daughter's judgement; nobody should try to curb her way of thinking. He had no problem with the way she wrote her articles, the inherent logic behind them; they were her own opinions.

That day after her father returned, he sat in the drawing room and asked her to bring him a cup of tea. He told her everything that had happened as he sipped the tea. Then he caressed her head and said, 'My dear, whatever you do in your life, do so after giving it a good thought.'

After a long time, she felt the touch of his loving hand on her head. Had he been alive, would he have allowed her to leave home like this, struggling with her luggage? She had bought the only car in the family. Why didn't her mother say that if her elder brother was hesitant about driving her to the bus stop, they could hire a driver at least? Her mother perhaps thought of her family and the house, about the safety of her brothers. Surabhi Barua's eyes filled with tears as she thought of her dead father. Her elder brother had bought a plot of land; the night somebody put fire to the rented houses on that plot, her mother had told her it would be better if she kept away from the house for some time. Her brothers and sisters-in-law stood around silently. It was not difficult to understand that her mother's words were prepared after long discussions with the rest of the family. She deliberately told them that she had received a scholarship from the institute in the hills. Everybody was elated at the news, she knew, but pretended to be sad about her departure.

After buying the ticket, Surabhi Barua arranged her luggage in the open space, sat down on top of a box to wait until the bus was ready. An unknown young man walked up to her. Instantly, Surabhi Barua was alert like a mongoose, the quills standing up. She remembered Dr Bordoloi had suffered a torn cornea, that a young painter's fingers were chopped off and after he was beaten up with rods, his body was thrown on the road. Surabhi Barua could feel droplets of sweat trickling down her body even in the cold. A gang of young boys would follow him any moment now and they would shout in unison, she feared. A damaged eye, a few chopped-off fingers, a head broken by rods and bleeding. Surabhi Barua stood up. The young boy was standing next to her now.

'Baidew, I came from Guwahati last night by the overnight super bus,' he said.

'What can I do about it?' Surabhi Barua's voice was sterner than she meant it to be.

He came nearer and said, 'Sir has sent me."

'Which "Sir"?'

The boy uttered a name in reply. The professor was almost under house arrest now. For the last three months he had not been able to step out of his house; it was anybody's guess how long he would have to live like this. Some others like him who thought on the same lines were living like the Jews under Hitler. The person who had sent the young man to her had gone to the bazaar one day and got beaten up; he had returned home with eight stitches on the forehead.

'I have bought a ticket for the same bus as yours. I'll keep an eye on you. Sir has asked that you stay the night at his place. Our duty will be done only after settling you in the train,' the boy said. He got up and boarded the bus which had just entered the depot. Surabhi got her luggage together and walked towards the same bus.

'Baidew, please let us help you with the luggage.' Surabhi Barua found that some of her students had come too.

One of them had a neatly packed bag. He gave it to her and said, 'Jonali and the girls have prepared some snacks for you to take along.'

The tender-faced first-year student asked almost in a whisper, 'Ma'am, after you finish your studies, will you stay back and work there?'

Surabhi Barua understood that it was a question all of them wanted to ask.

'No, I'll come back.'

'Ma'am, when will these things be over? We've heard that this year even the exams may not be held. Is it true?'

'Sometimes these things happen, everything goes awry, there's chaos everywhere. People as a group make mistakes,' she said.

'They try to gag the mouths that speak the truth,' the face of the B.A.-final student hardened as he spoke.

'People will learn to tell the right from the wrong. Why not? Wait until that time comes, be ready. I will too,' Surabhi Barua told them.

The boys were lifting the boxes one by one. 'Baidew, we'll write to you,' they said as they put the luggage in the boot of the bus. They handed her a pen and asked, 'Will you write back to us?'

As she took the pen, streams of tears flowed down Surabhi Barua's cheeks.

No Escape from Hell

MY DAD IS AN ATM

My father is an ATM. I can draw money from there at any time. Yes, those were the words written on the T-shirt. The words were in white and the garment was pitch-black in colour. A young man of around seventeen or eighteen was wearing the tee. The words in white attracted the eyes immediately. The boy looked quite smart and robust. It was easy to guess that he belonged to a well-to-do family and had easy access to whatever he wanted. What did the boy do? He must be a student in a good institution in a city like Delhi, Bangalore, Hyderabad or Chennai. After he finishes his studies, he would surely get a job offer with a salary of more than one lakh rupees. His father must have made a huge donation to get him admitted into a premier institution. Now, why was he approaching a rundown kiosk which only sold betel nut and knick-knacks? What was he buying? He was rich, with a father like an ATM machine. Was he buying chocolates? Nowadays, you get tins and packets of expensive imported chocolates even in small localities. But still, people bought them at prices that could've bought you gold in the olden days. And because people bought them, they were easily available too. He must be buying them for his lady love, or as people called them these days, his 'girlfriend'.

What would she be like? Which popular actress did she resemble? Or perhaps she could be compared to some beauty queen. If she didn't have some special quality, why would he choose her? Oh yes, he bought something alright, but it was a small packet. What was it that he had bought? You get curious. Look at the bike parked nearby. It was shining proudly under the sun. The colour was also very bright – like the yolk of an egg. The front portion was like two wings of a bird. It must be brand new. And why shouldn't it be? His father was a rich man. The bike must have cost a lot. Now the boy was walking towards the bike. His face looked a bit blurred from here. Only the writing on his black T-shirt was clearly visible – MY DAD IS ...

I AM SEXY

A girl was standing near the bike. She could be between fifteen and sixteen years. But her full figure made her look older. It was not difficult to guess that she too had been brought up in the lap of luxury. In the first blush of youth she looked like a butterfly in flight. She was wearing a narrow-cut pair of jeans that emphasized her legs. Her hips were rather full, hinting that she could have been eating a lot of fatty food. The jeans hugged them tightly. It seemed that if she moved too much, the foreign-brand trousers would burst at the seams. A sleeveless white shirt tried hard to cover her full breasts. The white of the shirt displayed some writing in black. The words moved here and there as if they were pebbles on top of hills but one could read them well nonetheless. Frankly, if you looked at the girl, the first thing that caught your eye would be the pointed breasts and then the large-sized words that would not escape your eyes –

I AM SEXY
IT'S A CRIME
PLEASE ARREST ME

Now the rich man's son got onto the bike. The girl was on the pillion seat. They waited at the petrol pump to fill the tank up to the full. There was enough space behind the girl to accommodate, if they wished, another person. And then they whisked off.

Where were they going? What was so urgent that the boy drove at such breakneck speed? The 'criminal' girl had been 'captured' by him. For them it must be an old game. Their bike left the outskirts of the city and now rode up the hilly road. The breeze made their shirts cling to their bodies and their words were in a playful mood – expanding, contracting with the wind; 'MY DAD ...' 'I AM ...' They did not stop at all. The cost of today's trip could perhaps manage the monthly food bill of an ordinary middle-class family. You wonder, does the rich father give his son this much pocket money every day? Suppose his father was not an ATM but rather had an empty powder tin where he kept his change? Could be, and most likely too. Even then he had to supply cash to his son who wore a T-shirt that made him seem filthy rich – because he was his son. Not unlikely. It was a possibility. And the girl, who herself announced to the world she was sexy, inviting arrest on that count, when she left her home in these clothes, didn't her parents object? Perhaps she didn't care; she might as well have sashayed out in her high heels as she left them staring after her. At what time of the night would she return home? Or did she stay in a hostel in the city? Perhaps her parents were hoping she would get high marks in the next exam and they would then invite some friends for a meal to celebrate.

It was difficult to guess. The only sure thing was that there were two shirts. One was hanging from a young man's body that carried the line, 'MY DAD IS AN ATM' and the other bore the enticing message, 'I AM ...

There was no ambiguity in these writings. It was as clear as the sun. One could see the words even from a distance.

A DAO TIED TO THE HALF-BROKEN BICYCLE

The corner where the half-broken bicycle was standing was rather dark. A dao, sharp enough to clear a jungle of bushes, was tied at its back. Often the streetlights of the suburban town did not work. Even today, two of them were off. Only the lights streaming from a shop a little further up helped illuminate this corner. This shop selling expensive motorbikes had come up recently. Now, the vehicles in the outlet shone under the bright lights. In the middle there was a red bike which kept rotating on a huge disc. When people walked by the showroom, they couldn't help stopping for a moment to admire the smart bike.

Inside, you could see a middle-aged man and a young man. The older man was wearing a faded white shirt, and a green-bordered *gamosa* was hanging from his neck. The young man was dressed in a pair of jeans and a T-shirt. The man was wearing a half-worn pair of flip-flops. The boy, however, was wearing Reebok sports shoes, obviously fake. Looking at the hands of the older man it was obvious that he was used to hard labour. The boy was busy with his mobile phone, which was also a knock-off, easily available in the market. Although from a distance, it looked 'genuine'. The man and the boy were talking with the salesman in the shop. Somehow, from a distance, the three men standing under the bright light looked like characters from a play. In a way, a scene was being staged there. Look, another character has joined the group. The new person was a professor at the local college. His name was Arnab Kalita. He had come to get a bike for himself. Actually, he had already made the necessary payment but at that time he could not get the blue-coloured bike he was looking for and so had to wait a couple of days. Today he had come to pick up the bike of his choice and in the process, he had become the fourth character in the play.

The elderly man and the young man had a tribal look. It was obvious that they belonged to the main tribal community of the area. Now, as earlier, the old man and his son were involved in an intense debate. The son had told his father that the bike would cost around 50,000 rupees. The father had agreed, though he could barely manage that amount. But now, the son had chosen one that cost 70,000 rupees. This was the reason father and son were having an argument. The conversation went like this:

Father (loudly): No, I won't pay a rupee beyond fifty thousand. I won't.

Son (less loudly but adamantly): You must. I'll buy that one and nothing else; it's my choice.

Father (ready to pounce on his son): Either you take the one you had chosen earlier or let's go!

Son: You'll have to buy me that one.

Father: I have given you 50,000 rupees by selling my land; now I only have 20,000 left.

Son: You'll have to buy me that one.

Father: Your mother has been diagnosed with a stone in her stomach, don't you know? I need this money to take her to the hospital in Guwahati.

Son: The old woman has been taking medicines here. Why do you want to take her to Guwahati?

Father: Why didn't you die at birth?

Thus the argument went on in one corner of the showroom. All the people present there – the employees, the owner who was sitting at the cash counter, the college professor who was sitting next to him – couldn't help looking at the father-son duo, though they were busy with their own matters. Suddenly the voices leapt to a crescendo. The son was looking furious; his eyes became unusually red. He was ready to plunge at his father. His father ran to stand near Professor Kalita. The other employees were now getting agitated too.

'What are you doing? Do you want to kill your father?' Kalita intervened, quite nervous now.

The eyes of the son were red and bulging. The boy who seemed to have just crossed his adolescence looked drunk. What kind of addiction was this? For a motorcycle? Was it possible that the hankering for a bike could overpower one's better senses? The boy seemed capable of doing anything; his whole posture announced that. Looking at his hardened eyes, those standing around the shop felt the hair on their napes stand up. The owner was now desperate to get rid of the father and son. People feared these sorts of young men like poisonous snakes or man-eating tigers. They had recently witnessed many incidents after all. The employees looked towards the owner for instructions. As soon as he gave the signal, they would try to throw the pair out. They inspected the boy's shirt surreptitiously. Was there a bulge underneath? They had lost some colleagues, who ended up blood-stained on the floor, who like them had tried to earn money honestly to manage two meals a day. But they saw that though the boy was almost attacking his father there was no weapon. Thank God!

Kalita recognized the boy. He was a class eleven student in the college where he taught. The professor was in charge of the college magazine this year. A few days ago, a group of students had held him hostage demanding that the magazine should carry more pages written in a particular language, and that it should feature those sections first. They were very rough in their behaviour. This boy was also part of the gang. He stood behind the leaders without saying anything. During class one day he had a heated exchange with him. The boy was busy with his mobile phone and Kalita had asked him to stand up, scolded him for not paying attention and instructed him to walk out of the classroom if he was not interested in the lecture. Last week, when the terminal exam was on, he saw a page from a cheap 'help' book slyly pushed in. Ninety per cent of the students in the college were like him; he was not an exception.

Kalita now approached him, held his hand, and said, 'Are you going to leave your father alone or not?'

'*Bhag hiyache*! Get out!' the owner too gathered courage from the professor's intervention. 'Get out of the shop! If you want to buy the bike, do it, or get the hell out of here! Don't try to show off your gangster tactics here!'

The employees now encircled the boy. They found that the father was taking out a bundle of notes from a gamosa tied around his waist. The son walked like a hero and paid 70,000 rupees for the bike he was bent on buying. He finished the paperwork and then drove away on his brand-new bike. All this time the father sat in a corner looking devastated. Even after his son left the place, he sat like this, beaten.

Professor Kalita approached him. The owner sent one of his employees to bring some tea and sweets for the old man and a glass of water. The man seemed to recover a little.

'Why did you give him the money? Why does he need such an expensive bike at this age?' Kalita asked, still angry with the boy.

The question was on the minds of the others too.

Now the man stood up. He went outside and came back pushing a bicycle. The rusty cycle had a long dao used for clearing undergrowth in a jungle tied to it. It looked very sharp.

He sat down on the floor again. It looked as if he was really crying. 'He would have cut me up if I didn't. He was the one who had tied it to the cycle while we were coming here. Had I not given him the money, he would have murdered me.'

He looked up now and addressed the people who were standing around him, shocked, and said, 'I didn't want to sell the plot of land. But he tied me to the cot for two days, and one day even to the areca nut tree because I had refused.'

Now he was weeping profusely, 'He will cut me up, he will do it, I assure you. He can do anything.'

His face contorted with pain. 'If I die who will look after my ailing wife? My two daughters will die of hunger, or he will kill them.'

The dao shone under the bright lights of the shop.

The man got up slowly. He pushed the bicycle with the dao and slowly went out of the shop. Outside, the darkness of the evening soon hid him from view.

I'M NOT SELFISH BUT I WANT EVERYTHING

The girl who was wearing a kurta with these words emblazoned on it in uppercase was tall but a little thin. She was fair with eyes dark and wide. At first glance, the girl looked quiet and well-mannered but if you looked a little more closely, you could see that her eyes reflected some innate restlessness. The kurta she was wearing was rather old; it was worn over tight flower-printed trousers and tied at the knee. She was lying on her bed in her room. On one wall of the room were pasted a variety of cards. On the rack next to her bed was a row of soft toys. She had received all these items and the cards from Shivaji Chaliha. Who knows why his parents named him Shivaji? Now that name had disappeared under the abbreviated Shiju. It would be difficult to know how a name like Shivaji turned into Shiju. Anyway, he was the one who had given her all these expensive gifts. Around the neck of a teddy bear hung a necklace, a monkey's arm was adorned by a bangle, the rabbit had a pretty nose-ring. She had received all these presents while spending time with Shiju on moonlit nights in a star hotel while a soft melody played in the background. Shiju, however, did not have any earnings of his own. He received a fat amount of pocket money from his parents. His father was a powerful politician and rolling in moolah. So it was natural that being his son, Shiju could afford to give his girlfriend costly presents which were now proudly displayed in her room.

The girlfriend's name was Jonaki Saikia – she was her parents' only daughter. She too has discarded her beautiful name, meaning firefly, to Jiki. Everybody in her circle, including Shiju, called her by that name. Snehalata Saikia, mother of Jiki, was a school teacher. Her father worked in a bank. They had studied together in the university and become friends. They have been married since and been together for the last twenty years.

When Snehalata was pregnant, both of them wanted a girl. Every day when she lit the earthen lamp in the prayer room, she requested, 'Please, God, let me have a daughter.' The couple had even decided on the name for the unborn child. They were very happy when she arrived. The child gave a lot of trouble during meals. The mother had to gather around playthings to coax her to eat. Her hair was dark like the wings of a crow. Her parents did not allow her hair to be cut and so, even at the age of three her hair was long and flowed down to her waist. Her mother tied it with a ribbon and also adorned it with colourful clips. They bought dresses in various colours and prints for her. Her father wrote down meticulously in an exercise book all the dates she did something new for the first time.

It was a Friday when her mother Snehalata discovered the strips of birth control pills in her room. She was not well that day and had taken leave from work. Already her daughter was boldly going on 'dates' with Shiju in his red car. She had cut her night-black hair into layers. Her hair highlighted in Muga-brown streaks fell on her forehead, and tapered to a lighter tone at the back. By the time she alighted from the red car in her newly acquired hairstyle, it was quite late. The company's name on the car shone under the streetlight.

Snehalata was waiting at the gate. The long, stylish car stopped a little way ahead. Jonaki's father was not at home; he had gone out to get something from the shop. But Snehalata knew that he was out looking for his daughter. The number plate of the car bore the signature 'JIKI'. The logo on the car announced it was a Volkswagen. The parents had often passed by the showroom on the way to their offices. That corner used to be a *kasuoni* full of long yam plants that thrive in watery soil. During the rainy season the water drained out to the low-lying area. The leaves of the yam plants remained almost submerged during this period, but the road remained unhindered even during the heaviest monsoon. Without anyone noticing, the kasuoni disappeared one day. In its place came up a field; on one side a little hillock was also built. Tamarind trees and flowers made the mound green. A glass-covered house came up on the hillock. The place was brightly lit up. Within a short time a lawn and a flower garden also came up there. Under that glass-covered shade entered a horde of cars. People looked, astounded, at the models, at their colours, their smart appearances. The imported cars changed the look of the locality. The shops and business outlets around the area were compelled to change their facades too and painted them in bright colours to keep up with their new neighbour. The banks were giving loans generously; people had more money too. Sales figures of the Volkswagen cars soared thanks to plenty of ready customers.

The car which dropped off Jiki at ten minutes to ten was one of those. As she got down from the red car, her mother looked at her hair in surprise. In her western clothes and newly dyed hair, she looked like a girl from the country where this car was manufactured. She did not say anything to her daughter, who said nothing to her either, except informing her, 'I've already eaten.' Then the girl went to her room and locked the door. Her mother could smell fermented grape juice as her daughter passed her by. That day, her parents spent the whole night sitting on the verandah. They did not speak a single word. It was dark so they did not see each other's tears, or pretended not to. They sat in the same position until dawn broke. Next day Jonaki, or Jiki, got up from her bed at eleven in the morning.

Jiki went to college but she spent most of her time outside the college premises. When she used to return around five or six in the evening her parents were happy; they could have dinner together, though these days she seemed disinterested in the home-cooked food. They assumed that she had eaten in some restaurant before heading home. Even while at home, she mostly spent her time in her room with the door firmly shut. When she emerged from the room she always carried her expensive crimson-coloured cell phone, obviously of foreign make, in her hand. Her mother knew that it was not the one her father had bought for her.

Meanwhile, Jiki's room was getting crowded with more and more gifts. Her mother observed everything but pretended not to. Frankly, she and her husband could not recognize the girl with gold-streaked hair in those outlandish clothes. The house slowly fell into a kind of impenetrable silence. The only sounds that broke this silence were the ringtones of Jiki's mobile phone, the songs played on the computer and the tinkling of the ankle bells she had started wearing of late. Looking at her anklets her mother recalled an incident. When her daughter was thirteen, and she was still known as Jonaki, she had asked for a pair of anklets. Snehalata had objected, telling her that they symbolized slavery. She had narrated the story of the women in the harem of Mughal kings who wore them; her father had told the story of how Taslima Nasreen's father had broken her bangles with a stone, and uttered those famous words: 'Become a human being, a real human being, and leave these behind.' Jonaki sat with a dark face wrought with unhappiness for a long time.

Snehalata was a bit curious, though it could be considered unseemly by certain people, but Jonaki was her daughter. She wondered whom this girl talked to for hours, when she did not like to exchange even a sentence with any of her relatives. Who gave her so much time? Shiju? The boy who was the son of the stinking rich politician? One day, she and her daughter entered the bathroom at the same time. There was only a thin wall between the two bathrooms, a clear sign that it was an attempt to save on the loan money borrowed for the construction. As usual, her daughter carried her mobile to the bathroom. Sometimes she spent more than an hour there. The room was full of all kinds of body care products. Snehalata was getting used to it now. She could hear her daughter crying, after which she swore at someone viciously as jealousy coloured her words. Apparently, Shiju had gone somewhere with one Rithika for company. Snehalata finished her shower quickly and came out of the bathroom. For the next two days, her daughter barely emerged from her room.

After a week, the red Volkswagen came to stop at their gate again. The road in front of their house was newly built but rather narrow. Shiju's huge car blocked half the way and created problems for the pedestrians. Shiju showed his displeasure openly at the inconvenience and parked his car in the playground of the high school a little distance away. It was a Sunday. Snehalata had cooked a few of her daughter's favourite dishes. When Shiju arrived she led him to her daughter's room. Soon she could hear hysterical crying from behind the door and a male voice trying to appease her. After that, there was a long silence. Then Jiki came out of her room, her golden hair open, and ready to leave with Shiju. She introduced him to Snehalata. Snehalata looked at him. Golden hair, light brown eyes, fair, almost six-feet tall, a body obviously toned at the gym and nurtured in a home with all the luxuries. He was wearing a blood red T-shirt on which was written in black: M D KING OF KINGS. Next to it was inscribed a crown in a deep golden colour. The 'king of kings' soon led her daughter to the red car. Somehow Snehalata was reminded of the snow-white tiger she had seen at the zoo. Handsome, but very dangerous.

A few days later, Friday came, a day when the silence was broken into smithereens, when the smoky volcano spewed fumes up to the sky. Snehalata had taken that day off too as she was not feeling well. Husband and wife were now suffering from high blood pressure. There was no one at home. She entered her daughter's room. The maid had said that she smelt something like a dead rat there. How could her daughter stay nonchalantly with such a bad odour in the room? Perhaps she was not even aware of it. So Snehalata went in with a broom to inspect. She found that the smell was coming from a dead lizard pressed to the door hinge. Then she thought of making her daughter's bed. Under the mattress she found a polythene packet with strips of a tablet. She then searched the room from corner to corner. The used strips were in another packet in the wastepaper basket. She also found used tubes of a gel meant for enhancing one's breasts. The packets bore the picture of a bare-breasted girl with golden hair and blue eyes. The tubes were also tied together.

Snehalata sat immobile with the packet of tablets in her hand. Biman Saikia looked surprised when he found his wife sitting still, as if she was in a trance. She looked extremely stricken.

Snehalata confronted her daughter even before she could enter her room. Fanning out the strips of tablets in front of Jonaki's eyes, she demanded, 'What does this mean?'

Jiki answered without batting an eyelid, 'Simple, I have physical relations with Shij.'

'Where have you come from now? Where did you go with that nincompoop? What have you been doing during the day?' Snehalata had lost her poise to extreme anger.

Jiki seemed even more defiant as she answered, 'I was at the Taj. His father has given that hotel to him. We have a room there.'

'Why have you become this way? You are Kuntibala Chaliha's granddaughter ...'

'Please stop it! I have heard enough of these meaningless words. My great-grandmother was the first woman graduate from the undivided Darrang district, my mom had a first-class career which she sacrificed for her daughter. Why didn't you pursue your career? Who asked you to take up a teacher's job so that you didn't have to send me to school alone? Who asked you? Me?'

With each word Jonaki uttered, her golden-coloured hair danced, her breath smelt of drinks.

Snehalata slapped her hard and shouted, 'You wastrel! Why didn't you die at the time of your birth?'

Snehalata became hysterical and went towards her husband who seemed to be rooted to his chair. Saikia felt his head reeling; he was picturing his colleague Niranjan Sharma's half-paralyzed body after the stroke. Everything around him seemed to move in circles. He held on to the chair forcefully.

His wife was asking him as if she was possessed, 'Tell me, tell me, why has our daughter become like this? Where have we made a mistake?' Her voice was unrecognizable, dry like a half-burnt piece of wood.

Snehalata asked her daughter again, 'Don't you feel ashamed that you have allowed your body to be used like this? Aren't you scared at all?'

'Your moral sense had made me almost frigid. Do you hear me? I was on the verge of frigidity. I had almost lost Shij. You know, every girl is crazy about him. Rithika was simply aggressive. At any cost I want Shij to be mine, only mine.'

She was speaking to her parents in a language from beyond the seas. It seemed like burning cinders. She was walking to her room now.

Snehalata was crying, 'Ma, O Ma! Look at your granddaughter! Look how the devil has taken over her senses. This devil is going to bury her alive.'

'Shij is an angel!' Jiki shouted.

Now her father got up from the chair and told his daughter, 'Please go away with your angel and let us live in peace.'

'I will go, certainly. What have you given me? I got everything from Shij. I hate you people and your hollow idealism.' Her steps were unsteady as she entered her room.

One morning, Jonaki informed her parents that both she and Shiju had decided to go to Cleveland to study hotel management. On returning, they planned to turn their Taj into a world-class hotel.

Snehalata became increasingly agitated. Her health started deteriorating and she was constantly in a foul mood. She had dark circles under her eyes due to sleepless nights. Her blood pressure shot up day by day. Her limbs trembled involuntarily all the time. Her colleagues almost forced her to take time off for a month. They advised her to go for a thorough check-up at a good medical institution outside the state.

Biman Saikia tried. He took her to a lodge in a forest for a few days. But even there, they discussed their daughter all the time. He held her hand when he led her to the cool portico encircled by a lattice net. They spent their nights wide awake, unable to sleep. Snehalata's throat and lips were parched all the time. Her husband brought glasses of water and fruit juice; she drank them and tried to listen as he spoke calmly. He was not a garrulous person but that day he talked for hours.

'Try to understand. Face the situation. By trying to run away from the truth, you are only torturing yourself.'

'From what am I trying to run away?'

'From changing times. When we were in college we were always together, isn't it?'

'Yes.'

'You didn't even like me to hold your hand. That was due to your upbringing. It was rooted in the cultural and social values you inherited from your grandmother Kuntibala Chaliha – a school headmistress. But if it were a western country and you behaved the same way, the relationship between a boy and a girl wouldn't have lasted. Yet I myself didn't think of you as unusual.'

'He thought my daughter was, though,' Snehalata said slowly.

'Time has changed, whether we like it or not. When you were young, we could count on our fingers the number of cars in town, which is now a city. Could you think then that these foreign cars would be common in our city today?'

'His car, the big red car, with her name on it.' Snehalata's tearful words trailed off.

'Not only the cars, many other things have arrived – like a floodgate opened. Who can block its flow?' His voice was trembling as if portending a disaster.

'The colour of their hair has also changed. Everything has changed.'

'What will you gain by thinking about it? When you are ill, who will look after you? Your parents are being cared for by your brother, my own parents are with my younger brother in the village. Do you know why he stuck to the low-paying job?'

'Nobody has to look after me. I'll stay in an old home, but my daughter ... my dear daughter, my Majoni ...' Snehalata started weeping. 'I understand everything, but she ... my Majoni ...' she trailed off, wiping her tears as she looked at her husband. He seemed to have grown old suddenly within the last few days.

'Can't we go to their house? Before they go, if not a wedding at least if we could have an engagement ...'

Biman Saikia stood up. He seemed very angry now, 'That's why you women have remained women.'

'Yes, I am a woman, and I am a mother. Isn't she also a part of you?'

Her husband got angrier and said, 'Listen well! Your tradition, your family, culture – nothing can hold her back. Let her live her own life and let me live mine too.'

'But is that a life? The life she has chosen? I don't want to give my daughter's hand to that dacoit. He has chosen her, but I haven't chosen him. He has ensnared her somehow. You are her father. Can't you take her away from his clutches?'

'When birds learn to fly, they go away from the nest. She is also getting ready to fly away. You can't keep a bird that has learnt to fly shielded in a nest.'

'But all the girls are not like her. Why has our Majoni become this way? Why has she let herself be devoured by the white tiger? He is eating her alive.' Snehalata leaned back on her chair and started weeping again. 'He'll leave her one day, I tell you.'

'This is not the verandah of our home. Let's go to the room.'

Other guests at the lodge were looking at them now, albeit furtively. A few even showed displeasure. The night became darker.

As Snehalata lay on the bed, Saikia tenderly spread a sheet over her thin body and said softly, 'Before she leaves I will hand over all that I had saved for her education and marriage. This will be my last duty as a father to her but after that, never ever mention her name to me.'

Now he cried, silently; only his contorted face was witness to his pain.

This time, Shivaji, Shij or Shiju did not make the mistake of driving into the narrow gully to reach Jiki's house. He sent the driver to collect her luggage. However, he came to the gate where Snehalata and Biman Saikia were waiting. Jiki did not try to touch her parents' feet by way of farewell. The tight pair of jeans impaired her movement. One could not see her eyes; they were hidden behind a huge pair of Ray-Ban shades. She looked very happy and excited. The boy joined his hands in a namaskar to them. He was wearing a banana-leaf green T-shirt over a pair of blue jeans. The words emblazoned on it in bright yellow were easy to read, even from a distance:

EVERY GIRL IS
ICE AND SUGAR
BUT MY GIRL IS
ICE AND VODKA

Snehalata and Biman Saikia stood at the gate until the car disappeared from sight. Then Saikia brought out his car from the garage, small enough to drive through the narrow road. Its colour was white, his daughter's choice. But later, when she became Jiki of the golden hair, she felt ashamed to ride in this small car. He asked his wife to get into the car and locked the door of the house and the garage. Snehalata was surprised to see that on the backseat there was a huge basket full of fruits, sweets and packs of biscuits.

'Where are we going? What are these?' she asked.

By now the small car was on the main road.

'My daughter has gone away today … and you are going for a picnic?' her voice broke in sorrow. These days, Snehalata spoke in this voice all the time. When Jonaki was a little girl they used to go out like this on holidays with a picnic basket.

'Get out of your comfort zone; people don't live only with their own concerns. Do you remember something?' her husband said.

'What?'

'When Majoni was quite young, one day there was a huge storm. There were many big trees where we used to live.'

'Yes, many branches of the trees broke. There were quite a few bird nests too that fell down in our courtyard. Jonaki and I picked up the half-dead, disoriented birds and looked after them. We had managed to save the parrot chicks and then one day set them free. Majoni was happy to see them fly away but sad too.'

These days Snehalata suffered from this preoccupation. If she recalled some incident from the days when her Jonaki was young and happy with them, she did not stop and went on talking.

'I am trying to talk about the birds who fell down with their nests that day,' Saikia said.

'Do you want to go to the orphanage? When Jonaki was young we used to go there with sweets for the children on her birthday. She loved feeding them. She had even taught them a song once ...'

Saikia stopped the car on one side of the road and said to Snehalata, 'Please move to the backseat now. This patch of the road is rather rough. The items in the basket will get dislodged.'

She did as told and held the basket tightly.

'From now on, we will come here every Sunday. There are lots of things to be done for the children here but only a few hands.'

Saikia drove carefully. Snehalata held on to the basket with extreme care.

A Warm Jacket for the Son

The house stands in the middle of a big compound. It is constructed in the style of the old Assam houses. The tin roof has now turned reddish with rust; the woodwork is infested with termites; a few glass windows are broken and pages of newspapers have been used to cover the gaps and ward off the draught. Sadly, the effort to cover up the naked frames has not succeeded, and the paper leaves have been hanging like the broken wings of birds. The plot in front of the verandah is edged by a half-broken bamboo fence.

Once upon a time there was a flower garden here. A few bald hibiscus flower trees, a couple of thin-stalked rose plants without leaves, a dwarfish tree that bears the aromatic *tagar* flower, and a few half-dead trees without leaves which are unidentifiable, announce lamely that at some time in the past, there used to be a flower garden here. Only the *tarua kadam* tree, with small flowers that look like yellow cottonwool balls spreading its thorny branches all over the place, proudly indicates that, yes, there used to be a beautiful garden here. The kitchen garden in the backyard and the pitiable flower garden also seem to suggest the presence of goats, the voracious eaters. Except for the thorny plants too difficult to negotiate, every other plant has been under attack.

You are right. You can now see a flock of goats munching on the leaves and stalks. The smell of their dung, small rounded balls in black, and urine overwhelm the nose immediately.

Even a cursory glance at the house and the compound would tell you that the goats have been reared to offer some relief to the economic condition of the household. To the west of the house, under a tin shade, a pile of firewood can be seen. Next to it is a weighing scale. The morning sun falls over the plants, or rather the stalks that the greedy goats have turned them into. With their woebegone leaves the plants look quite lonely. Just like the dried trees gasping at the onslaught of the goats, a couple of emaciated children, a woman and a man resembling them – their parents, most likely – stand around the pile of firewood. These people live in a slum at a little distance. They come in the morning to this house in Ananda Nagar, a locality for the rich and sophisticated, to buy firewood. They cannot afford kerosene or cooking gas; the jungles around town from where they could have collected firewood have also disappeared.

The neighbours are not very happy that these people from the fringes of the town visit their locality. Who knows what kind of people they are? They could steal anything if they got the chance, though until now nothing has happened. Although two expensive cars and a motorcycle have been stolen from the neighbourhood, the privileged people of the area have not accused the slum-dwellers openly yet. So despite facing some hostility, these people have been coming to the house of 'Goat Saikia'.

This is a nickname the people have secretly bestowed on the present householder, Hemanta Saikia, the only son of late Alok Saikia, who was the head clerk at the Jamunamukh Tea Estate, and his wife Kuntibala Saikia. Actually, he does not seem to fit the moniker with his smart get-up, but he got it anyway due to the flock of goats his wife has been tending at home. The name Goat Saikia, however, is uttered only in whispers. After all, it is a cultured, sophisticated locality. Most of the people here are deemed to be successful in life. There is a certain sense of pity, of disdain and ridicule attached to this name they have bestowed on him. His father had built this big house during his lifetime on a plot of four *kathas* in this rather upmarket place. In the morning when Hemanta or Goat Saikia goes out, well-dressed and handsome, for an adda at the tea stall on the *chari-ali*, people comment unkindly behind his back. There is a reason for this too.

Hemanta Saikia is known for his tall talk. He behaves as if he is above the hoi polloi. One day, while he was at the tea stall, its owner Sujit Biswas had mentioned the rusted tin roof of the Saikia house and suggested, 'Saikia, why don't you paint the roof?' Frankly, there was a hidden agenda behind the clever businessman's jab. His son had just become a franchisee of a leading paint company and opened a big showroom. He also took orders for painting houses. But Hemanta Saikia, in his usual bombastic style, replied, 'Oh, why should I waste money on painting the rusted roof? I am thinking of building a new house after demolishing this one built by the old man.' Then he went on jabbering about a list of things he intended to invest in – tiles, marble, running water, going as far as geysers and air conditioners. Meanwhile, his wife somehow manages to run the household and pay the children's school fees by rearing the flock of goats, stitching clothes, knitting sweaters for people and selling firewood.

Today also you could see his wife busy with the chores. She opened the corral gate for the goats, then swept the courtyard, and was now carrying buckets of water from the other side of the road. His mother, Kuntibala Saikia, was taking care of the customers who had arrived to buy firewood. Who else would do it anyway? It was still midnight for her precious son Hemanta Saikia. He usually got up late. She was around seventy; perhaps you could add even a few more years to her age. She has been suffering from a strange illness for some time. Every six to seven months, her blood becomes putrid as if it was poisoned. Her hands and feet swell, even the eyelids become heavy with the swelling. Once the body receives fresh blood transfusion, she recovers and continues well for the next six months or so. It has been seven or perhaps eight months since the last transfusion.

Kuntibala noticed in the morning that her ankles showed signs of swelling again. Still she stood near the weighing scale to keep an eye. None of the customers could afford to buy more than a day's need. But she depended on them to keep the business going. In the past she often received big orders when there was a community feast or some other celebration. Those days were gone now; everything was done with gas cylinders these days.

Kuntibala had started the business herself, almost by chance. At that time her son was sitting around the house looking for a job after finishing his graduation. It all started almost innocuously. The *koroi* tree in a corner of the compound had fallen due to the onslaught of a storm one day. She borrowed money from her younger daughter and employed a labourer to cut down the tree into small logs. There was some feast in the *basti* at that time. Someone saw the pile of wood drying in the sun and asked for some. The next day, a few others from the slum came asking for wood too. Even after the pile was finished people kept on coming, looking for firewood. This gave Kuntibala an idea. She started buying firewood from a wholesaler and then sold it at a profit. That was the beginning.

Her son did not approve; he felt ashamed and showed his displeasure. But Kuntibala did not listen. How long could she ask her married daughters for money? There was a time when she was used to a comfortable life as the wife of the head clerk in the tea garden. What was the use of thinking about it now? She was also quite upset to see the plight of her son. Her heart sank as she looked at him. Such a handsome boy, so presentable, yet he could not manage to get a job. An officer's job would suit him perfectly, she often thought. She had not kept track of how his elder sisters, her four daughters, passed the exams and promptly got jobs. She was too busy looking after her son who had arrived after a long wait. Her husband, by this time, had retired but he kept up the same lavish lifestyle, cutting into his savings. Kuntibala's days revolved around her son. What a beautiful child he was! When she went out with him for a walk, people asked, 'What do you feed him?' Immediately after his birth the nurse had said, 'Baidew, look! Your son has come with white talcum powder smeared on his face. So fair!' True, looking at him Kuntibala felt inordinately happy.

To tell you the truth, Kuntibala did not have to carry on with her firewood business anymore. Her four daughters sent money to her regularly. Her daughter-in-law was very hard-working. She managed a lot – looking after the goats, chickens and ducks, stitching clothes, knitting woollens and so on – to contribute to the household expenses. The house was already there; there were enough kitchen utensils, mattresses, and all the things needed to run a house. If her son could earn something that would have been enough. The sisters did not trust him with any responsibility, neither did his mother. He was unemployed – what could he do anyway? So even with her ageing body, Kuntibala continued supervising the firewood business. Just for her son. If he needed something, he approached her. When he came to her like this, his head bowed, asking for money, Kuntibala felt as if her heart would break.

Ah, when his father was alive, how he fulfilled his son's every need. A son after four daughters – what a joy it was for him! When the boy was born, as per custom, he generously distributed fish in the neighbourhood. But now his father was gone. Who else could her son approach, Kuntibala reasoned. If he asked his sisters they would grumble, no doubt. And his brothers-in-law – their husbands? Useless, lazy, good-for-nothing, sly, wicked – all these adjectives were readily used when they talked about him. When she heard these words, Kuntibala felt a pain shooting up her chest. Was he so bad, really? He didn't drink, didn't take drugs, he didn't have a girlfriend, he married the girl his mother had chosen for him. Why did people utter derogatory comments about him? So he was not a doctor or engineer, so what? *All of you are established in your professions, why couldn't you manage a job for him? All of you girls are well-to-do; you have your own house, own cars,* she thought. When she remembered their households, her old anger surfaced from time to time. These days they did not send the money in his name either; they sent it to her daughter-in-law.

Kuntibala finished selling the first lot of firewood. These days, she found it difficult to sell even that much, and had to wait the whole day looking out for customers. Sometimes, however, three to four lots were sold off, enabling her to fulfil her son's wants. She looked at her daughter-in-law carrying water in buckets and felt sorry for her. There was no running water in the house. The woman had to work so hard. Earlier, she helped her with the household chores but since the illness took over, she has not been able to do so. Sometimes she thought it would be better if she died. But when her son came to her and requested hesitantly, 'Ma, do you have some money? All my shirts are old and torn,' she felt that she should live a little longer. Who would give her dear son money to buy shirts when she was not there? If he asked his wife she would only lose her temper.

Kuntibala grumbled silently. Her anger at everybody – her daughter-in-law, her daughters, their husbands, was swelling by the day. She almost said aloud, 'I am here, his mother. They better not forget.' She felt as if her body was being invaded by mustard seeds in hot oil. The sons-in-law were such influential people, yet they couldn't help their only brother-in-law find a job. And the daughters, what did they give him? True, they sent some money at the end of the month to her daughter-in-law to help run the household. It was like throwing the skin of the banana after eating the fruit. Did they think of investing some money to open a hotel in their dear brother's name? He was brought up with such care, how could he sell rice and curry in an ordinary restaurant patronized by common people? No, they did not think about it. True, there was a burglary at the cosmetics stall he had in his name. But was it his fault? Should he have been sleeping on a mattress in the shop? Let them do it for their own children and husband, let them sleep on mattresses in the shops if they liked, but not her son. Never!

By the time Kuntibala finished selling firewood for the day she realized that her old health problem had made an appearance again. This time she had fortunately kept well for eight to nine months. She put the money aside. Then she asked her daughter-in-law, who had just returned after selling off two goats, in a quarrelsome tone, 'My daughters send money every month, you also get money by selling the goats, yet I have to wear this tattered sador. Why?' Her daughter-in-law looked at her and wondered where she had got this visibly worn-out sador? She knew her mother-in-law had a boxful of clothes sent by her daughters. She also bought her clothes with her limited income. After all, despite her ill health she helped around the house. For this she was grateful to her mother-in-law. The old woman also took care of the demands of her good-for-nothing, pompous husband.

When he went out wearing pure white pajamas like the wings of a crane, a kurta with Lucknow-style *chikan* work and a pair of Kolhapuri sandals, she knew immediately that he had coaxed some money out of his mother. A few days back the old woman's sister had come on a visit. Her mother-in-law had held her sister's hand and cried copiously, requesting her help in arranging a job for her son. Kuntibala seemed to be more concerned about her son than her own health. Her sister promised to try and left a good sum of money with her. This new kurta-pajama was financed by some of that money, she surmised.

In the past, people in the family took Kuntibala's request seriously, but nowadays they only became irritated. In effect, doing something for Kuntibala's son meant getting blamed. Her sister's husband had arranged a job for Hemanta as a company representative in a hilly area. Hemanta had returned home within a month, saying he was suffering from fever. Kuntibala blamed her brother-in-law for a long time, even in front of others. How could he send Hemanta to a jungle to earn money? Thank God he had come home in time. The husband of one of Hemanta's sisters had also tried and with his influence got Hemanta recruited in the sales department of a company. When Hemanta was on an official tour in a small town, a terrorist was gunned down in the hotel where he had been staying. The police had ordered the hotel to be evacuated. Hemanta left on the night bus to reach home the very next day. He was in such shock that he could not even talk much. He was married by that time.

In front of his wife and mother, the strong-looking man was trembling like a banana leaf in the breeze; his temperature shot up and his face became unusually red. It took some time for him to recover. He then described in a trembling voice how the body of the extremist was lying in the room next to his and how the policemen had dragged it out. He also revealed that every person in the hotel was interrogated by the police. He announced that he was not going to continue in a job that involved touring and staying at different hotels. His wife had tried to reason: this kind of incident was not going to happen every day and that he should not take a hasty decision. After all, the job was quite well-paying.

Kuntibala had reprimanded her daughter-in-law in no uncertain terms. So she wanted only money? Didn't she worry that she might become a widow in the process? Kuntibala put a handkerchief soaked in cold water on Hemanta's forehead and brought warm water to wash his feet. In between she muttered words of support for her son. No, Hemanta should not continue with this type of a job. She even burst into tears, saying that if her husband were alive, would he have sent her son on such a mission? Never! She even complained about her second son-in-law, who had arranged this job, in front of relatives. Thanks to the gossip, the words reached him soon. He heard that Kuntibala even said that he had arranged this job for Hemanta out of jealousy. Otherwise why didn't he let his own brother take up this particular job? No wonder that these days nobody offered to help Kuntibala's son. They would rather help with some money so that the household could run.

Presently, Kuntibala's daughter-in-law asked her to have a cup of milk mixed with water and two biscuits. The old woman jumped up in anger, 'What are you giving me? When I was in the garden I used to wash my hands with milk. Oh, what fate! At my age I can't even have a piece of fish or a cup of real milk.'

She kept on lamenting her fate. Perhaps she was crying too. Her daughter-in-law looked at her from a distance. God knows what took over the old woman from time to time. True, she could not afford the milk without adding water, but at least she had fish on her plate every day. Who cared that the bedsheets were worn out and needed changing, or that the old curtains hung desolately? The son had to have fish for lunch and dinner. This was the only job, that is, going to the bazaar to buy fish, which Hemanta did eagerly. Her mother-in-law always gave money to her son made from the firewood business so he could buy fish. When he returned from the bazaar Kuntibala herself cleaned the fish and she almost always cooked the curry too. For the last few days she had not entered the kitchen, though. Her heels had started swelling up and now the swelling had even crept up her ankles. The daughter-in-law did not say anything and went about her chores. When Kuntibala was ill, only a stupid person would argue with her. Let her say what she wanted, how long would she live anyway, thought the daughter-in-law.

Kuntibala had started the day complaining about an old sador and now she seemed determined to continue, spreading out the tattered piece of cloth as the day progressed. The grievance about the morning cup of milk was done with; now she began with the bathroom. As she carried a bucket of water from the hand-pump, she looked like she would fall down at any moment. As she went to the bathroom, she continued to spew vile words against the world at large, 'Hei, is this what I have lived to see? Is this a bathroom? We don't have your kind of bathroom with marble floors. You jab at the switch and lo! there comes out either cold water or hot water. Okay, we don't want your kind of bathroom but at least arrange to have a tap. But who will do it? Who cares? Is this a house? It's a pigsty. People don't live here, only pigs and cows do.' Her daughter-in-law knew that all these abuses were aimed at her daughters, their husbands, brothers and sisters, sisters-in-law, brothers-in-law, and so on, but now she too was losing her temper. She had believed she was marrying into a well-to-do household whose head was working for a big company. But now look at how much she had to toil! Did her father or her brothers bother about her state of affairs? And on top of everything, this old woman was at her throat for no fault of hers. Her patience from the morning disappeared and her temper gathered heat like the midday sun as she said, 'Who asked you to carry the bucket? Your maidservant is here, don't worry – I filled a bucket in the morning and have kept it in the bathroom. Go have your bath!'

Presently, the old woman started sweeping the bathroom with a broom made of dry coconut leaves, her arm supporting her waist. Now her daughter-in-law really blew up. She shouted, 'Have you lost your senses? Why do you behave like a child? Don't you remember you broke your waist while sweeping the bathroom floor? How much trouble you had given to everybody! If you don't want to have your bath in this bathroom, why don't you go to your daughter's place?'

It seemed that the old woman was waiting to hear these words. She came out of the bathroom and created a ruckus. 'Of course, I'll go! Why shouldn't I? I'll go a hundred times! They are my own children too. I'll definitely go by tomorrow.'

Spent, she entered the bathroom to have her shower. From the bathroom window she picked up leaves from the *bhedailata* creeper climbing the bamboo fence next to it. When her daughter-in-law went to have her bath, she ground some ginger and garlic and added them to the chopped leaves. She then dipped them in a mixture of *pithaguri* rice powder and fried them into a few savoury chops. When her daughter-in-law came to the kitchen she found her breakfast was laid out and in a corner of the plate were a few crunchy bhedailata cutlets. She could feel tears moistening the corners of her eyes. She recalled how one day she had mentioned that she loved this kind of cutlet. From then on, whenever she could, the old woman fried them for her. Like today, even though her legs were swelling up and she found it difficult to sit down.

'Why do you bother?' the daughter-in-law said softly as she bit into the snack. Yes, one had to admit, there was something special about her mother-in-law's cooking. Whatever she made had a special taste.

'Why do you say that, my dear? There was a time when I cooked so many dishes, entertained so many people for lunch and dinner. Now for my own daughter-in-law ...' Kuntibala's voice broke with unshed tears. How could she be angry with her mother-in-law? She saw that she found it difficult to get up. Leaning on her daughter-in-law, she walked slowly towards her bedroom. She opened her big box. She emptied it of all its items. She folded a mekhela, two sadors and a few other things and packed them in the box. She knew that in the evening one or two of her daughters would call. They did so every day. So by evening all of them would come to know about their mother flying off the handle in the morning, the swelling of her feet, and the rest of it.

Kuntibala was limping now. Despite her condition she had finished selling the firewood. Yesterday her son had asked for money to buy a new pair of sandals. Yes, he needed them badly, she agreed. In this hot season how could he go around wearing shoes and socks? In her mind's eye, she could picture her son wearing the new pair of sandals. His feet were pinkish and soft, like a woman's. No, even women seldom had such soft feet. Look at her daughter-in-law's, or even hers, with the heels rough and strips of lesions running across them. She heard that men with such lotus-like pink heels were lucky. The old woman felt her chest heave with an old sadness again. *What does my son have, tell me! Nothing. He doesn't have a motorcycle to go around, or good clothes to wear.* She wanted so much to buy a warm jacket for her son, like the ones her sons-in-law and grandsons wore. He would look so handsome if he had one. She sighed. She wanted to do so many things for him!

At these moments, she remembered her husband and felt her anger rising again. What did he do when he was alive? He enjoyed good food and feeding his guests. What did he do for her son? When he was alive the land price was low. Couldn't he have bought a plot near the road and constructed a row of shops for renting purposes? Look at Hari Mandal's son; his father had wisely invested and now with the rent from the shops the son was enjoying life to the hilt. The image of Hari Mandal's son wearing a nice jacket and riding a red motorcycle floated into her mind.

She saw that her daughter-in-law and granddaughter were carrying water in buckets from the tap on the other side of the road. Her granddaughter took after her mother; she had not inherited her father's good looks. Her nature was also like her mother's; she did not talk much and went on with her chores silently. She would soon start menstruating – Kuntibala knew how old she was. But she looked as thin as ever, with no sign of a maturing body. As usual, as she looked at the thin girl Kuntibala felt a bit crestfallen. Then she looked at her daughter-in-law. By now she should have called one of her daughters. Which one of them would invite her to stay with her? Last time she had stayed with the second daughter. Going to her place meant visiting all of the other daughters as well, since they had all settled down in Guwahati after moving around other towns in the state due to their husbands' postings. All of them were well-settled.

Kuntibala had once suggested that their brother too come over to Guwahati after selling off the property in this town. After all, a big city had more prospects. Surely, he could manage to do something – he was still young. But her daughter-in-law had put her foot down: she won't go anywhere, nor allow the house to be sold, but her husband was at liberty to go anywhere he wanted to, she said. By now, she had borrowed money from a self-help group, cleaned up the pond in the compound, bought a few ducks and now their number had increased to a gaggle. Most of the people in Ananda Nagar bought eggs from her. It at least paid for the essentials in the kitchen. After enjoying an omelette made with two eggs, Hemanta Saikia would go out to join an adda session at the tea stall.

Nah, there was no sign of anyone making a call, Kuntibala thought to herself. The daughter-in-law was not very keen to trouble her husband's sisters even when there was some problem at home. She would say repeatedly, 'They do a lot for us; why should we trouble them at the slightest difficulty?' Even Kuntibala had asked her not to call unnecessarily. The swelling had been increasing; she could also feel her head spin from time to time. She knew very well that if the treatment was postponed she would be bed-ridden quite soon.

She remembered how once she was so ill that she had almost stopped breathing. Her son had wailed, 'Ma, Ma oi, what has happened to you?' When he heard the *ghrr-ghrr* sound coming out from her throat, he himself had collapsed.

Poor thing, he must have remembered his father; he too had made this ominous noise before dying. Meanwhile, her daughter-in-law and granddaughter had called the Mritunjoy ambulance service and taken mother and son together to the hospital. When Hemanta Saikia gained consciousness, he started crying, 'Where am I? Where are you taking me?' But his daughter scolded him and asked him to keep quiet. Oh, she had taken after her mother all right, she did not hesitate to speak rudely to her father. Her son had been brought up with love and tenderness. He couldn't bear to see people suffer. Was it his fault? But being his daughter, her granddaughter did not hesitate to speak rudely in front of others. She looked at her granddaughter still carrying water in buckets. Her old irritation welled up again. Both mother and daughter were busy with the chore but Hemanta Saikia was waiting for a cup of tea.

Ah, perhaps he was afraid to ask his wife even for a cup of tea. In the past, when their brother asked for something, his four sisters had competed with each other to pander to his want first. Now, she could not go to make the tea either. The man from the firewood supplier was unloading the truck. She could not move from there. If she didn't keep an eye on him, he would find a way to cheat her, she knew from experience. Today Kuntibala bought more firewood than usual. Even though she would be away, the business must go on. After buying the firewood she would still have some money left. That amount she would leave for Hemanta. Whom could he ask for money anyway? Who would lend him money? The whole world was his enemy. At least, if she left behind enough to tide him over during her absence, he would have his daily expenses taken care of and she could rest in peace. She knew if she gave the responsibility of selling the firewood to her daughter-in-law, she would do it.

Kuntibala waited but none of her daughters called to ask her to come over. So they hadn't heard about her state of health. She waited until the van that delivered the wood left and then started scolding her granddaughter, 'You don't pay any attention to your father, do you? Why? This is what you have learnt? Haven't you seen your father has been waiting for a cup of tea for so long? Don't you know that your father has to have a strong cup of tea in the morning laced with ginger and bay leaf, otherwise he will have a headache the whole day? What kind of a house is this? Even when there's a young daughter like you, your father can't get a cup of tea on time?'

'Aita, Ma will make the tea soon. Let us finish collecting the water. Today, they say, they will supply water only for half an hour.'

'Oh, it's more important than giving a cup of tea to your father? Go see how your aunt's family members drink tea together in the morning sitting on the balcony!'

She emphasized the word 'balcony', referring to Hemanta's elder sister's family. No, even now nobody said, go then to your daughter's house if you like it so much. The younger daughter had not sent word about arranging a doctor's consultation for her, and that she should come over. Nobody said, 'Your middle daughter, your *maju*, has called; they will come to fetch you. Give me the clothes you want to pack; I'll wash them now.' All this meant there no phone call had been made.

Now the old woman addressed her son, 'Why are you waiting for a cup of tea like a stork waiting for fish? Don't you have your limbs? If I die, who will look after you?'

As it was, he was not getting his tea on time and now his mother was going on and on. Hemanta Saikia got irritated and replied, 'Why are you shouting so much in the morning? Keep quiet!'

His mother got even more furious and challenged him, 'Why I am shouting, huh? Who are you to shout at me? I am the only one you can shout at, right? Go wear your wife's mekhela sador and make your tea in the kitchen.'

Now her son really lost his cool and said, 'What's biting you? I've heard that you've been behaving childishly like this since yesterday.'

'Oh, have I? Has anybody bothered to enquire how I have been suffering? I can't even walk properly, my chest feels as if something is sitting on it.'

'Your feet are swelling, your chest is hurting, but what do I do about it now? Tell me what I should do.'

The old woman saw that her son sat down with his head in his hands in utter distress. Whenever he had to tackle a problem or there was something that needed to be done, he sat down like this. The fair skin on his face changed colour, his eyes welled up. Oh good, now he was holding the phone in his hand. The old woman cocked her ears – yes, he was calling his eldest sister. Hemanta Saikia did not have to worry about his wife or daughter; if there was some problem, they solved it themselves. But if there was something concerning his mother, the easiest thing to do was to call one of his elder sisters. And today was no different.

His mother walked silently to her room. As she had emptied her suitcase, she emptied her money bag too. She knew she would return with the bag filled with enough money to sustain the family for some time. She took the clothes she would not be carrying to her daughter-in-law along with the money, and instructed her about the pile of firewood that would last for three months. Her daughter-in-law knew whom this money was for. The old woman got ready to leave home with the almost-empty suitcase and empty money bag.

Kuntibala's eldest daughter did not come to fetch her, she sent the car instead. She avoided coming to this house because she had had a fight with her brother in the past, as well as her parents. She herself was a high officer in a bank. Her husband and children were all well-settled. As soon as she finished her graduation, she appeared for a banking examination. In fact, her three younger sisters were guided by her and they followed her instructions without question. The problem was with the brother. She had used her contacts to get him a job in a tea garden, but he had quit and returned within a month. He had complained that he could not live in the garden at the foot of a hill – it was too lonely. Her parents accused her of disregarding her brother's welfare. How could she send him to work in a place known for extremist activities?

She had tried her utmost to get her brother the job of a Welfare Officer, but her mother complained for a long time to her three other sisters that she had sent him 'to die' in a godforsaken place. From then on, the eldest daughter stopped visiting her parental home, but she did perform her familial duties. Like today. She sent the car as soon as her brother called. If it were the other three sisters, Hemanta would have accompanied his mother, but he did not go to his eldest sister's house. His wife could not go with her either, since there was no one to look after the ducks and goats. So Kuntibala went alone in the car. To be honest, these days Hemanta Saikia did not like to visit any of his sisters, so his mother was getting used to travelling on her own in the car.

Kuntibala fell seriously ill at her daughter's place. She had been right, her old disease was making an appearance again. She was almost on the verge of death. She did not know who admitted her in an expensive nursing home, who waited by her bed at night, who bought the medicines. She did not try to find out either. Even in the past, her daughters had gone out of their way to look after her when she was ill. This time too they did the same.

After some weeks, Kuntibala recovered enough to walk around the house. Medicine, good food and care helped her get back on her feet in three months. Her daughter had brought her small bag at the time of going to the hospital. Now she put the few things she had brought along in this bag. She started filling the empty suitcase with new things. Well, they were not new but used, leftover items. A white coffee mug with red flowers which they thought of throwing out because it showed cracks, a couple of expensive T-shirts her granddaughter had abandoned because she found them discoloured, a few pairs of socks her son-in-law did not wear any more, a pair of shoes her grandson had left behind to go study in Bangalore, two pairs of jeans, a tube of shaving foam still half full, and so on. So within a month, the corners of her suitcase filled up. Her money bag too was replenished. She would have to buy medicines and good food after returning, the daughters reasoned. They also bought her a new suitcase and filled it with clothes for summer and winter.

Kuntibala checked both the bags regularly. Especially during the afternoon when there was nobody at home and even the maidservant had left. She opened the bags and enjoyed arranging and re-arranging all the items. Some new items had been added of late – a pack of use-and-throw shaving blades, an aftershave lotion, a men's body spray, a bottle of hair gel. In between, Kuntibala was invited to stay with her middle daughter. Theirs was a small family. Both husband and wife worked, and their only son had joined a private company. He had to travel a lot for work. All his things lay about in his room haphazardly. Now it became almost an addiction for Kuntibala to enter her grandson's room during the afternoons. The house was empty at this time of the day. Her room was just across her grandson's room. His name was Siddhartha but everybody called him Sid. Kuntibala could not pronounce it properly, so in the old style she addressed him as 'Bopaitu', my son.

Kuntibala's eldest daughter and husband were careful about the things in the household and kept tabs if anything went missing. Their two daughters were no different and even checked if their hankies were kept in the designated place. But her middle daughter's family was much more relaxed and did not keep track of things as much. Their son Sid was the same. Kuntibala thought that he looked like a prince. His parents were quite well-to-do and now he had been working too for the past six months. She heard that he was already earning around 90,000 rupees a month. His company also took care of his work-related expenses. When she was staying at her eldest daughter's place she heard that when he was still in college a famous American company had recruited him. This was quite a trend these days, she was told, when bright students did not have to wait for the final exam to get over to get a job offer. Really, this boy was lucky. He could afford to buy new things every other day, use them if he liked, or throw them out half-used if he so pleased. As soon as you entered his room, there was a whiff of a nice perfume. On the dressing table there were various body care products for men. If he came back from a tour of Delhi and was leaving for Bangalore next, he abandoned the old set, even if half-used, and bought a new set. Good, Kuntibala was happy that God had bestowed on him a life to enjoy.

So, out of his neglected items, she picked up a bottle of body spray, a piece of expensive soap, and some other things. These were just lying about and nobody was going to miss them anyway. The old woman's suitcase was getting fuller and fuller. There was a cupboard in Siddhartha's room that stored his warm clothes. He did not bother to lock it. It's not like he had the time to do it anyway! He was always in a hurry, running to catch a flight or a train. One day, one of the doors of his cupboard was open. Kuntibala peeped in and was astounded. The hangers, the shelves and drawers were heavy with all kinds of warm clothes – sweaters, coats, jackets. How many warm clothes did a man need, she wondered. As her eyes ran over them, they lingered on a handsome jacket. It must be of a foreign make, she thought. He had gone abroad for a month recently, she knew. She felt it – ah, how soft! Inside there was a lining of fur and outside it looked as if it was made of deer skin. She was sure when a man wore this jacket even the coldest night of the month of *Puh* would not bother him.

When the people left for work, Kuntibala would take out the jacket. Ooh, how beautiful! If a handsome man wore it, it would make him even more attractive, she mused. She often sat with the jacket in her lap; its smell and softness kept her mesmerized. In the meantime, she kept the small treasures she had collected on one side of the suitcase and kept the other side empty. The day before she was to leave for home, she rolled up the jacket and stuffed it into the empty space. Then she locked it and put the key in her money bag. It was summer now, and it would be a long time before people thought of bringing out the warm clothes. By that time her grandson would buy more clothes, she was sure. He definitely wouldn't miss his jacket with so many new clothes in the cupboard pushing it into a corner, she reasoned.

By now, Kuntibala had taken turns to stay in the houses of her four daughters. She was not very successful with her mission in any of the houses besides this one. When she was at her eldest daughter's house, after she picked up the half-finished shaving foam there was a great deal of searching and enquiries. Kuntibala kept the key of her suitcase tied to her sador. When she said that she saw a young boy near the bathroom window one day, the enquiries stopped and there was talk of making the gaps in the grilles narrower. The second-youngest daughter was a homemaker and spent large parts of the day at home. The youngest daughter had arranged for her to stay in her grandson's room, where he used to stay before moving to Bangalore for his studies. From there she could collect only a few discoloured T-shirts and a pair of jeans with their zips missing. Thus she could fill up her suitcase with only knick-knacks at this house. When she entered her grandson's room, Kuntibala felt as if she had entered Alibaba's cave. *Shisim-phak* – open the door, and there! So many things to choose from. She saw, in her mind's eye, a handsome young man approaching her, scratching his head and bowing, as if trying to say something but unable to do so.

She lost her senses and packed this and that in her bag. Nobody noticed anything; nobody searched for anything lost. One day, Kuntibala picked up a money bag from the table. It looked quite dusty and there was no money in it either. This was the only time that Siddhartha had asked his mother if anyone had seen the money bag, as his credit cards were in it. Kuntibala did not understand what this credit card business was but figured it was something important to her grandson, who otherwise never bothered to find out about the other missing things. Kuntibala took the money bag out of her own bag without anyone seeing and pretended to search for it under the table where she pretended to have found it. The happy-go-lucky boy hugged her and said, 'This is my Aita after all!' and then shouted at his mother, 'See, Ma, Aita has found it!'

Kuntibala then asked him, 'Bopai, if you don't need this money bag, you can give it to me. I can keep the money here. Usually my handkerchief is enough to hold whatever I have. Now what money I have is actually what all of you have given me.'

Siddhartha created quite a ruckus, shouting, 'Ma, Aita doesn't even have a purse. Have you bought her any gifts? She says she will be going back soon.'

That day both mother and son went shopping and bought many things – mekhela sador for Hemanta's wife, churidar set for the daughter, and sets of clothes for Kuntibala. When she held the packet containing a costly shirt for Hemanta Saikia, Kuntibala cried, saying, 'Why did you spend all this money? You have spent so much for my treatment and now all this!'

When he saw his grandmother crying, Siddhartha was a bit surprised. What was wrong with her? Was there something amiss? Kuntibala wanted to go home straightaway. Her daughter-in-law had called to inform that the firewood stock had finished. She had to buy a new lot. Not to worry, Kuntibala thought. The money her daughters gave her to buy medicines and so on would be enough to buy firewood to fill a mini truck.

She got ready to go home. She would go in the car provided by the eldest daughter. The driver Bolen was familiar with the route. He was looking forward to this trip because the old lady's daughter-in-law always greeted him sincerely. She served him lunch on a bell-metal plate with utmost respect, and presented him with a gamosa each time. The daughter-in-law felt happy that she could at least do this much. She was grateful to her husband's sisters because they stood by her and the household. Her husband was useless, everybody knew that, and the old woman needed lots of medicines. She felt sad that she could not even ask them to come for a meal. The sisters did everything but they too somehow did not find time to visit her. So from that side, Bolen was the only one who came to her house. Bolen too felt at home here. He too brought along something always; sometimes he stopped on the way and bought a fish. On arrival, he would request her, excited, 'Bou, please bring the *moida*, the curving knife! Let me clean the fish first.' Hemanta Saikia would join the conversation. Whenever he visited, Bolen stayed overnight – they wouldn't let him go.

Bolen arrived early in the morning. Kuntibala asked him to put the two big boxes in the boot. The car was big, so there was no problem. When the big box was brought out Kuntibala looked up and down. Of course, this house was not like her eldest daughter's, where the people woke up early and started doing physical exercises. This family would keep awake until midnight, talking or watching TV; if guests visited, they wouldn't leave before eleven. Nobody woke up until eight in this house, not even the maidservant. She had made the tea the night before for Kuntibala and kept it in a flask. Now Kuntibala shared the tea with Bolen.

When her daughter and the others got up, they saw that Kuntibala was already dressed and waiting in the drawing room. All the daughters called to find about her health and bid her goodbye. The eldest daughter spoke to Bolen and gave him instructions. Kuntibala got into the car.

Kuntibala was going home with her big boxes. She knew it was her last journey to her daughters' city. She had heard what the doctor had said; at this age it was not advisable to operate on her chest. Her hands and feet would be swelling from time to time; there was nothing they could do about it.

She closed her eyes and saw a handsome young man wearing a beautiful jacket passing her by. A lovely perfume emanated from his body, and he was smiling a little. Aha, he smiled the same way when his father gave him something. Kuntibala wanted desperately to see that smile, half shy, half hesitant, as he scratched his head, before she died. She asked Bolen, 'Bopai, how much time will it take to reach home?'

'Say, three to four hours, at the most.'

'Okay, not much longer then.'

'Aita, shall I increase the speed?'

'What did you say?'

'Shall I drive a little faster? I thought you might feel uncomfortable, so I've been driving slowly.'

'No, no, go faster. It's better to arrive by midday.'

Old Kuntibala smiled in satisfaction and said, 'I've taken so many medicines, so many injections – is it for nothing? I feel absolutely fine.'

Bolen increased the speed of the car.

SCREAM

The newspapers draw a picture of a hillock ...

Every morning, the newspapers build a hillock in front of me. This hillock is not green, nurtured by sun and rain; it's coarse and heartless, made of hard, black stones. On this hill, not even a handful of moss grows. It is unable to keep in its womb the sparkle of a spring. Not a single blade of grass peeps from its crevices. It is a hill built out of anger and crudeness. The morning sun wants to visit my flower garden. The flowers wait for him the whole night. The creepers seek out the rays with their soft tendrils, the sunflowers stretch their necks towards the east as they wait, ignoring the creaking pain. The white roses wait, a little crestfallen, for a little of the sun's first ray of pink to smear them, without which they feel hesitant to bloom into full glory. The patch of land where the *no-baji* flowers, looking like decorative jewels, get excited. Not much time is left for nine o'clock when the sun will shine on them; at this moment most of the buds are half asleep. The tree with flowers that look like powder puffs little girls use, sleep peacefully too, offering rest to the leaves for the night. Without the warmth of the sun they still feel a bit groggy. Like this, all of them wait for the sun to appear in the sky. The sun too wants to brighten the kitchen garden in the backyard with its golden light. The raw papayas wait; sunlight will soften their skins, change their green skin to orange and make them soft and moist. The mood of the comb of bananas is restless too. Without sunlight it will become dry and make the skin appear serrated. The lychee tree begs for a bit of red colour, the *kordoi*, however, wants some yellow, while the ribbed gourd flowers want a darker shade of it.

Who doesn't want the warm rays of the sun? But the cruel hillock shuts it out and casts a shadow over all. The darkness drills cruelly into my heart. But I am compelled to face the dark hill standing just in front. The heat burns the body, the throat becomes dry and the chest feels heavy and suppressed with the hill's weight. There is no shade, even a little, to give relief.

Every morning, the newspapers create this heartless hill in front of my eyes. It looks at me, cruel and relentless.

Another massacre ...

The headline in the newspaper in big font on the front page stares at me. A row of dead bodies covered with white sheets accompanies the story. The people were on their way to their workplace. Nobody knew why they were asked to disembark from the bus they were travelling in. Caught unawares and still wondering why, they turned into lifeless lumps of flesh in the next instant, shot unceremoniously.

Mentally retarded woman gangraped, the next headline reads. A picture of a body wrapped by a reed mat dumped under a lamp post illustrates the story.

Woman burnt to death for dowry. People performed the last rites on the very courtyard of the accused. The picture shows a burning pyre.

Bomb blast at the bus depot. Thirty dead, more than hundred injured. The picture tells it all, the place replete with scattered limbs. Another picture shows human limbs and a head hanging from the fork of a nearby tree.

Three extremists killed in an encounter, four escape. Another headline. The picture shows three healthy young male bodies carried on two bamboo poles like they were carcasses of pigs.

University building burnt to ashes due to arson.

Old couple murdered in daring daytime dacoity. Money and jewellery worth ten lakhs looted.

Inebriated students of well-known institute caught red-handed.

Political leader arrested, caught in compromising position with young woman.

Youth commits suicide by jumping from night bus unable to get job even after paying bribe.

Son murders mother with axe.

Supporters of bandh set fire to more than a hundred vehicles. Passenger inside bus burnt to death.

Silt from flood covers thousands of bighas of fertile land.

Farmer commits suicide.

Sonjuri village about to disappear due to erosion.

Some other news on the first page is relegated to the corner, the font size gets smaller and there are no accompanying photos.

I try to scan the news on the second page. I concentrate on some inane news about houses and properties on sale, mainly to forget the dark hillock that looms on the first page. Here, descriptions of personal experiences try to catch my attention from the midst of ads for jobs. They are stories washed in tears, told by old and middle-aged people, of their long journey and how life cheated them. Broken dreams, broken homes and the sighs of desperation bring the cruel hill back to me again.

Son disowned – the letters stare from the dark background.

...By notice at the Notary Court, I, Manik Bora, announce that I disown my eldest son, Robin Bora, for torturing me in my old age. From this day, he is barred from laying claim to any of my property, including land, cash and savings.

One whole column is devoted to the agony of a father cutting off bonds from a loved son. Other such appeals on the page reflect some other stories of devastated families, bitterness and unshed tears. Of couples mourning the remains of families they had nurtured. The young men and women meanwhile point fingers at their old parents and curse them heartily. This should have been the best time in their lives but their minds are full of black soot – the colour of the cruel hill.

Newspapers, TV, radio – all conspire to build up the hill in front of me. It prevents the sun from reaching me. Though unwilling, I have to climb up that stony, rough hill every day. My heels bleed, I find it difficult to walk. My body burns with the heat, thirst makes my throat constrict, I can't see anything through the haze. I find darkness engulfing daylight. I drag myself up the hill. I shout, silently, give me shade, give me water, give me light. The more I shout, the more tired I become. Like a tendril of a gourd creeper I search for the sun helplessly. Like sunflowers devoid of sunlight, I bow, depressed; my neck pains looking down at the ground all the time. Like a raw papaya waiting hopelessly for the sunlight to moisten its breast, I turn stone-cold. I am like a bud unable to bloom for lack of air. I try to breathe deep, drawing air from my lungs.

The hill seemed far away
It's so near now, crushing me

I am afraid of the heartless black hill. But I can't avoid confronting it. Suddenly, without warning, it grows in front of me, casting a shadow on my surroundings.

That day, the hill reached my doorstep, easily walking through the grassy passageway to my house. Instantly, my house was submerged in darkness. Not a stream of light could penetrate that gloom, and my house filled with an unbearable musty smell.

In that dark atmosphere smelling of decay, I was pinned down. He walked boldly to my drawing room. Whichever side he moved to, that rotten smell of unwashed clothes, sweat and bad-quality liquor travelled with him. Forget entering our home, at some other time, this man would not even dare to talk to us on the street, mainly because he cheated us and owed us money; he had promised to get a gas cylinder when it was in short supply. So now he avoided us. We scolded him often for his heavy drinking. He was becoming like a poisonous mushroom growing amidst a waste heap. Whenever we encountered him, we found him half asleep and reeking of cheap liquor. A foul smell assailed the nose when we passed him by. Whether in summer or winter, he was always seen dressed in khaki shorts and a dirty gamosa wrapped around his neck. His khaki shirt was worn out but we could still read the Lakhimi Gas Company logo stitched to the pocket. Once upon a time when the shirt was new, it had buttons, and he wore matching khaki trousers. He used to work for the gas company at that time. With his pushcart he delivered the cylinders to households and collected the empty ones. But once he started drinking heavily, he began cheating customers. Complaints reached the management. He lost his job. Now his preoccupation was to beg for money from people and spend it on his drinks. He looked pale like a candle. His eyes, feet and hands were swollen. I see him often lying unconscious by the roadside. One evening he was seen lying naked by the railway station, only the khaki shirt covering his upper body. Somebody threw a jute burlap over his body on finding him like this. Flies often settled on his open mouth. People sometimes peeked at him and commented, 'Is the drunkard dead?' No, he did not die. Once he sobered up, he came home and exerted his masculine power over his poor wife, who managed the household by working as a maid in people's houses – washing clothes and kitchen utensils.

And today, this man entered our house boldly and reached as far as the kitchen. My husband and I were having tea sitting at the dining table. The TV was on and showed relatives of the people massacred after being pushed down from a bus, being interviewed. A young woman was hugging two infants to her chest and wailing incessantly. She was unable to utter a word as the reporter asked her questions. A couple of men belonging to the extremist group that wanted to establish their own state and running amok in the process, were also seen on the screen. Their body language, the way they spoke and jutted out their jaws towards the screen made them look like robots. They did not look like ordinary people with a heart. They defended their act without remorse. The anchor was reading out a statement from the extremists taking responsibility for the killing.

Our eyes were fixed to the screen when we heard his voice, 'I want money.' We jumped up in shock.

'What money are you demanding now? You have cheated us of cash for two cylinders.'

He did not seem to pay attention to our accusation. He was not asking for the usual ten or twenty rupees for buying liquor; he wanted ten thousand rupees! My husband asked him to get out of the house immediately. His reaction was to take out the dao, wrapped in a worn-out gamosa. He looked at me and threatened, 'If something happens to him, don't blame me.' His eyes were red. He stood defiant and challenging. The look in his eyes was of utter hatred. Then suddenly he went away, leaving behind a cruel hillock in our midst. The foul smell pervaded the air long after he had left.

Thus the hill, the one I hate and fear, comes near suddenly sometimes, without warning. It suddenly sprouts near the dining table, by the divan next to it.

~

Sometimes the hill appears far away. How far? My birthplace is 300 kilometres from here. That place near our town, landscaped by green hills and a river, is not too distant, at least in my mind. During our schooldays and later in college, we went there many times for picnics. I remember one particular school trip. We travelled in a station wagon. There were six teachers who accompanied us and only two men in the group. One was the driver, but the car was driven by Miss Dorothy Kennedy, an American teacher. The other man was his assistant, the handyman. We reached the beautiful spot with the salubrious air, cheerful streams and orange orchards. There were other picnic parties as well. Many young men were part of these groups. They cleared a place for us with utmost respect. They looked admiringly at the healthy tribal girls who carried baskets of orange and firewood for lighting the temporary stoves. And at our group too, especially our golden-haired foreigner teachers. The boys waved at us cheerfully, bidding us goodbye when we were leaving. When the wheels of Dorothy miss's car got stuck in the sandy bank of the river, some boys brought a wooden plank so that she could drive the car on it and towards the pebbled path. We waved goodbye to the boys. Our teachers – we addressed them as 'Miss' – asked us to thank them. When we waved at the young men, our eyes locking, we felt a thrill we had never experienced before. The memory of that excitement at the cusp of adolescence and youth remained with us for a long time.

In that very place, a senior professor in a local college was in charge of the girls' hostel. He was to retire after two years. Now he too witnessed the sullen hill growing slowly in front of his eyes. He could not bear the ominous shadow of the hill and had sent a report on the whole experience to the newspaper. That hill I knew so well – pretty and green, the dancing spring, orange orchards, the silver sand on the river bank – until I saw the ugly stone-filled hill emerging and a dark veil covered everything.

It was almost a duty for the professor to take out the girls of the hostel for a picnic every winter. For many years he had been doing it, but for the last couple of years he almost feared this responsibility which he had enjoyed earlier. So that winter he had taken the girls to a place where a waterfall danced its way down to the valley. The girls were singing and cooking their lunch. Thankfully, there was no other picnic party visiting that day. The girls were thrilled to have the hills and its surroundings to themselves. They were responsible young women; perhaps in a year or two they would get married and manage their own homes. Already they were acquainting themselves with the problems that could arise while taking on future responsibilities as homemakers. But today, they shook off all these thoughts and became like young girls touched by the first bloom of youth. They seemed like daughters of nature abandoning all earthly worries. The professor insisted that they should wear their uniforms even if going out for a picnic. Even today they were wearing churidar-kameez sets in blue and black. Now they tied their dupattas to their slim waists. The contours of their bodies, now prominent, emphasized the charm of youthful figures. Like fairy queens of the forest they were dancing, singing, and preparing their food. The driver and the handyman were helping them dig an earthen stove. First came the tea. Then arrived rounds of fried luchi and potato curry. The girls had also carried with them home-made sweets. The professor ate sparsely and soon declared that he was already full. The girls' mood was euphoric, like the perfectly ballooning luchis. They laughed in joyous abandon and at times it seemed even the sound of the running water from the spring was overpowered. And then they appeared. Eight to ten young men driving down in a convoy of Boleros and Tata Sumos. They were young men no doubt, but their looks did not reflect the healthy handsomeness seen in men of their age. All of them had had quite a few drinks, it was obvious. On seeing them, the professor jumped up, throwing his book to the ground. The driver and the handyman who had taken out the detachable seat from the minivan and were resting under the shadow of a tree, grabbed two tree branches lying near them. The girls who were freely running around immediately covered their bodies with whatever they could find. The whole atmosphere suddenly became gloomy, as if covered by a dark cloud. The tension in the air made it difficult to breathe. After a few minutes arrived a convoy of motorbikes. The bikers parked their vehicles in such a way that the girls seemed to be ensnared – like wild animals about to be killed.

The girls ran towards the professor and stuck close to him. The trees, the sky, the birds bowed in shame. The young men instructed the driver and the handyman to go sit inside the bus. Then they addressed the professor, their voices inebriated, 'Uncle, let us young men and women have some fun. It's best that you too get inside the bus or you could wait in one of our cars as well.'

'Uncle, come to our car.'

'Uncle, we have good stuff. Have a sip.'

'Hei, give our uncle that imported stuff.'

'Uncle, this is a question of young bodies. Don't blame us, okay?'

The professor asked the girls to move into the bus immediately. They ran without even looking at the food they had cooked. The bus started making its way down the pebbled road. The cars and the bikes started following them. Vulgar words, body language making no secret about their intentions, followed them. At times, one or two bikes would come very close to the bus and sometimes the cars would catch up as well. They threw words at random to the professor, 'Uncle, leave that fair girl for us.'

'No, no, I like that dark one.'

'Uncle, the one with the big boobs is for me, remember.'

The girls started weeping. One or two of the more courageous ones asked, 'Sir, shall we teach them a lesson?'

The professor asked the girls not to sit near the windows. He sat next to the driver and told him that he should not stop at any cost. Around them the silent jungle was watching. The professor suddenly remembered that the police officer in charge of the local thana was once his student. Every year, before leaving for picnics, the students were asked to write down the phone numbers of the local thana and the nearby hospital. Now, the professor's student himself picked up the phone. He arrived at the scene with a contingent of policemen almost in the nick of time, as the boys were trying to block the bus from the front. As soon as they saw the police force, they scooted. At the thana the police officer offered a cup of tea to the professor who was sweating profusely even on this winter's day; his shirt clung to his body. He said, deeply traumatized, 'You know, all these boys come from so-called well-to-do, educated families. They haven't completed their studies. They don't do anything, just laze around. But the people in power support them. Common people don't dare to complain about them. They fear them as people do man-eating tigers.'

The officer bowed his head and admitted, 'Sometimes we too have to face their ire.'

So the girls, the professor, the driver and the handyman returned home, each carrying in their chest the burden of a black hill. As soon as he reached home, the professor entered his study and describing the events of the day, composed a letter for the 'Letter to the Editor' column, trying to push away the ugly hill from his chest. He knew nothing would change but he felt his chest getting a little lighter nonetheless.

The hill thus lives on. Sometimes it comes near, sometimes it moves a little farther. But there is no respite from it.

I stand facing the huge hill
I feel small, insignificant.
To win over this feeling, I kick at it hard
But I only feel smaller, more helpless.

~

When I open the window near my desk, I can see a *simolu* cottonwool tree. Its roots are as big as a small elephant. Believe me, at night it seems as if a baby elephant is sleeping there. When the tree starts flowering, hundreds of birds come to rest on its branches. They suck the honey and sing in great joy as if it were a festival. The colour and the birdsong move the tree too and when the buds burst, it looks as if hundreds of butterflies are flying around it.

That day, a group of young men arrived in their fancy cars and bikes accompanied by a few labourers carrying axes and saws. They wanted to cut down the tree. People knew these boys; they were afraid of them and avoided all confrontation. The men had taken a contract to build a multi-storeyed building somewhere in the city and now needed the Simolu tree logs to build the roof. They had taken over the sky, air, river, hills, trees with the power of their guns. Who then would dare to challenge them?

I was mortified. The hundred-year-old tree would be destroyed thus in a moment? How could I be a silent witness to this heinous crime? So, I protested. The boys looked at me angrily, they spoke to me rudely. I begged the people around – please look, the tree will be cut down any moment. The red simolu flowers would turn into drops of blood on the branches and the trunk. The tree would be dismembered soon. The men showed me papers with the stamp of the ruling party. We, the people, were like mere ants in front of these people who ruled with the power of guns. They told me, not only the government agency, even the people of the locality had given permission to cut down the tree. A woman shouted, 'When the cottonwool from the seeds fly in the air, it dirties our house. I have to sweep the floor again and again.' Somebody supported her, 'When the flowers fall on the ground it becomes too murky and makes it difficult to walk.' The axes and saws were ready to strike. What do I do? I felt helpless. Should I go and hug the tree? I remembered how those women from the hills hugged the trees and saved them. I could feel the rough feel of the bark on my skin. A few red flowers fell on my body. I could feel the heart of the tree racing in fear.

'Is this woman mad?'

'You go home, don't interfere unnecessarily.'

'Ask this woman to leave this place.'

'You'll pay for it, I tell you.'

'If something bad happens to you, it won't be our fault.'

'The tree will be felled, be sure, but you will too.'

The tree lay on the ground, decimated. The flowers stuck to its branches for quite a few days after, looking like clots of dried blood.

~

The structure of our salary has changed. We were to receive some amount long overdue. But to receive our rightful due was not so easy; the amount the employees under the powers-that-be demanded to make a smooth payment astounded us. Forget about the overdue amount, unless a percentage was paid from the monthly salary, it did not reach us in time. Whom do we tell? Who would believe us? How could one expect anything from an administration that fed on gun-power and blood flowing from its victims? I tried to say these things but was stopped. People blamed and reminded me, 'Only talking about idealism won't fill your stomach. Every country has its own rules. Unless you compromise, how can you hope to live in this country?'

Eventually, all these accusations made me realize that perhaps they were right. After all, even the life I lead now has been bought by paying monthly EMIs. The matter of the unpaid salary was not significant enough to cause headaches.

These days, I bring home my salary all right, but only after paying a high interest. I am getting used to it, like others, as something as normal as having a glass of water with my meal.

I feel as if I am an earthworm, or perhaps an insect
I try to distance myself from this feeling of self-annihilation
But even amidst a crowd, it chases me, surprising me
I stand again in front of another hill

And discover, I am but an earthworm, or insect, or at the most,
a colourful butterfly.

~

Let me tell a story. Of an old man. He had a patch of land. The land never saw a speckle of light. There was a small hill in front of this patch and made it damp. He planted a row of cabbages but the plants just grew tall without bearing any fruit. The old man became depressed. He tried everything – he cleaned the weeds, dug the soil around the roots, fertilized it with cow dung, but look, no result! Then he planted two rose bushes. They too grew lanky but sadly, no luck with the flowers. Whatever he planted just grew tall but nothing came out of it. Poor plants, they tried hard to survive and grew as if reaching for the sky. The old man could feel their cries touching his heart. They wanted sunshine, they wanted light. When they grew too tall, the thin trunks bowed down, unable to bear the weight. The old man felt his heart give way. One day, he decided to dig up the hill. He went on and on without stopping and then finally, he achieved his goal. The gloomy patch of land now basked in sunlight. The old man once again planted cabbage and cauliflower. The short and thick plants showed off healthy cabbages and cauliflowers resting on their breasts. The potatoes flourished under the soil, the turnips looked like big-sized wood apples. The rose bushes dressed themselves in red. And thus, the adamant old man became a legend.

The old man didn't like the hill
It blocked the sunlight.
The old man started digging the hill
The old man was not an earthworm, nor an insect,
Or a frail colourful butterfly
He was a man.

~

The river reaches the valley at this point. Here she is at peace, without any turbulence. After carrying the stones and pebbles from the hills and depositing them at the riverbed, she is now happy to take a break. All she wants is to flow at her own pace. But the hungry eyes have discovered the stones lying at the riverbed. Countless trucks carry them, day in, day out. The ugly screeching *ghrrr-ghrr* sound from the engines intrudes into the neighbourhood. They have dug the riverbed in such a way that the river has gradually flowed towards the populated areas on the bank. There is a purpose behind this. If the river is closer to the habitations and the main road, it is easier to approach and the cost for renting the trucks comes down.

Holding the coffee cup in my hand, I watch helplessly from the verandah the procession of trucks carrying the stone chips.

I had an invitation to attend a *shanti biya*, the customary mini-wedding on attaining puberty still observed by many families. The girl's mother told me that her almanac predicted she could become a widow and so there was a fifteen-day fast to eliminate the bad omen.

The highly educated mother was a relative of mine. I went dutifully with a gift for the adolescent girl who was sitting dressed in silk mekhela sador and wearing jewellery, and had a sumptuous lunch with rice and fish curry.

Yes, I have learnt to accept all these things, and my skin has become like a rhino's – difficult to penetrate.

I watch the news on the TV screen about the mother of a girl who was gangraped and then murdered. She is crying as if her heart is breaking. In between I go to the kitchen to stir the chicken curry.

At another time, I listen to the beautiful rendering of a song and then read the news running on the ticker below: a village disappearing due to the erosion of the river; a landless farmer committing suicide. A new song starts – a young pair of lovers dance around the flower garden, their lustful body language makes no bones about what is on their mind. Again, the news tickers tell us about a village, chunks of soil disappearing in the water, and about a farmer who died after consuming pesticide used in potato fields.

~

The boy was brilliant at studies. The young man slogged quietly and established his credentials even at the university level. He would get his law degree in another year. Meanwhile, he passed the Civil Services exam at the first attempt and was among the top-ranked on the Assam Government's list. He even organized the bribe money that might help him secure the job. The people in power collected the money but he did not get the job. He was good at maths and was under the impression that this formula was simple. He had never made a mistake while solving a maths problem. As a student now trying to find an answer, he lost his mental equilibrium. He tried to find an answer in his room's ceiling fan and a plastic rope, ending up as an inert body. His tongue hung out of his mouth; people could not look at his eyes, they bulged out from the sockets. He hung like that from the fan on top of his desk throughout the night.

I went to his house and handed over to his mother the customary food items people take to a home in mourning. Before leaving, I involuntarily looked up to the gold-coloured fan from which he had hung himself.

The old man who dug the hill was adamant, foolish
But I am not a fool; I am shrewd, educated, worldly-wise
I don't like to face problems or sorrow
And so I withdraw into myself
Like a delicate flower closing its petals.

~

It was an evening of the monsoon month of *Sawan*. Even for a rainy day, it was unnaturally dark. The rain poured incessantly.

The place was near the bus depot. Water flowed through the roads and almost stopped the city from functioning normally. The commuters stopped wherever they were. Within half an hour, the roads looked almost like flowing streams. There was a girl at the bus stop. She was returning home from work. The Scooty she was driving stopped midway because of the onslaught of the rolling water. Soaked thoroughly by now, she somehow dragged the Scooty a little way down so that she could park it near the footpath, but it refused to move after a point. Actually, it was standing rather in the middle than the side of the road. She could see that the bright yellow seat was slowly disappearing under murky water. Her brother lived abroad, her father had died two years ago, and only her old mother was at home. Who could rescue her now? She called her mother and informed her that she would be late coming home owing to work pressure, but mainly to reassure her mother that she was fine. She knew that until she reached home her mother would be standing by the door scanning the road. Their pet dog would be standing next to her too. He would cock his ears for familiar sounds. He started shaking his tail as soon as she reached the turning near the house.

Her churidar-kameez now clung to her body. She tried to cover herself by wrapping the wet dupatta around her body and sat cringing on the cement bench at the bus stop. There were a few more people waiting. Behind the bus stop, construction work for an embankment was ongoing. Several labourers were engaged in digging the earth. Their conversations reached her ears. Now they were silent too. Suddenly the electricity went off. The whole area plunged into darkness. It was difficult to imagine the road in front as it looks during daytime, as angry rivulets formed.

Their car stopped near the bus stop too and they took shelter under the roof. They immediately saw the girl shrinking in one corner. The darkness of the evening gave them other ideas. The evening progressed to night. Despite knowing well what was happening, the people around her kept quiet. It was only he who protested. Who was he? Just a thin young man, still a student in college. He tried to block the boys. By now the water was receding but the lights were yet to appear. The people under the shade started leaving one by one. He also thought of the same thing but the ruffians jumped on him to attack. One or two of them were aiming for the girl. She screamed and screamed in utter terror. Hearing her, the labourers who were working behind the bus stop abandoned their chore of preparing roti and vegetable curry for dinner and grabbed whatever they could get hold of – spades, hoe, and other miscellaneous tools. Seeing them, the men ran away. Had it not been for the young man and the labourers, she would have ended up like a skinned deer – bloodied. Or, a dead body wrapped in a mat and hidden in the boot of their car. Her mother would have waited the whole night near the door. The dog would have laid at her feet whimpering. And the girl? Lying somewhere in a pit or dumped in a marshy land – an unknown body – a victim of gangrape. Perhaps after a few days, she would become a news item in a corner of the third page of the newspaper accompanied by a hazy picture. She was lucky; that night there were a few men protecting her. They had spines unlike slithering earthworms, insects or colourful butterflies.

The adamant old man possessed something
That I do not have
The hill chokes me.

~

The people of Assam were celebrating the harvest festival of Bhogali Bihu. Rich meals with fish and mutton curry, flat rice and yoghurt with jaggery filled everyone with the spirit of celebration and enjoyment even if for a night, as they forgot about all the other things. Even on such an occasion, people of a particular village were fasting and remained awake the whole night. For the past sixteen years, they have been doing this – fasting on the Uruka night of the feast. Yes, it was sixteen years ago that a group of terrorists swooped down on the village when the women were roasting pitha and frying fish for the Uruka feast, and killed the innocent people, shooting them like birds. The food lay scattered on the kitchen floors. The rice on the plates waited for the fish curry. Those who wanted their own state killed them on this festival day in the month of Magh after a good harvest. That night the people did not add fire sticks to the celebratory *meji* made of piled up firewood. They lit twenty-one pyres.

Since that year, the villagers have observed every *Uruka* day of the *Magh* Bihu by fasting, though all over the state people celebrated with feasts and bonhomie. They lit earthen lamps in remembrance of the dead and sat in vigil throughout the night. They did not drink even a drop of water during the vigil.

All of them knew who the killers were, from where they had come, and due to whose benevolence they now roamed free. Not even a scratch has appeared on their skins. They still roam free, walking around the village without giving a damn. The meals they have – an abundance of meat and fish curries, and the liquor – have fattened them like pigs.

And these people sit around the earthen lamps, their hearts breaking. When the whole state breaks into celebration, they huddle in groups. Their resentment, their grief, slowly create a dark hill. An angry hill bereft of water, lacking a cool shade under which to rest.

Will you give me
Your hand?
Does the hill choke
You too?

Author's Note: The above lines are from the poem 'Tuchchta' which appears in Rajen Kalita's poetry book *Swapancharita's Padavali.*

The Half-burnt Bus at Midnight

Right in front of the police station at the chari-ali, a road forks away from the national highway. Further down this road, the traffic thins. Instead of shops and bazaars, you see paddy fields on both sides of the road. After a while, you can spot a river which runs alongside the road all the way through. Sometimes it looks on from a little distance, then it disappears altogether as if in hiding, then it appears again, flowing coolly along. Beyond the stretch of green fields, the hills take on the hue of peacock feathers. The paddy fields, the sky and the hills dazzle the eye. Occasionally, a rainbow arches right across the sky. The river borrows a bit of the rainbow and mixes the colours on its own liquid palette. When the river flows through the leafy banks of trees, it turns green; the sky adds a tinge of orange in the afternoon; amid the sand banks, it looks brown and sombre. From time to time, it turns sharply, like a dancer bending her waist, then decides to flow on.

Two rows of simalu trees flank the river near the bridge from where it flows straight on and disappears from the roadside. During the flowering season, when the birds flit joyously from flower to flower, sipping nectar, the trees look as if they are covered by a quilt flecked with bright red patterns. When the seeds burst with cottonwool, the trees appear to be covered with snow.

The little town begins where the row of simalu trees end.

The little river girdles the town – flowing serenely by the backyard of a house, the window in another, even the front doors of some other houses. At the crack of dawn, when the sky awakes in a flush of pink, schools of small *jaoria* fish too wake up in the stream only to disappear underwater as the day gets brighter. The river keeps the town well watered and the trees a lush green. Upstream, the river starts playing hide-and-seek among the emerald carpets of tea bushes and then it gets slimmer and swifter, then ducks for cover at will.

The people who live on the banks of the river are like a flock of chickens without the mother hen. Nobody has given them anything. Unused to privileges of any kind, they do not demand anything and probably believe they deserve nothing either. They get by, making do with whatever is within their reach, and somehow manage two meals a day. Of their own accord, they have kept the neighbourhood clean. The bridge has been waiting to be completed for the last two years without any progress and they have managed, or tried to, with the unsteady temporary bridge built by the contractor of the project. During the rainy season the road gets speckled with potholes deep enough for a duck to swim in. If people have to pass by that patch they somehow avoid the deep holes and the cars and buses. Sometimes a few people get together to fill up the worst of the potholes. They are careful to look after themselves around the temporary bus stop and bazaar, avoiding any kind of trouble. Whichever political party declares a bandh, they observe it; they are watchful to never get into an argument or strife and are hyper-conscious not to get involved.

So life continues in this way. The waves of conflict from outside invade their equanimity from time to time; they go away after a while like a flood that leaves behind destruction. The people keep to themselves for some time and then slowly venture out. After all, they have to fill their stomachs. Like floods sweeping away some, these conflicts also take away a few; those who are left behind reminisce about the others and organize the funeral rites. After a period of time, all that is left of them are memories. And the town carries on, with its ups and downs. During the Chhat Puja festival they light up the place on the bank with bright bulbs; loud film music blares from the microphone. On the morning of Bihu, they take the cattle to the river to give them a ritual bath; during the wedding season, women, accompanied by a 'band party' go to the river to collect water for the ritual bath of the bride, they perform *shraddha* for the departed soul on the bank, and immerse the idol of the devi after the puja is over.

On the days when trouble brews the army puts up temporary camps on the river bank. On these days people avoid the ghats, though they are more convenient, as this is where they usually wash clothes or have baths. Instead, they go up the river or use the tubewell in their backyard for the daily chores. Thus the people have learnt to cope with life in the town despite its rickety bridge and the road full of potholes. The schools and colleges hold exams, a few get through with high marks while some don't manage to pass. Some die, some are born – in short, life goes on in its own way. Money allotted for the broken bridge and uneven roads collects in the big city to be spent by some on cars too big for the lanes, and luxurious multi-storeyed buildings. The people look at these buildings, talk among themselves and then abandon the topic as useless.

However, sometimes the town with its winding river becomes impatient. One day, a boy returning from school was abducted in broad daylight in the heart of the town by a gang of bikers. As the drama unfolded with a demand for lakhs of rupees, all the townspeople came out to the streets. Though they might seem simple and yielding, at times they could prove to be obstinate too. However, because it is more peaceful compared to towns and villages in the vicinity, it has been expanding quite rapidly. New houses have been coming up in the open fields and the bank of the river. The higher part of land on the bank is already full; now houses have been built even on the land at river level, as if in a frenzy. After all, this river, slim and calm, has never caused any trouble. Well, one should never take it for granted; the water level might rise some day, it is a river after all. But for the moment there is no problem; if something happens one will see. With this thought in mind, little cottages have been coming up, their small kitchen gardens almost levelling with the water. The people living here treat the river as if it is their own pond in the backyard. Placing a stone slab on the water they have drawn out their own space, their very own ghat. How much garbage would the poor householders generate anyway? Theirs are not big houses or hotels that will produce tonnes of plastic waste every day. They are poor no doubt, but they have their own toilets. So all they use the river for is washing clothes and having a bath. The river does not mind, it takes that much grime nonchalantly on its way. With the moist touch of the water the trees on the bank – coconut, jackfruit, betel nut, among others – have grown rapidly creating a border of green on the bank.

Every family member living in the little cottages takes part in running the house. If the husband goes to stand in line to buy biscuits from the wholesale shop to be sold at a little profit back home, the wife leaves home to work in somebody's house as a part-timer maid or to the bazaar to sell *moori*. Most of them cannot afford to send their children, especially the boys, to college. After passing the school final or even before that, the boys take up some job around the place. Most of them work in car-repairing garages or bakeries or as salesmen in shops. The people here are grateful to the town that somebody has not come out with a gun to shoot them dead and that they are still alive. In the evening, the earthen lamp lit at the base of the basil plant in the courtyard of every house reflects against the water like garlands of light.

One does not come across houses big enough to attract attention in this part of the town. The few which are to be found are in the centre of the town. The only big house in this area belongs to Ramgopal De. Ramgopal has left behind his original home under duress. Actually, all the people who have built their little houses on the bank of the river have been driven from their original homes in different villages. Like them, Ramgopal had also left behind his, fearing the ethnic cleansing some people took part in while seeking their own land, and has now settled down here. Everybody calls him 'De babu'. He had sold off his paddy fields, house, everything, at a ridiculously cheap price before moving here. He opened a garage to start his life all over again. Besides repairing damaged cars, he has also started another business. He buys broken cars and buses, almost beyond repair, makes them as good as new and sells them in the market. Often he buys abandoned passenger buses because they are too ramshackle for use, then builds a new body, repairs the engine, and sells them to an interested buyer. At times he even buys buses auctioned off by the government agencies.

Most of the boys who work in De babu's garage belong to the houses on the riverbank. Ramgopal started prospering quite soon. Like his neighbours, Ramgopal is also grateful to the town. Well, there are those who come from time to time to collect money from him. Wherever one lives, there will be a class of people who will squeeze money from him, he knows. But isn't he lucky that someone hasn't come to burn down his cottage or shot and killed his family members? His two sons have grown up here. Now the older one is studying for a medical degree while the younger one is studying computer science. So he feels thankful to the little town. In fact, most of the people in this town are new settlers who have come from different parts of the region after leaving their homes for some reason or the other. In the last decade, lots of people from the interiors have arrived fearing for their lives, bought small plots of land and built new houses. They belong to different communities, all looking for a new beginning. The little town by the river has not turned anyone away. The elephant herds descending from the hills do not come here; even those with their guns cannot come to blatantly kill the residents. Yes, from time to time, a body is found by the roadside, a bit of looting and demands for money go on surreptiously. But who would consider these little incidents dangerous?

The real danger is heralded by the ones with two legs. They could shoot down everyone in sight as if people were birds; they could light the houses on fire if they fancied. So the people remain fearful – like cattle after escaping from a burnt-down shed and now so scared as to fear even the hint of a red cloud. So they prick their ears instantly even if the sound of bursting crackers comes from a wedding party arriving at the bride's house. *Has anything happened? Is there trouble somewhere?* – they worry. But then life goes on with all these discernments, fears and hopes. The rice stalks ripen in the field, the simolu trees flower, the silver fish play in the river, trees full of ripe mangoes and jackfruit, orange and lychee, bow with the weight of the fruits, the new moon appears, the full moon washes over the countryside, the dhol beats welcome the Bihu, the dhak resounds with Durga puja, the *ciphun* flute is heard during the Baisagu festival, men and farm produce congregate in the weekly *haat* as always. Yes, life goes on.

One day into this town entered a bus at midnight. The bus approached the road, which veers away from the national highway near the police checkpost at the chari-ali. The bus could not progress on its own steam; a truck was pulling it. The silence of the night was rudely disturbed as the bus laboured down the road.

The lights from the cars on the national highway had obliterated the soft light of the full moon, but this lonely road was flooded by moonlight. The trembling leaves of the coconut trees took on a silver hue under the sky. And the river? It was as if it had plucked the moon from the sky and gathered it in her breasts. The water sparkled with its silvery waves. At twenty minutes to one, the bus arrived on the bank of the river with a screeching sound. But now the moon resting on the breast of the river suddenly disappeared. The silver colour vanished too. The bus was being dragged along the riverbank. Wherever the truck-drawn bus passed, the water of the river turned dark; the sky above the water became dark too. There was no moon, no stars; what remained was only an inky-dark, impenetrable sky. An odd putrid smell came from the river water. Like the odour of clotted day-old blood. Under the dark sky as the bus went on, the water of the river became red – the colour of blood.

The truck stopped after some time. The driver and his assistant got down for a wash in the river. They had come a long way after all and needed to freshen up. They could not see any habitation around. When the driver braked to stop the bus, its front part banged into something. In any case the bus was in a shambles. Now a burnt splinter of wood from the bus fell into the river. Immediately the silver fish floated up to the surface, all dead. How did the fish die suddenly? Was it because the river got filled with blood and they could not breathe? Or was it because the moon disappeared, and darkness covered the earth? Once again, the burnt bus pulled by the truck was on its slow journey along the river where it played hide and seek with the road. Wherever the shadow of the bus fell on the river, the water became blood-red in colour and the fish died. As the bus tore through the midnight silence with its screeching *ghetleng-ghetleng* sound, the fireflies in flight above burnt to ashes and vanished into the jungle.

The truck took a turn. It was difficult to manouevre the bus tied to its rear. But the road was empty so it could somehow be managed. At that point, the river also took a turn. At that junction, one could see a sizeable sandbank. The land here remained fertile all through the year. Even today it was so. Newly appearing green seedlings of wheat carpeted the soil. As the bus followed the truck at this turning, its shadow fell on the sandbank. Instantly a fire seemed to burn everything. The little wheat plants went up in cinders as if a jungle fire had scorched them. The leaves became black and crumpled. Its young stalks sank to the earth. Within a minute the green stretch ensconced lovingly in the midst of the river lost its lush cover and took on an ugly black hue.

Now the bus was travelling underneath a huge banyan tree. The ancient tree's branches had sprouted roots that penetrated the earth. It was a really huge tree. From here the wide paddy fields stretched for miles. After a tiring day in the field, the farmers took rest under the shade of the tree. They shared lunch and exchanged the news of the day before returning to the fields again. The trunk and branches had many hollows where different kinds of birds made their nests. Next to the tree were paddy fields. The tree provided shelter, so it was natural that the birds built nests in it. But now something happened to the old tree. It could no longer offer protection to the myriad birds it had sustained for so long. As the half-burnt bus went on its way underneath the banyan tree, the birds fell down one by one as if they were seeds. The birds looked shell-shocked and lay spreadeagled on the ground. A big family of *salika* fell on top of each other in a pile. Flocks of parrots, sparrows, bulbulis, *mou-pia*, lay in clusters on the grass below. Like the *kopou* birds of north India which drop off one by one in the peak of summer, these birds of the ancient tree also fell off one by one from the branches. It looked as if life had been sucked away from them by an unbearable heat.

Darkening the sky and the water of the river, killing the fish, burning the fireflies, impaling the birds, the half-burnt bus went on towards the little town. At the edge of the town is an old pond. A thick cluster of lotus flowers has floated in it for ages. The leaves entangle with each other, the flowers pop up one after another adoring the moonlight. Today the white and red lotuses were in full glory under the silver moon. But as soon as the bus reached the spot, the lotuses started looking unnatural. It was as if a wind hot enough to melt metals wrapped itself around the blooming flowers. Before the eyes could blink, the flowers withered and came to rest on the leaves. But how could the leaves hold on to the flowers? They themselves crumpled up in the heat. By the time the bus left the spot, the beautiful lotus garden in the pond was gone.

The truck was speeding up a little now. The driver must have been tired after the long journey and wanted to get home as soon as possible. The screeching sound was getting louder – *ghetleng-ghetleng* – it went. Now one could hear its approach from the rows of the simolu tree. But these trees were sturdy. Not like the delicate lotus or the tiny birds, nor like the little fish in the river which could be killed with one slight of the palm. They had sturdy trunks and strong branches. But were they strong enough to save themselves from the poisonous gas emanating from the burnt vehicle? Now as the bus passed by the road, their leaves wilted as if singed by fire. The strong gas poisoned the trees to their roots. In a moment, the branches which were playing with the moonlight and breeze, bowed down in anguish. The row of trees died instantly. The burnt leaves gathered into knee-high dumps beneath.

At last the bus arrived in the little town. It was almost dawn now. People were slowly waking up. On the right side, from where the road led to the town there was a small, tidy house. Even a cursory glance would reveal that the family had moved in recently. The coconut plant was young, the banana plant had just one flower and the pomegranate tree was yet to come up to a proper height. Like the young plants the family had a little baby; two new teeth had just appeared in his otherwise empty gums. He slept by early evening; so now he was awake and playing on the bed. As he felt tired, he started crying. His mother was still sleepy and wanted to hush him by putting her nipple in his mouth. Just then the bus crossed by their house. Suddenly the milk froze in her breast, depriving the baby of his only food. The baby started yelling and the mother looked on helplessly.

The bus rambled on in the half darkness of dawn. Down the unsteady bridge, down the broken road, it went.

There is a very old paddy field around here. People live on its other side. The river goes through the open field in a straight line from this corner. The field has already been ploughed. On some patches rice saplings have been planted but most of them are still muddy from the ploughing. The sun from the east had just touched the field when the bus arrived at the spot. The freshly ploughed field filled up with ashes. The black earth looked grim and ugly. The bright light of the morning looked like plumes of smoke. The newly dug field ready for planting should have had a moist, earthy smell; instead it now smelt of ashes from burnt houses and smoke.

But the bus went on, that half-burnt bus.

The black ash made the mud sticky. The frogs living in the field perished; their white bellies lay upturned to the sky. They started giving out a putrid smell that filled the air, making it unbearable to breathe.

The bus was now skirting the field. A few minutes ago a flock of white cranes had landed on the field. Now their white wings too were spattered with black soot. Then one by one they dropped on the black earth, their necks twisted at an odd angle. The white flock of cranes were now dead.

As the paddy field was left behind, the houses appeared. Most of the people were still sleepy. The bus had rolled down several horrendous patches of road while passing the villages and got a drubbing. Now while coming across a big crater on this road where after the rains a duck could swim, the bus jumped at the impact. A loose piece of glass scattered into smithereens with a loud noise. A few people who were feeling too lazy to get up though they were awake found their chests pierced by the sharp shards of glass. They could feel the pieces lodged in their hearts and doubled over on their beds with intense pain.

The bus left the main road unable to go ahead; the bridge in front was half complete. The people somehow went across the temporary bamboo bridge but was it possible for a bus to do so? So it took the road on the side of the reserve forest. It is a government reserve forest. The jungle is full of *saal* and *segun* trees. There are other trees too and underneath are bushes of dhekia ferns. As the half-burnt bus made its way by the forest, the thick leaves of the saal trees got burnt and soon an acrid smell like burning tobacco leaves drifted through the air and assailed the senses. The bark of the trees became black and the fern leaves turned into cinders.

Destroying the forest thus, the bus went on. Bypassing the broken bridge, the bus emerged on the other side of the main road. The river too emerged at this point.

The air was heavy with moisture; perhaps it was going to rain. The dancing dragonflies indicated as much. The soft morning light fell on their transparent wings and reflected the hues of sunlight. They went flying up into the air, waited for some time and then started flying again horizontally. But as the sound of the bus heralded its arrival, the dragonflies died, burnt. Within a second their thin wings crumbled and put an end to their dancing frenzy.

So it went on, this terrible bus, destroying everything on its way.

The crows started cawing from their nests. The street dogs woke up from their slumber and started barking. 'What's happened this early in the morning?' some people wondered and opened the window to check. If someone caught sight of the bus, he or she could not open their eyes any more for they started smarting. They splashed water on their faces. In agony, some wondered whether to blindfold themselves or put some medicine in their eyes, and before long they realized they were losing their vision.

The bus was still rolling along. Its destination was De babu's garage.

The boys were coming out of their houses on the edge of the river, houses where the earthen lamps lit in the evening at the base of tulsi plants reflected like garlands on the water. It was early morning, too early, in fact, for them to start working. But today their boss had asked them to start earlier than usual. A new job was coming up. The *malik* had already bought the material for the seat covers, bundles of rexine and leather, steel sheet and other knick-knacks needed to convert a broken-down bus into a new one. In fact, De babu had arranged to bring a few more half-burnt buses for repair work. After all, these kinds of buses were not so common. He was expecting a good profit. The young men were approaching from the direction opposite the oncoming half-burnt bus. They seemed very enthusiastic. The job meant some extra money for them. Which meant they could fulfil some secret desire. They handed their regular earnings to keep the home fire burning but this money could buy a pair of jeans, a cell phone, a pair of shoes perhaps. So those boys teetering between adolescence and youth got up early without complaint and were chatting happily.

The bus had by that time reached De babu's garage. The young boys could see it from a distance. A half-burnt bus with a long body blackened with soot. Even in this state, it was easy to see that the bus was a luxury bus meant for long-distance travel, comfortable and smart. They were sure that with their experienced hands they could make it look new.

The young men approached the bus with hammers and other instruments. Two of them slid down under the bus, two went to the front, another two were by its side. They were ready to start. But as soon as they touched the bus they were turned into stone. Yes, those fresh young men standing between adolescence and youth turned into statues.

That bus which had entered the town at midnight aiming for De babu's garage had come from a place that had reverted to an uncivilized age. The community that wanted its own state wanted to establish its right over others and had called for a bandh. The bus had entered the area early in the morning. It was full of passengers. The morning was bright and sunny. Under that bright sun the bus was burning furiously. Not a single passenger could escape. The windows and door of the bus were shut tight and a can of petrol was emptied on the vehicle. Even before the fire caught properly, the poisonous gas asphyxiated the little children in the laps of their parents. On the lonely road the bus burnt unattended. Before fleeing the scene, the attackers had aimed their rifles at the bus; the bullets came in torrents. Of course, not a single passenger survived. By the time the police, the military, the administrators and the fire brigade vans arrived, the people inside the bus were dead, their bodies reduced to clumps of burnt flesh.

Yes, the half-burnt bus entered the town at midnight.

The Auspicious Day

27 November 2011. This was a special day according to the Hindu almanac and extremely auspicious for weddings. After examining the positions of different planets the astrologers declared that it was one of the best days to get married. The capital of the country was agog with the preparations. Even the newspapers reported that on this day there would be almost 35,000 weddings. The whole city seemed to have turned into a big wedding venue. The huge population of the city was in an animated state. Hundreds of cars were ready to ferry guests and merrymakers. The city looked like a new bride, bright and beautiful.

Look at that wedding venue. In front of the gate are two mermaids. In their hands are two lotus flowers. From the flowers spout two colourful fountains. The carpet that leads to the inner court is a soft blue, matching the colour of the sea, the abode of the mermaids. At the centre of the courtyard you can see a huge white fish tinged in red; its tail moves from side to side and from its mouth spouts a fountain of coloured water. The table, laden with a variety of foods, looks like a boat, creating the impression that all these goodies have been churned up from the bottom of the sea.

The latest trend in the city is to have 'theme' weddings. Everything is taken care of by the event management companies, not to worry. For example, a birthday party could be organized around the fairy queen. On the grass lawn surrounded by high walls to ensure that prying eyes are kept at bay, the fairy tale unfolds. Amidst the flowers are tiny flower princes and princesses. From amidst them rises Cinderella, her pumpkin buggy, one shoe of the high-heel pair left behind in her hurry. In this way, children of the rich and powerful celebrate their birthday parties in the colourful world of fables. This fashion has now spread to other celebrations. As in wedding venues. If one has flowers as their theme, the other has the sea. You shell out the heavy-duty bill and hey presto! Get everything to your taste done to perfection. These days, institutes to train workers who can give shape to the dreams of customers have sprung up everywhere. Just make a phone call and relax.

Tonight, the lane near this park was reverberating with loud music. The lights dazzled the eyes. The groom, in a golden outfit, was riding a white horse. His face was covered with strings of small garlands. Behind him was a young man. He had a *kirpan* in his hand smeared with vermillion. As the music got louder, he swayed the kirpan rhythmically in the air. Was it a groom on his way to get married, or was he on an expedition to defeat enemies, you wondered. You couldn't be blamed for thinking wryly that it was more like a charging army than a wedding procession. Well, he was indeed a prince who was on a journey to win wars. Somewhere, a princess was waiting, confined to a lonely island. The members of the band party, wearing sherwani-kurtas in red and gold, revved up the music to a frenzied tempo. Their headgears too were a golden colour. Golden fringes hung from their shoulders. Under the piercing light the band with their drums and clarinets looked as if they were musicians in the Mughal court. One of them held an eye-catching placard which shone invitingly. It announced that though they looked like musicians from the Mughal court, they actually belonged to this technology age. They worked for modern-day companies trading in music for such occasions. Written in big fonts, both in Hindi and English, the placard announced, 'Har Nand Dhalwala Private Ltd' with the cell phone and landline numbers thrown in for good measure. Even the email address was printed: har-nanddhalwala@yahoo.com.

In the next lane too, you could see another groom's party on its way. The same music, the same placard, 'Har Nand Dhalwala Private Ltd' with its cell number, email address, and so on, was in evidence, the only difference being that this groom was not riding a white horse. He was in a Mercedes Benz. The red car was almost immersed in flower decorations.

There, yet another buggy came up carrying a bridal couple. The ornamented carriage was also nearly buried in flowers. You wondered from where so many flowers had appeared in a city where there was not any empty space between two houses. Actually, the city is supplied by a huge flower market from the hinterlands. Today that market was overwhelmed by thousands of orders. Of course, the price had shot up too. But who cares, the most important thing was to get hold of the desired posy. Otherwise the wedding venues would look bare. Who could bear even to think of that? After all, a wedding happens only once. And this is a city where the average income per person is one of the highest in the country.

So it was not surprising that the flash of money sparkled everywhere. Look, a groom was now throwing currency notes merrily. Hundred-rupee and 500-rupee notes were flying in the air, carrying the message in no uncertain manner about arrogance born of money and power. The groom was also wearing a garland of thousand-rupee notes. Amidst the flying notes a woman lifted her hands to the sky in a dance *mudra*, her diamond and gold bangles tinkled and shone. If figures from history – Chengiz Khan or a Sultan Mahmood of Ghazni – resurrected themselves now and invaded this city, they would have managed to carry sacks of gold and diamonds after slicing through wedding venue after wedding venue.

But the fear of the invaders was absent now, so the people had no worry while turning the capital into a huge wedding venue. Not a single wedding hall or hotel was empty. The illuminations turned the city into a fairy land. Look at that star hotel. At other times too it attracted attention with its bright facade, but today it was dressed like a bride in a dazzling sequin outfit. Its parking space was overflowing with cars, which spilled over to the kerb outside jostling for space.

It seemed that the best food items in the world were piled together on the platters. A tempting aroma wafted in the air. A thriving market supplying the food worked behind the scenes. Like the flowers, their price too had sky-rocketed but so what, the city was in the throes of celebration. Even the trees bowed down with the weight of fairy lights entwined around their branches.

So on this *suvodin*, this auspicious day, when 35,000 weddings were taking place in the city, the frenzy of activities was reaching a crescendo. Understandably, the police were in a tizzy organizing the traffic and managing other logistics. Not a single policeman could go on leave. The department, in fact, had to rope in extra personnel. Their problem multiplied with weddings held in the farmhouses on the city's outskirts. At the wedding venues on rent or hotels at least there were allotted parking spaces. When one spent lakhs of rupees on one night some privileges had to be provided. But at the farmhouse weddings cars had to be parked on the road itself. That created a real problem for the policemen on duty as they had to run around trying to accommodate the huge luxury cars. On the other hand, the police department had made a rule that private farmhouses let out for weddings, could not have parking on the main road. Now, what to do? After all, how could people travel from this corner of the city to the other without a car? And then there was another problem; the police had also made it mandatory for the event to be wrapped up by eleven p.m., which was almost impossible. After the bride was led to the holy fire of the *hom* for the wedding ritual and later when she bid adieu to the parents as a sad tune played in the background, it was usually past midnight. So though the police department had made certain rules, was it possible to comply? Hence the policemen faced a hundred problems.

There were also logistical problems with so many weddings happening on the same day. Look at the beautiful four-storeyed building in red and white under the gulmuhar tree. It is known as Amarjit Manjil. Three generations of the same family have lived here. On the top floor live the grandson and his wife; both work in well-known MNCs. On the floor below live their parents. The father has a clothes mill in the suburbs. The mother is a homemaker. On the ground floor live the patriarch Parminder and his wife Amarjeet. However, the old couple does not stay here all the time. They visit their village where they own a considerable expanse of fertile land. Obviously, they are quite rich. Now a wedding was on the cards for this family. The old couple's granddaughter Surinder was getting married. The groom lived in London; his family had been running a flourishing business for two generations now. The plan was to hold the function in a five-star hotel with all the paraphernalia. But it was all in vain. The family could not book a venue in time, not even a guest house for a night. The problem was that the wedding was fixed at very short notice. By then all the venues were booked. So they took permission from the authorities and held the function in a plot next to their house.

However, the family of Ashok Khosla was luckier. They could manage to have their wish fulfilled to hold the wedding at a star hotel. Of course, they too are well off. Khosla has retired as a high-ranking officer in the army. All his four sons are well established. They have taken advantage of globalization well. Ashok Khosla would sometimes feel surprised by the salaries offered by companies. At such a young age his sons received such a huge salary! You must admit that the MNCs pay very well indeed, never mind the workload. The youngest daughter of the Khosla family was getting married. She planned to place an order for her *lehenga* at Bride's Beauty, famous for their exclusive designs. For a good reason. Besides making the bride look exquisite, the heavily embroidered crimson outfit embellished with gem stones and golden thread would also announce the family's social standing. But alas, BB had been overbooked for six months already. So she had to wear a lehenga from another boutique which saddened her no end.

The availability of priests posed another problem. Thirty-five thousand weddings would require 35,000 priests, right? All of them would be following Hindu rituals. How was it possible? On this day, the son of a powerful political leader was also getting married. With so many years of playing the field of political imbroglios, the father had no problem in organizing everything to his satisfaction. The only problem he faced was how to book a priest. So from among his fleet of cars, he gave one to the priest so that he could arrive in time. The priest was extremely happy. He was also arranging for a puja to the god Shani two days prior to the wedding to appease the god who, he found, was angry with the politician for some reason. Naturally, the priest stopped taking on any other assignments. Thus on the auspicious day, the priest became the owner of an i10 car, besides pocketing his high remuneration.

There were also unexpected problems involving the groom's horse. Members of the 'Save the Animal' group objected to the practice of the groom riding a horse. A few households conceded but most cocked a snook at their demand. So protests, as well as grooms arriving on horses, happened side by side.

All these events turned the capital's atmosphere exciting and euphoric. Look anywhere and you would be caught in the dazzle of money. During the Mughal era this city was known for its luxurious lifestyle. Rich objets d'art in many hues shone like a peacock's fan. Today on this suvodin the medieval royal court seemed to have descended on this modern city. Even the seats for the bridal couple looked like the peacock throne of Shahjahan. The reception area looked like replicas of Sheesh Mahal or Khas Mahal. The groom was dressed like an emperor and the bride like an empress. There was one difference, however. During the Mughal durbar days, this luxurious lifestyle could be found in a limited area where the royal lived. The other areas inhabited by commoners were ordinary, even impoverished. But today in this modern city the Mughal court culture seemed to have spread all across the city.

You hear that there are some more wedding dates this month. The tabloids have reported that altogether one lakh weddings would have taken place during this time. Out of them were today's 35,000. A leading newspaper carried the report on the first page, 'Wedding industry generates 1,90,000 crore business.' Difficult to believe? But why? Can't you see the game of money played all around?

Despite expensive lights flooding the city, there were nooks which continued to wear their usual look with a few fixed lights here and there. The educational institutes, hospitals, government and private offices, bus depots and Metro stations, for example. They have not been touched by the fever of celebrations. The railway station also looked the same. The trains went up and down, the same lights blinkered on the platform, the passengers moved in a hurry as always, the same stalls with displays, the same porters in their red shirts, the same huge clock, the same TV screen. The same odour too, as also the garbage in the corners, the same group of young boys, dirty and bedraggled with sacks on their shoulders trying to salvage something usable from the waste bins.

This was a busy time at the station. Quite a few passenger trains came and left. Like on other days, Rajul was running up and down the platform with his sack hanging from his shoulder. He was twelve years old. His home was in one of the poorest areas of the country. His family was just as poor. He was the eldest in the family. He read up to the level the Sarba Siksha Abhijan enabled him to. Then the family sent him with his uncle to this city to do *dhanda* and earn a living. His uncle stayed in a slum; his family too got left behind in the same village. He introduced Rajul to his 'profession', which in reality involved retrieving objects which could be of use from the garbage bins. This was a job which did not need any educational certificate, no training, no permission. Just foraging through the things passengers threw away was enough to provide for two meals a day. But even here, one had to know the intricacy of the trade – what to pick up, what object to give to whom, who would buy the things he collected. Rajul's uncle explained all these things to him. Now he could manage on his own. On his arrival, he first stayed with his uncle in a shed covered by a blue plastic sheet. It was shared by four other men. Well, 'staying' was an overstatement. After labouring the whole day, they just spread sheets on the floor and went to sleep. After two months Rajul decided to stay on the platform. After the hot and humid shed of his uncle, it was a better option with taps for water, lights and fans and a more open space at his disposal. The winter days, of course, were torture. He dreaded the winter nights. Rajul worked hard; he did not have any bad habits like other boys in the group. They were addicted to different kinds of drugs. Their earnings were spent on Dendrite. A few could not spend a night without the powder that came in small wrappings. Thankfully, Rajul was free from all this. He nursed a small dream in his heart. If he could save a little, he would buy a handcart and ferry ice, lemon and water. He had observed that in the hot summer, lemon juice and ice sold very well. In the winter, he would ferry fried peanut and savoury pakodas. Perhaps one day he would have his own shed in the slum. Then he could bring his mother from the village to stay with him. When he thought of her, his mind strayed. His mother was in such a dire state back home. But the formula never worked. Like the distended plastic bottles he collected, Rajul's dreams were misshapen. The discarded bottles were later broken into pieces by stamping on them. Sometimes he felt his heart was like that – breaking into pieces. He had confided about his dream in only one person, his friend Lalu. He had promised to stick by him in his venture. Lalu said he would roast the groundnuts, deep-fry the pakodas, and prepare the sherbet too in the summer. Sometimes at night as they lay on the platform they drove the handcart in their imagination.

But the maths never added up for Rajul; the handcart seemed like a distant moon. At the moment with winter knocking at the door, the most urgent need was to get hold of a warm jacket. At the most, he earned a hundred rupees a day if the picking was good. But it was rare to get so many abandoned bottles in a single day. He had to buy rotis for lunch and dinner too. Besides, he had to send money home. His mother waited for it. Without his money the other members of the family could go hungry. With great perseverance he was able to save only a hundred rupees. Now it seemed even the jacket was like a distant moon to him.

Recently he had made a change. He stopped buying rotis from the stalls. Instead he and Lalu jointly bought a griddle, two plates, a knife and a spoon. Lalu was an expert at cooking. He planned to buy a pot for cooking dal. In the evening on the footpath leading to the station, Lalu and Rajul started their 'household'. They collected, along with the bottles, plastics and papers and concocted a stove on three brick slabs and roasted the rotis. True to his word, Lalu managed to get hold of a pot to cook dal. So now they had the luxury of sitting comfortably on the footpath polishing off rotis with freshly cooked dal. Afterwards, they retired to the platform for the night. As soon as they spread the jute sacks that were their beds and lay down, they were fast asleep. During the day, besides running around collecting the bottles, they had to walk ten to fifteen kilometres carrying the sacks to reach the *thekkadar* – the contractor. Who would allow them to board a bus with their dirty sacks even if they paid the fare? They were barred from travelling in any kind of public transport. So they walked and walked, dragging their half-worn sandals.

Rajul liked to watch films on the TV screen on the platform. In one film he saw Sunny Deol beating up a policeman. From then on Deol was the favourite hero for both of them. If a film with Sunny Deol was playing on the TV they tried to catch a few snatches at least. They hated policemen. The police harassed them at any available opportunity. And look, Sunny Deol beat them up! How could he not be their hero? One hundred per cent!

The city opened up so many avenues for earning a living for them, and for this they were grateful. If they had stayed on in their village, how could they have managed to have hot roti and dal just by picking up discarded water bottles? Besides, where would there have been so many bottles back home anyway? Rajul and Lalu did not read newspapers. Had they done so, they would have come across a report on the number of boys like them. This capital city had 1,00,000 ragpickers. There were pictures accompanying the story. The dirty clothes, their clothes either too small or too big, their bodies emaciated. Like them.

However, the auspicious date of 27 November was going to touch their lives favourably too, Rajul and Lalu were sure. They knew that the next day there would be a good haul from the waste bins and the railway station footpath. They looked forward to a good income.

On the TV screen, a Sunny Deol film was on. Lalu and Rajul were watching it in fits and starts as they snoozed. They put the bottles they had picked up during the day in the sack and then had their roti and dal. They saved a couple of rotis for the next day which could be washed down with water from the tap on the platform.

Lalu loved to show off his culinary expertise while cooking dinner. Today he had brought a packing box. A fire with polythene and frayed paper was not strong enough to roast the rotis; the wheat in it remained half cooked. Today he would have the luxury of a fire lit with real wood. He had also bought half a kilogram of mixed dal. Rajul bought two onions in the evening. Both of them enjoyed chopped raw onion with the simple roti-dal meal.

Ashok bhaiya was rather fond of Rajul and Lalu. He needed their help sometimes and enjoyed their company too. Like them, he had left behind his family behind in a distant village. Last summer he suffered from a terrible bout of dysentery. But for Rajul and Lalu he would have died. People like him, even Rajul or Lalu, could easily become *bewarish laash* – unclaimed bodies.

After dinner, Rajul and Lalu bundled up their little 'kitchen' in a sack and set it up near Ashok bhaiya's stall. Rajul often teased Lalu about his passion for his household.Throughout the day, though he ran around, if he got something of use for his little household, Lalu would sprint and drop it in his sack. Rajul sometimes suspected that he ran around to check if the sack was still there.

When the incident took place, both Rajul and Lalu were either snoozing or watching a Sunny Deol film after their meagre lunch. They had collected the plastic bottles and flattened them too. By evening they would deliver them to the *thekkadar*. Meanwhile, they were thinking of the dal they would enjoy at night. Ah, all those varieties combined – arhar, chana, moong, masoor – to be cooked on a fire made of real wood from a packing box. They could not imagine this luxury back home. Rajul had not told Lalu that he had bought, besides the two onions, a small pack of mango pickle from Sita bai who sold them in the railway compartments. He kept it hidden under his too-short sweater. Hidden between the shirt and the sweater, the polythene pack with mango pieces, swimming in oil, was safe. At times he touched the pack and thought how Lalu would jump with joy at the surprise. He imagined how he would suck at the kernel for a long time.

He looked at the half-asleep Lalu and smiled. On the screen Sunny Deol was thrashing an anti-social and then threw him on a cart full of watermelons. Ah, how nice to see the man's face looking helpless amidst the pile of watermelons. Rajul was about to clap his hands in glee when it happened.

A man jumped in front of an incoming train. Nobody knew who he was or from where he had come. And why did he jump like this? To commit suicide, of course! Why did he want to take leave of this world? The people on the platform were caught off guard as it happened in the blink of an eye. The man was cut into pieces by the moving train. The head fell on one side, the legs on the other side and the arms on another. The police arrived blowing the siren. The railway track with the dead man's limbs lying about was closed for traffic. Platform number 4 became crowded with onlookers trying to catch a glimpse of the gory sight.

Rajul and Lalu joined the crowd too. It seemed that the scene from the film they were watching with blood-red watermelon pieces scattered about was now transferred to the track. Rajul averted his eyes immediately; his head seemed to reel. Lalu had already left the scene. So Rajul decided to follow him too. But then he heard a policeman speak and stopped. A 500-rupee note was held between his two fingers. Lifting his hand above, the policeman announced that whoever picked up the limbs of the dead man and packed them in a sack would get the money as a labour fee. Nobody came forward. Another policeman brought a plastic sack. The first policeman was still holding up the reward of 500 rupees firmly between his two fingers. Rajul's eyes were glued to the note. A warm jacket! If he got this note Ashok bhaiya would give him the jacket promptly. He did not even allow Rajul to touch that expensive thing. That jacket with leather outside and fur inside. One day he begged Ashok bhaiya to take it down from the top shelf just to touch it. Ah, how soft it was! Whenever he opened the store in the morning, Ashok bhaiya always hung this jacket on a hanger, along with a woman's coat and a few sweaters to attract customers. The other clothes, less important, were spread on the cot.

Rajul made up his mind. He suddenly went up to the policeman. He folded his hand on his chest and said that he would do the job. Rajul stepped down on to the track. The people on the platform moved to the edge to watch.

At first, Rajul hung the plastic sack on his shoulder, getting ready, as if he was going to pick out discarded things from the waste bin. He first saw an arm, the fingers splayed; one of the fingers had a silver ring and on the side of the arm there was a tattoo with some writing. As he tried to pick up the arm Rajul felt faint; the arm looked like a scaled piece of fish, the colour of the skin like the watermelon in the film. He closed his eyes and picked up the arm and put it in the sack.

He then went for the other arm; it was broken into two. As he tried to pick up one part his stomach churned, he felt like throwing up. Again he closed his eyes and put both the pieces in the sack. He looked unusually pale. Drops of perspiration lined his forehead. His hands and feet shook. An unusual throb went up his spine to the back of his head and down. He was trembling, the people on the platform could see. They were now silent, dumbstruck. Suddenly a shout broke through the silence. It was Lalu. He had by now put two dry chillies in his precious sack. There were a couple of carts with the chillies that had come by another train, and he picked up a couple from them. Just imagine, a thick dal with a seasoning of those chillies – hot, aromatic. Now the only thing left was to deliver the bottles to the thekkadaar. He was annoyed with Rajul. What was taking him so long? Then he came to know from Ashok bhaiya that Rajul had volunteered to collect the dead body, or rather the decimated limbs. Was he mad? Now looking at Rajul he was struck dumb. Who was this boy? He felt scared. Rajul was standing near the corpse; by his side was a sack. Within such a short time, between Lalu going to Ashok bhaiya's stall and returning, how had this boy, his friend, changed so much? Lalu shouted and tried to jump down on to the track but a policeman held him back immediately. Lalu tried to say, 'Stop doing this.' His voice could not carry the message, his tongue was stuck, unable to move. People could make out from his half-said words that he was asking Rajul to drop immediately this horrible task. The policemen dragged him away as if holding onto the tail of a dead rat and locked him up in their van. From there too Lalu kept shouting.

But Rajul was oblivious to any sound coming his way. Now he was trying to lift a leg by its knee. A bone was stuck to the track. He dragged at it but was finding it difficult. He felt a veil of mist covering his eyes. He somehow put the leg in the sack. Now he approached the body, without a head, but with the other leg still intact. His stomach churned again; he was unable to touch the body. He vomited on the track. Somebody was shouting – well, it was the policeman, advising him to take the money and have a bath. A passenger added that Rajul should buy a packet of joss sticks after the bath and go to a temple. It was an unnatural death after all. A few others agreed; if he did not visit a temple, this thing would trouble him all his life. And he would have to offer a proper puja too. Rajul did not hear any of it. The only thought running through his mind was that he had taken up a job, and he must finish it.

Throughout his short life, he had been stalked by the same refrain – finish the job, only then would you have a roti, otherwise you would go to bed hungry. For his young body that could digest even a stone, this fire of hunger was all-consuming. So finish the job somehow, this is what he had learnt. Finish cutting the wheat, finish the weeding, finish picking up the plastic bottles, flatten them with your feet, deliver them to the thekkadaar, finish searching for bottles in the waste bins and compartments. Finish, finish, finish – and have the roti to eat. Otherwise everything stopped. His brain was unable to think of anything else at the moment. Only this message went on hammering in his head – finish your job, otherwise you won't survive. You'll die of hunger, you'll die of cold.

Look, Rajul had put the headless corpse in the sack. Someone from the crowd on the platform shouted, '*Shabbash beta, bahadur bachcha!*' Bravo! Brave boy! But Rajul did not hear anything. The voyeuristic spectators did not realize that Rajul was losing his ordinary senses, he was like a zombie mechanically doing what he had to do. Only Lalu could understand the turmoil inside him. Listen to how he was shouting incessantly – 'Rajul bhaiya will be finished, the wicked policemen have made him into a living dead, Rajul bhaiya will be killed by the policemen.' Caged inside the police van Lalu continued howling thus.

Now Rajul went to pick up the head. It was lying face down on the track; Rajul pulled at the hair and turned its face up. The eyes were open. Two eyes, not moving, the steady eyeballs stared at Rajul straight in the eye. What a cold, lifeless look! Rajul looked at the eyes once and then he started screaming. He started frothing at the mouth. The policeman with the 500-rupee note in his hand brought Rajul up from the track. Now the spectators started blaming the policemen. They used the young boy to do what they should have done. Why did they tempt him with the money? The man who was advising him to light joss sticks at a temple now created a hullabaloo saying that the 'thing' had possessed Rajul. The policeman made Rajul lie down on the platform. But he went on howling like an animal. White froth dribbled from his mouth. His eyes became red. He moved in circles on the cement floor, his arms and legs thrashing in the air. It seemed like he was about to die. The policemen were now scared. They carried him inside the van. Even there he did not stop screaming. The van was now moving. And what about Lalu? He was thrown out of the van. He was sitting by the roadside and crying. Rajul bhaiya was finished, he had become rotten, he was now a part of the waste. How he had planned to share the mixed dal and roti with Rajul that night.

After the police van left, platform number 4 went back to its regular routine. The sack with the dead body was removed, and transferred to its destination. The signs of the turmoil were wiped out. The trains started running on the track which had been closed temporarily. The passengers, the luggage, the porter in red uniform returned to their normal schedule. Only Lalu stood forlornly standing by a pole. He felt bereft, and did not feel like doing anything.

The van left the railway station behind and entered the city precincts. Its progress was slow. It had to stop at many points as the exuberant bridal processions blocked the road. They had tied Rajul's hands and feet and thrown him into the back of the van. As the van went through the city's populated areas it seemed as if it was going to be swept away in the euphoric mood of the evening. Rajul was still screaming but the music from the bands accompanying a groom's party drowned the sound. Even the policemen sitting in front could not hear his cry, a cry like that of a pig being slaughtered slowly. The odour from his body was unbearable. But the fragrant air outside from people wearing expensive perfumes somehow helped to smother it.

The hospital was still a little further away. The van continued the journey, breaking through the river of celebrations. By the time the police van with Rajul arrived at the hospital, it was evening.

The polythene packet with the mango pickle remained unharmed between Rajul's too-short sweater and shirt pocket. The onions had by now disappeared somewhere from his pant pocket. Only a few onion skins remained.

The Man Who Planted Palm Trees

The gentleman had just completed eighty years. The very next day while stepping into eighty-one, he suffered a stroke. Luckily, doctor and hospital were both available. He was saved in time, but the left side of his body showed that the stroke had left its mark behind.

I decided to visit his house to enquire after his health. Though this is a city, the approach road to his house was too narrow to drive through. It took me exactly one and a half hours to find a parking spot. This gave me a headache. By the time I reached the house it was almost eight in the evening. I felt guilty about disturbing the old man at this late hour. But I had to come today; the next day I was leaving Assam for a long stint outside.

The house looked dark. The old man had two sons. The elder one was a doctor and lived in the main house with his father, while the younger son lived in Delhi. Wasn't there anyone in the house, I wondered. I had heard that the younger son and his family had come to stay with his father. Had something untoward happened in between? My heart skipped a beat. It would be a great loss if he died. For a long time this man has been a legend in our city. If I could not meet him for some time, I felt something was amiss in my life. Each time I returned after meeting him I felt a sense of fulfilment. His positive words inspired me and for some days at least, I could get a whiff of fresh air in this atmosphere poisoned by negativity.

I stood uncertainly on the stairwell with my mobile phone switched on. Why was everything so silent? I couldn't see Bhola, their black dog with patches of white either; he came out whenever I visited and sat near the armchair on which his owner rested. Sometimes the old man talked to Bhola too. He described his various activities in details.

Somebody must have heard the doorbell. Tilak, the stay-at-home help, opened the door.

'Grandpa is sleeping,' he said. He asked me to sit, switched on the fan and went inside.

'No, no, he is not sleeping. He's reading a book,' a plump boy of seven or eight said as he entered the drawing room through the drawn curtain. His eyes danced mischievously. He must be the offspring of the younger son from Delhi, I surmised. He looked at me directly.

'Are you a friend of my grandpa?' he asked.

'Yes. I am.'

'Do you know, these days Grandpa walks like a penguin?' He demonstrated the walk by dragging his feet, imitating a penguin.

I could now hear a pair of sandals approaching us. And there he was. He dragged his left foot. It was true, he walked differently now. The defect left by the stroke was not difficult to see.

'Look, look, Grandpa is walking like a penguin!' the naughty boy clapped his hands in glee.

'If I am a penguin, you are a sparrow.' His voice was the same, alive and spirited as usual.

'Sparrow – you mean those which come to sit with the salika birds and eat biscuits Grandma gives them?' the little boy asked after giving it some thought.

'But sparrows don't walk, they jump like this!' he said and started jumping, criss-crossing the room.

'What are you doing?' his grandmother came running from inside the room. Her hair was all white and parted in the middle. Bright red vermillion smeared the parting. On her forehead between the slightly curly hair was a red spot as big as a one-rupee coin. She was dressed in white mekhela sador; only a narrow woven border on the sador broke through the whiteness. The 'sparrow' was jumping near the table where numerous trophies the old man had received were displayed. They could have dropped to the floor at any point.

'Oh, oh, he will break everything now,' the old woman trembled at the thought. But the little boy did not pay any attention; he was too busy playing the sparrow. The daughter-in-law entered the room now wearing a light blue saree. Her husband followed her. He looked like a replica of the old man in his youth. The little boy did not listen to his mother. His father now picked him up. The boy looked at me and said, 'You know, Grandpa got all those prizes.'

He got down from his father's lap and stood near the table but was now more careful. His sparrow-like jump stopped too. Pointing to the trophies he said proudly, 'My grandpa has received these for writing books.' Everybody in the room smiled. Now arrived a lot of food: luchi, curry, sweets. The little boy went inside and returned with an A4-size sheet of paper and pointed out, 'My Grandpa has written this.' Showing us the paper he commented like an adult, 'It looks like a computer printout.' We couldn't help laughing again. Now his eyes fell on the sweet which I had set aside, as I excused myself from having two sweets in one go. His grandmother guessed what would follow next, and pulling his hand, tried to persuade him into going to the living quarters inside. She was limping a bit.

'What's happened to her?'

'Oh, what's new? She fell down,' her husband seemed rather amused. His wife was about to leave with her grandson in tow but now stopped. The old man smiled as he said, 'Once she broke her ankle falling down on the courtyard; another time she sprained her ankle while getting down from the bed. This time she has hurt her knee.'

'So what? Have I not looked after you despite that?' the old woman seemed slightly angry.

'If you fall one time, it's an accident, even twice perhaps. But if you fall down thrice you can say it's habit,' the old man said and smiled. We couldn't help smiling too.

The old woman looked at me and said, 'You know, I fell down, but he couldn't lift me up. If you fall one time, it's an accident, even twice, but if you fall down thrice you can say it's a habit!' She imitated her husband perfectly, in tone and gesture.

All of us burst out laughing.

'Why are you complaining? There was no one at home. Who took you to the doctor? This old man.'

'That day Deuta in fact drove the car himself,' his elder son said, his voice betraying his anxiety.

'Oh, is that called driving? I can see the clinic from the verandah itself.'

'Please don't do it,' I said. I was really worried for him. Just think, in this city where even finding a parking spot is a matter of luck, this old man was driving his old Fiat car! It gave me the jitters.

'Don't worry so much. All of us have to go one day. So do we sit at home afraid to step out? And at this age some health problems will surely assail us. As they say, it depends how you treat your body and whether you accept its quirks.' The old man sipped at something Tilak brought for him. For us there was tea.

'See, I am ready. I am ready to bid goodbye to this world. I have got everything that I wanted. I am a thoroughly happy man,' he said.

By now, his wife came back to join us. She was looking at her husband without blinking. She looked a bit tired. She had perhaps put her naughty grandchild to sleep.

'Though she has a habit of falling down from time to time she is not a bad woman,' he said.

'Yes, I am not a bad person. It's you who are bad. You know what he did that day? He smoked a cigarette standing in front of the paan shop at the chari-ali.'

'Deuta, what am I hearing? You are a heart patient, remember!' the doctor son sounded really worried.

'He was standing there, arms akimbo like a young man and smoking; Tilak saw and reported to me,' his wife complained.

The old man looked down, smiling shyly and said, 'Nobody lives forever. I tell you all, get ready to say goodbye to me. I have got everything I wanted from this life.'

'You got everything?' I blurted out, as I could not forget the innumerable betrayals he had suffered.

'Yes. After all, I won't get the Nobel Prize, that much sense I have. But many readers of Assam have liked my books. Otherwise why should the publishers approach me? In my personal life too, I have been lucky; I've got what I strived for.'

I remembered the difficult days in his youth. He could have easily said, 'The best days of my life ... went through the grind,' and so on. But he did not seem to nurse any bitterness.

'And my two sons have not done anything in their life to cause me sorrow,' he said as he looked at both his sons sitting there. But who could cause sorrow for the man with an innocent face like that of a child?

His elder daughter-in-law brought a glass of water and some medicine for him.

'And I am happy with both daughters-in-law too. Both of them are doctorates – one in English, the other in Physics. But see how they respect and look after their mother-in-law who is not even a matriculate. The old woman is not bad either.'

'Okay, stop it,' his wife seemed shy at such praise. She scolded him mildly, 'Oh, how you go on! He has come from such a distance to see you and you are only talking about yourself.'

'Yes, you are right. As I am getting older, I seem to be talking more about myself. Actually, it's winding-up time, that's why.'

'No, please don't think it's time to wind up,' I objected.

The old man kept thinking for a few minutes. Then he said, 'At the age of ninety, Marquez wanted to start all over again. Have you read his *The Memories of My Melancholy Whores*?'

'Yes, I have,' I said and waited with bated breath to hear what the old man might have to say about the book.

'Listen,' he said as he arranged his hearing aid.

'Do you know what the hero of the book wanted to give himself as a present on his ninetieth birthday? A virgin prostitute. He brought an adolescent seamstress from a poor family.'

'But the whole book has been written from a man's point of view,' I interjected. I had a problem with the book and expressed it.

'But you can look at the book from another angle. That young girl could be a symbol of the old man's love for life.'

We discussed animatedly for some time Marquez's depressed prostitute.

'Have you read Marquez's autobiography?' the old man asked and brought the chair nearer to us. He rearranged his hearing aid. 'What a lovely title – *Living to Tell the Tale*. The character of the old granny is unusual, isn't it?'

'Yes, she told the doctor that after the eye operation she could see everything clearly.'

'The things she described always had to do with her bedroom. In the hospital she described everything about her bedroom.'

As the old man talked about the world of *Living to Tell the Tale*, we were all spellbound, caught in the web of that world.

The old lady asked her husband to eat something. I felt mortified that I had spent more time than I should have. *Oh, how could you*, I scolded myself. I came to enquire after the well-being of a person who had recently suffered from a serious ailment. I brought out the fruit juice packs I had brought for him.

'What have you brought? Oh, for a sick patient? Please pour some for me,' he requested and gave the grape juice pack to his elder daughter-in-law.

'Have you read Pamuk? Which ones have you read? I have placed an order for some of his books. They should arrive soon.'

I apologized as I got up to leave. 'Sorry I have taken up too much time. I actually came to enquire after your health,' I said.

'Oh, come on, stay a little longer. We have our dinner late,' the old man persuaded me to spend some more time with them. He then pulled a stool near him and put up his slightly swelling legs. He addressed his wife, 'Please bring the book by Doris Lessing lying on my bed. There is a slip of paper inside, you will see it.'

'Is it Lessing's *The Grass is Singing* you want?' she asked.

'Yes, the one with the white cover; there are two green strokes across.'

The old lady went out, still limping a little. Her legs must have been paining still.

'She is a voracious reader of Assamese and Bengali books but finds the English ones a bit difficult to tackle. I have to explain to her the subject of the book. Sometimes I have to translate some portions for her,' the old man said fondly.

'Seeing Ma and Deuta poring over books sitting on the bed, a neighbour's son had asked, "Are Kaka and Aita appearing for some exam? There are so many books!" But do old people like them appear for exams?' the younger daughter-in-law said. Again there was a round of laughter.

The old lady brought the book, along with coffee and biscuits. She gave the book to her husband. She offered me the cup of coffee and said, 'This book fills your heart with profound sadness, doesn't it? He had told me the story, translating it for me. Ah, that girl Mary! She tried to build a house, but what distress she fell into!'

I finished the coffee and got up to leave, excusing myself, 'I've spent more time than I thought I would. It's your dinnertime too and there must be cooking to be done.' The watch showed it was a quarter past nine.

Both the daughters-in-law and the old lady informed me that it was already prepared – dal, fried vegetable, fish curry and some other dishes, which were being kept hot in casseroles.

'I'll just wash the rice and cook it in a jiffy, don't worry,' the old lady said. She seemed to be eager to hear more about the book and was looking at her husband with her palm on her chin.

'Lessing chose a title that captured Eliot's poem very well. The empty room with no windows where the wind swirled is like Mary's tin house, hot under the sun, isn't it?'

'What were the lines of the poem?'

Who asked this question? Perhaps the elder son.

'I have never tried to translate poems. But somehow I felt like translating this passage into Assamese. But it's a very tough job, you know!' his father said.

His wife brought him the reading glasses and from inside the pages of the book she took out a slip of paper.

Paharar major ei poson dhora khorangtut
Seta jonor pohorat, ghanh bore gaan jure
Hamkhuri khai pori thoka kobor buror uporat, girja tor
kase kase
Sunyo girjatu, botahor basosthan etiya.
Eiyat kuno khiriki nai, duwa-rkhon henduli thake
Sukai jowa harbure kar ki soati-tu koribo.

In this decayed hole among the mountains
In the faint moonlight, the grass is singing
Over the tumbled graves, about the chapel
There is the empty chapel, only the wind's home.
It has no windows, and the door swings,
Dry bones harm no one.

The Wasteland, Part V

The old man stopped to catch his breath. He seemed a bit tired.

'A man's life sometimes turns into a window-less house where it becomes the home to the wind.' He uttered the words slowly. An air of sadness now pervaded the room.

'Do you feel unwell?' I asked, feeling guilty that I had made him talk so long after his ailment.

He did not open his eyes and muttered, as if to himself, 'That girl suffered a lot living with that useless man in that box-like house in the middle of the African desert.'

He pointed his finger at me and said, 'He won't let her become pregnant. Do you know why? Because he could not afford to feed his child. Afterwards she became so dependent on that black man.'

'He was the one who killed her, isn't it?' the old lady asked, her voice heavy with sadness.

'Her blood was slurped by a dog.' The old man's voice broke.

I watched the couple intently, wondering how they could put aside their own sufferings and bitter memories and now become one with that unfortunate woman in Lessing's book.

The ambience in the room turned sombre now. It was as if Mary's plight touched everyone in the room. Yes, this old man had brought the suffering of many people to a wider audience. In his story about that boy, Prahlad, the son of a demon king, an aberration in the region where he grew up. Quiet, polite, intelligent but always on tenterhooks because of his drunkard father. With his own diligence he had established himself. And then his father brought a new woman to the house. What an embarrassment! His father could not meet the expenses of the children; money was always short. The son took the responsibility of sending money to his father. A story of utter helplessness.

And then think of his portrayal of the jobless young men, their love and yearning, and disappointment. As that beautiful girl with a 'bad' reputation passed them by in her blue saree, the young men teased: '*Neel saree ninkaria srimati chole ... e ... e ...*' They gossipped about her character and her reputation with salacious enjoyment. And then, to add to their misery, a classmate who used to be rather in awe of them came back to the town as a doctor and settled down with his family. The smart young man was unrecognizable from that shy boy of yore. He invited his old friends for a meal and introduced them to his pretty wife. They discovered to their own astonishment that they found in her beauty a reflection of that ill-reputed girl. Later it was found that each of those frustrated young men, without revealing to each other, were trying to woo that same girl in the blue saree. The story ended with the young men pushed to the fringe of the society and their anguish.

The old man, who started writing only in his middle age, had told stories of so many people like us, of their sorrow and happiness, with incredible tenderness. He was the right person to talk about his dream of planting palm trees on the edge of the pond. The old man had started planting rows of palms there. People started commenting, 'The man must be mad; he is on the verge of death and now look, he has started planting palm trees. By the time they grow, he will be long gone.' Somebody dug out the saplings at night. The next day, the old man planted new saplings again and was seen taking care of them. He happily dreamt every night of the palm leaves shining under the moonlit sky.

Now he dragged his feet, in his grandson's words, 'like a penguin', as he walked to the inner quarters. He gave me a book and said, 'Read it. It's a collection of interviews of many famous people.'

I took the heavy volume from his hand.

'From Marilyn Monroe to Hemingway, you'll find many. You'll enjoy reading it. But remember it's not for keeps, you have to return it.'

'Sure, I'll return it after I come back,' I said.

'It was difficult to get the interview from Hemingway. You know what the interviewer did? He poured alcohol generously on his body, and pretending to be drunk, pushed aggressively through the group surrounding the legendary author. The interview that happened later became a memorable one. The interviewer and author became friends afterwards. And about Marilyn Monroe ... well, you'll see for yourself,' he said.

He walked me to the door to bid goodbye.

'You don't need to go down the steps,' his doctor son cautioned. The old man stopped on his way and and said, 'You know, my grandson was absolutely right, one hundred per cent right. That day I was watching this show about penguins on Animal Planet and it's true, my walk has become exactly like theirs.' As he said it we laughed with him.

He then disappeared into the room.

'Deuta's health is not that great. He is keeping himself alive only through his mental strength. His kidneys and heart are in bad condition,' the doctor son said, his voice reflecting his frustration.

'Who will talk about books like this when he goes away?' the old lady's eyes brimmed with tears.

'When Deuta is gone, who will visit us like this and spend hours into the night?' the elder daughter-in-law said heavily.

'We can't imagine this house without Deuta,' the younger daughter-in-law wiped her tears.

I left without saying anything.

It was drizzling a bit. At 10 p.m., the city was quieter. Under the light of the halogen lamps the slender raindrops looked like strips of Muga silk. They seemed to escape from bundles and spread like golden strands in the air. From amidst them a thin old man seemed to emerge again and again. This old man was the only one who could tell the story of the person who loved planting palm trees repeatedly; nobody else could do it. Somewhere he had written about the words of

Martin Luther King, that even if he was sure that the world would be destroyed the next day, he would still water the apple tree.

Yes, some people can. They can still plant palm trees, even while standing at the door of death; they can still water the apple tree knowing fully well that the world would be destroyed the next day.

The day after meeting the old man, I left Assam for a long time. I came to know that he had left this world peacefully in his sleep.

Did he dream of planting palm trees that night? Or was he watering an apple tree in his dream? One thing is for sure: that night he dreamt of something. And he left this world holding it close to his chest.

A Cup of Coffee from Aunt Brinda

In another year, Aunt Brinda or Brinda *khuri*, as we called her, would be seventy. Years of relentless labour had now resulted in a pain here or a pain there in her body. Sometimes when she got up from bed, an excruciating pain would shoot up from her waist suddenly; it lasted throughout the day, even a week sometimes. She had to depend on the hot water bottle and painkiller tablets in order to go on and manage the household work. She could not afford to rest. Resting meant that the whole household would come to a grinding halt. On some days, after cleaning the fish on the moida placed on the floor, when she tried to get up, her knee would give way. Afterwards she would walk with a limp. At night, when she retired to bed and found it difficult to stretch her legs, she often thought that as per the advice of the orthopaedic doctor from Guwahati, she must fill a sack with half a kilo of sand, place it under her feet and do the prescribed exercise. But by the time she wrapped up the day's work she did not have the energy, mental or physical, to gather the paraphernalia to give relief to her aching limbs. So it went on like this – the shooting pain in her waist while getting up from bed in the morning, the warning bell on her knees when she got up after cleaning the fish, the tingling sensation on the elbow while peeling the gourd, the arms almost failing to move while spreading the wet clothes on the clothesline. They had to be ignored and so the days and nights rolled on. The household counted on Aunt Brinda to go on, despite her pain.

Otherwise her grandson would be crestfallen. Jibon *khura*, her husband, would feel listless. Who would feed their hungry mouths? Who would look after the pair of pigeons? And the geese and the chickens, the pair of white peacocks, the doll-like Dimpy, a Bhutia breed of dog smaller than a chicken? And there was Rob, the black-and-white-spotted Dalmatian, too. When he stood on his hind legs he almost reached six-foot-tall Jibon khura's shoulders. And there were also the red-and-blue lovebirds in the cage. Who would fill the bowl with rice grains for the ducks, chicken and pigeons? And rice with milk for Dimpy, boiled meat for Rob with a bowl of parboiled rice, and for the lovebirds the special *koni dhan*? Who would do all these chores? Brinda khuri, of course! Sure, there was Nirmala bai who came in the morning and evening to help out, and stay-at-home Budhuwa. But without Brinda khuri directing everything, nothing seemed to move. When Nirmala bai offered rice to Dimpy, she refused to eat; she always forgot to – or intentionally did not – add a spoonful of Amul milk powder to Dimpy's food. When Brinda khuri reminded her, Nirmala bai would mutter angrily, 'You give rice and milk to the dog, that's not enough, now you even want to give away a share from khura's milk.'

Brinda khuri would scold her, 'Why do you keep on saying "dog"? Dimpy was his daughter.'

When this subject came up, Nirmala shut up immediately and with her head bowed, busied herself with some chore or the other. Sometimes when she washed the utensils in the shade outside in the compound, she wiped her tears, complaining, 'God! Why have you given so much sorrow to this woman?'

In the first half of her life Brinda khuri did not know what sorrow meant. She was the eldest daughter of advocate Naren Hazarika of Golaghat town. She grew up as if floating in an air of care and happiness in that prosperous house. People in the family addressed her only with sobriquets like *sun-joni*, my golden girl, and *majoni*, little mother, and so on. She grew up in the quiet, little town without facing any conflict. She went to school and college, learnt singing and embroidery, planted flowering trees and even learnt weaving from her mother on the traditional loom. She was like the *sthala padma*, or the cotton rose flower – but not the pink one of the afternoon coloured by the sun's rays but rather, like the pure white bloom of the morning. Brinda khuri was like that – quiet, soft, innocent. She could not use rude words, neither could she bear it if anyone spoke roughly. One day, finding the gate open, a stray cow and some goats entered the compound and all but destroyed the flower garden. Instead of shooing them off, Brinda started weeping, sitting on the staircase. Who could bear to see her crying? Everybody in the family came out and with a stick someone beat the animals too. But Brinda khuri snatched the stick away from him and asked, 'What's the point of beating them? Can you bring out the flowers from their stomach?' She could not bear the death of even a mosquito, arguing, 'Why do you have to kill it? You can drive it away.'

Then there was the case of the newly opened butcher's stall, not far from their house. Everybody in the family welcomed it; it would be convenient to buy the meat next door and one did not have to go to the bazaar. If guests arrived suddenly the young domestic help could run and buy a kilo of meat. But when Brinda saw the butcher dragging the goats to his stall, she cried copiously. One day she saw Futuki, the spotted goat at the next-door neighbour Rumi's house, being dragged like this. She ran to her father and begged that he should do something about closing the stall. Advocate Naren Hazarika was well known in the town. He complained to the municipality office and within a week the butcher was compelled to down his shutters.

This was Brinda khuri in her younger days.

At that time, she had passed the pre-university exam and enrolled for the three-year degree course in the local college. She passed the first exam with quite good marks; there was just one more exam to go before she could add the suffix 'Bachelor of Arts' to her name. But then the wedding proposal came from advocate Jibon Hazarika's house. Belonging to a respectable family, handsome in looks, he had just started practising as a lawyer after graduating from a college in Kolkata. What else could one want in an ideal groom? So she got married and came to take care of Jibon advocate's household. Eventually, she became a mother to three children, looked after her mother-in-law and father-in-law very well until their death, and took good care of her sister-in-law and brother-in law until they could be on their own. And now, after taking care of all these responsibilities, she stood at the threshold of seventy years.

Brinda khuri was quite interested in studies. She wanted to complete her graduation but caught up in the duties of a daughter-in-law and a mother in an extended family, she could not keep track of how the days turned into weeks, then months and ultimately years. But she was happy that her two daughters and lone son could finish their post-graduation from the university. Both her daughters had married into good families. Both of them stayed outside Assam. Earlier, they used to visit her every year. These days the gap between their visits had become longer due to various family commitments. Brinda khuri did not mind. She just prayed for their well-being and that at least they would keep in touch with her. When her son decided to join a local college she was overjoyed. Not only was he the youngest of the lot, he was the only son. Siddhartha was special to her. His nature was such that people could not help loving him. In fact, he had inherited Brinda khuri's nature. His heart seemed to have love for everybody. He was equally fond of animals and birds. An abandoned kitten from somewhere, a stray dog, a dove's chick falling down from a broken nest, a salika rescued from a cat's mouth – all these creatures crowded the home. The year he was appearing for his matriculation exam, he brought from somewhere a goose whose one leg had almost been torn off by a vicious dog. In between his studies he took care of it and by the time he appeared for the exam, the bird had recovered completely. It now followed him around. Everybody in the family teased him that on the exam paper he would only be writing about the goose. In reply, he only smiled. How sweet that smile was! When Binda khuri remembered that smile she could feel an arrow going through her heart. All the pain in her body seemed to gather there, like a storm, destroying every vein in her body. At these moments, she ran to her grandchild. Without any reason she kept herself overly busy with him. She gave him a bath for the second time, changed his clothes again though they were fresh, and fed him something though he was full. Slowly that oppressive pain seemed to subside.

Siddhartha had passed all the exams at the local college with good marks and then went away to a well-known university outside Assam. He was unfamiliar with the new institution surrounded by bright clusters of bougainvillea flowers. Though he could not relate to some of the things going on in the university, he did very well indeed. Simultaneously, he also got involved in something he liked. He gathered around him a peacock, a few parrots, a group of sparrows and a few dogs. After the long day in the university, he came back to the hostel to give them food that he bought with the savings from his pocket money. He did not notice that a girl was observing these activities and had even collected relevant information about him. Her lover from Haryana stayed in the same hostel as Siddhartha. She visited it often to have sex with him. The foods that Siddhartha found difficult to digest was ordinary stuff for her. This lover was her third or fourth boyfriend. Frankly, she was getting a little tired of him. Besides, he had decided to migrate to Canada; his family relations had a business over there. She knew that her lover secretly regarded her not unlike a car he would change every six months. This was when she laid eyes on the boy who fed the birds and animals. She set her target. She admitted to herself that she was not capable of getting a good job, but Siddhartha easily could. So she took help from the dogs to spread her net wider. She had gathered information about the boy thoroughly. The son of a prosperous family, he did not have any familial obligations, had good career prospects, and most importantly, he did not have a girlfriend. She kept tabs on when Siddhartha returned from his classes and kept a pot of cooked dalia ready. When Siddhartha gave the dogs biscuits she made her appearance. By that time her lover had flown away to Canada. Before leaving, he had presented her with a car. They had been together for two years. He spent generously when they went out together and found it easier to break off his relationship with her. For her it was not a big deal; it had happened before with her ex-boyfriends too. In fact, it was he who seemed to be more affected. But he was intelligent and realized that this girl would never fit into his family and she would never offer him a home either in the true sense. So he did not feel too guilty but nevertheless assuaged his guilt by presenting her the car.

She started arriving in this car with cooked *dalia* for the dogs and sat on the bench in the park where Siddhartha would normally sit. The dogs ran to her whenever she approached, wagging their tails expectantly. She even gave names to each dog. By now she had also changed the way she dressed. She used to wear revealing western clothes her ex-boyfriend bought for her. Now she started wearing churidar-kameez, even a saree sometimes. She stopped smoking openly. She came closer to Siddhartha through the dogs. She talked about animals with him. She also took the trouble of becoming a member of an animal welfare organization. One day she even took him to one of their meetings. Slowly, she was pulling the net closer.

The day she properly ensnared him in the net, she was wearing an onion-coloured mekhela sador. She had travelled far searching for the Assam Government's emporium to buy it. She then went to Siddhartha's hostel carrying a bird with a broken leg. She had made the hostel's helper catch the bird but the job of breaking its leg was her doing. She tied a hanky around the broken leg and arrived at Siddhartha's hostel with a face ready to burst into tears. She remembered that Siddhartha had told her about the goose he had nursed when he was appearing for his matriculation exam. That day as Siddhartha got caught in the net he jumped around like a restless *sol* fish in water, as if caught by a fishing rod but now released. So it was not difficult for her.

Eventually, she was welcomed to the house known as Jeutara Bhavan as a daughter-in-law of Jibon khura and Brinda khuri. In this cultured old family in upper Assam, she had to learn different forms of address for a whole lot of relations – mami for maternal aunt-in-law, khuri for paternal aunt-in-law, borma for elder mother-in-law, and so on.

The big house with a big compound had been built by Jibon khura's father. Whatever he earned he spent on buying things for the household. The house was always full of guests. Sometimes when there were no guests, the residents felt as if something was amiss – the house was too quiet. Jibon khura did not construct anything extra to embellish the house his father had built. Now that Siddhartha was getting married he added one room with an attached bathroom and an air-conditioner to the house. He understood that the girl whom Siddhartha was bringing home as his bride was fond of the good things in life. Siddhartha himself was rather surprised, wondering how this girl could be so greedy for material things. Her father Jibanath Saikia was happy to live a simple life. Through his calibre and hard work he had become a senior officer in a bank. When he visited their house Siddhartha was more than pleasantly surprised to find that her parents, her brother, were all quite down to earth and not show-offs in any sense. How come this girl who belonged to such a family was so different? Siddhartha's otherwise sharp brain failed to find an answer.

They had stayed in a city outside Assam when the affair started. So nobody in the family could guess that relations between the two had already seen fissures. She had roused his passion to a crescendo with her experienced body. For the next six months, he was like a person under a daze. When he emerged slightly from the all-pervading erotic obsession, he realized that things were not what they seemed to be. He also heard gossip about her past affairs. He was also not very comfortable with her habit of drinking and smoking. The day she went to meet her ex-lover from Canada and came back loaded with luxury items he had brought for her, Siddhartha decided it was over; he would put an end to this relationship immediately. He had made another decision; he wouldn't take up the job offer from an MNC with headquarters in London. He'd rather accept a job in the college in his hometown. He tore the job offer letter from the MNC to pieces. In the small two-room flat where he stayed the pieces blew here and there under the whirling fan. With them was floating a woman's body broken into pieces. Two breasts fuller than most women were rolling on the floor; in one corner of the bed her private parts were trembling for a passionate embrace; next to the pillow lay her full hips; from the ceiling hung a pair of eyes – like that of a newly born calf – restless, lively, as if without guile. He made balls from the newspaper stacked near his bed and threw them at those eyes. Wherever he looked those eyes followed him. The floor of the room was hidden under the barrage of paper balls. He could feel his mouth dribbling and moisten his pillow. Sometime later he hugged the pillow tightly. Soon the pillow was full of stains and he tore at it aggressively. But here too he saw a rounded hand with no ornaments – only full, plump, smooth skin. The hand always pulled away the pillow as the tensions peaked and Siddhartha, like a sol fish on a fishing rod, jumped up and down in the overflowing water. Then the pillow was kept aside and the hand got adorned with bangles. The calf-like eyes stared at him in amusement. Every time after sex, he was apprehensive, but she asked him not to worry, that everything would be alright. After some time, he got over his fear. He left everything to her discretion and became like an elephant caught in quicksand, unable to move.

In the closed room, amidst the paper balls and cottonwool from the pillow, Siddhartha lay, his cry half stifled like an epilepsy patient and his mouth frothing. The whole world seemed to him like a painting spoiled by dripping water. He stared at the books covered with dust. His scholarship was coming to an end. He did not have to appear for an exam again, but if he did not complete the course, he would have to return the scholarship money, which was a considerable amount, to the government. He wondered if he should dust off the books and start all over again. Just then there was a knock at the door. It was her. The landlord, people in the neighourhood, even shopkeepers, did not take much notice of her visits to his place; they were under the impression that she was his fiancée. She gasped as she saw him like this and wanted to clean the room. Siddhartha jumped from the bed and dragged her towards the door. He asked her to leave him alone. But she smiled and said, she could leave him all right – but what about the foetus in the womb? She demanded that the wedding must happen within a month. After that they would go away to London.

When she heard that he had decided not to take up the job offer, she sat down heavily on the bed and lit a cigarette. She smoked three and a half cigarettes silently and then said, well she could stay with his parents too, but the wedding must happen quickly. Siddhartha looked at the girl in red shorts and a sleeveless top with a tiger's head on the chest, and despaired that he would have to spend his life with this girl. A shiver ran through his body. He somehow managed to put on a kurta over his pajamas and ran away from the room. In the heat of the afternoon an obscene smell from the drain floated in the air. An intense desire to get away from the acidic smell felt like a hammer on his head. He saw an autorickshaw coming his way and jumped into it.

She waited for a long time for him and then left. In her own room, she did not go for a drink or cigarette. She took out the chillum and filled it with marijuana and pulled at it throughout the night before passing out. She was worried that she had to go back to Assam. Through a haze she remembered her father's stern face. That meant going back to his house, to the woman – her mother – who listened to him with utmost respect, and their lectures on good bahaviour. She had planned every step, like solving a simple sum, centering around Siddhartha. The answer was almost there but now everything seemed to fall through.

She had sprayed spit in a corner of the room when she realized that she had failed to hold on to Siddhartha, and looking at him she screamed angrily, 'You son of a bitch!' and then bombarded him with the choicest abuses she knew, her voice now cracking with all the screaming. Why did he say no to such a lucrative job in London? She was the one who had pushed him for it. And now all the plans were going to waste. She had already guessed that the tame pigeon was getting restless and ready to fly. Any moment it might fly out to the open sky. So she was tightening the knot at its leg. She had decided to bear his child after much thought. She had been cheated quite a few times, not anymore. She was tired, mentally and physically, and did not want to play another game, with another man. Siddhartha was her last bet. And she was succeeding too. She could not understand where she had made a miscalculation. Perhaps she was becoming overconfident by thinking that the pigeon had been tamed completely. Perhaps a little too careless. She knew that he did not like her drinking and smoking but she had put her foot down, saying it was her right to decide, she was a woman of this time and wanted the freedom to be her own person. So she continued with her indulgences. She did not change her style of dressing either.

But the relationship continued, despite the quarrels and other problems. To make it permanent she made other plans. One day Siddhartha told her that perhaps they should put an end to their relationship. He would never be able to offer her the kind of freedom she wanted. His parents, his relatives would think she was from another planet – she would never be able to adjust to their kind of family. It was better that she renewed her relationship with her ex-lover in Canada. It would be good for everybody – for her future, his own future. When she heard his voice, strong, assured and cold, she felt herself tremble to the core. Why did it happen like this? Why her? Was it a sin to look for a sophisticated, upper-class life? Why should she always lose out? People said that she looked like a model or an actress. She was not that bad at studies either. Then why was she losing out to others? The old anger and frustration that gathered in her mind once, between the years of adolescence and youth, shook her up again.

The old anger against her father escalated and dropped, depending on the level of her drug-infused consciousness. For as long as she could remember, the words she associated with her father were 'No', 'You won't be allowed', 'Not possible for me', and other such phrases. His only mantra was 'Study, study, study. Put your mind to your lessons and obtain good marks in your exams.' He did not like to spend money on anything other than study materials. He was quite a senior officer in the bank but he never allowed his children to enjoy a modicum of luxury. He always talked about how, being a farmer's son, he went to the fields for ploughing and later went to college, how he obtained the job in the bank on his own merit, how he graduated from college with only one set of clothing and a single pair of shoes.

She was bored listening to all this, day and night. Her brother was like his father, a bookworm and reserved by nature. What about her mother? Her opinion did not matter within the household. She seemed to be grateful to her father for whatever reason. The people from her family were very good-looking. Her mother was the only exception. Perhaps she had suffered from an inferiority complex from childhood and that's why she felt fortunate to have been accepted as the wife of a handsome, highly placed bank official. She inherited her looks from her aunts. She observed from her childhood the kind of luxurious lifestyle the families of her aunts and uncles enjoyed. In her cousins she saw the reflection of her own unfulfilled dreams. She grew up watching them wearing the clothes she craved, attending the birthday parties she wanted to throw, going to places she wanted to visit, eating the delicious food she hungered for. Sometimes they teased her too. They all studied in colleges and universities outside Assam and described to her, sometimes exaggeratedly, the kind of lifestyle they led and how she was out of touch with present-day realities.

She was in the last year of college then. Her cousin who was studying in a university in another state pitied her. She looked rather patronizingly at the clothes she wore, and was surprised that such a beautiful girl did not have a boyfriend. She laughed openly at her 'Victorian morality' in front of their friends, who too found her an anomaly. She bore it all silently. But inwardly she was getting fed up with her father's strict diktats, the house seemed like a jail to her and all the people there her enemies. She concentrated on her studies with the desperation of a sinking man holding on to a straw as the only means of escape. When she did well in her exam she insisted on going outside Assam for her post-graduation and even took recourse to fasting so her father would relent. She wanted to run away from the familiar atmosphere, the people she knew, and most importantly, the house she found so oppressive.

She did achieve her goal. On holidays, she often made excuses about the high pressure at her university to avoid visiting her family. She was like a person at a feast after remaining hungry for days. She changed herself completely, wanting to enjoy everything at one go. She wanted to become a model too. Though not successful, she found in Vinod Chopra the lover she craved. He was rich beyond her imagination, so what if he had a daughter not much younger than her? She was floating in the world of self-indulgence she had craved from a young age.

But look, today she was lying supine in a drug-infused haze, like a pig in a sty. Her anger at Siddhartha, a desire for revenge, made her burn with rage. Her cousin was now in England. She had arranged everything. She wanted to win the last battle, to piggyback on Siddhartha's bright future. That night, even the drugs could not make her forget the futility of her life, and she was burning all over. She was not sure whom she was so angry at or whom to blame. A deep hatred for everybody ate through her.

~

In this same mental state she accepted the new mekhela sador and the ring set with pomegranate-red rubies in traditional *jethipotia* style, resembling a lizard, at the engagement ceremony. The ring was a family heirloom. Brinda khuri's mother-in-law had given it to her at the time of her wedding. When she hugged her beautiful would-be daughter-in-law, Brinda khuri brushed off a tear of happiness from her cheeks. She got involved in arranging a fitting trousseau to welcome the bride. Jibon khura on the other hand got busy refurbishing the house. When they came to know within a short time after the wedding that a new member was joining the family, their happiness spilled over. A number of celebrations to commemorate different milestones during the pregnancy followed. The house in any case was always full of guests, now it was even more so. The daughter-in-law often complained that she wasn't feeling well and confined herself to the bed in her room. The relatives, even Brinda khuri, were a little surprised. How could a woman stay in bed day after day? Brinda khuri found her beautiful daughter-in-law turning dark like charcoal and sullen. One day she tried to explain that if she stepped out of her room and walked about in the open, perhaps she would feel better. She tried to repeat the advice her mother-in-law had given her to ensure an easier pregnancy and childbirth. But her daughter-in-law shrugged with impatience. This behaviour was becoming common and people in the house learnt to accept it. They feared her hard words, aimed at them like poisoned arrows. Brinda khuri cried silently in the prayer room blaming her fate – what they had imagined and what had actually followed. Every night she could hear from her room the sound of quarrels, of things thrown and glasses being broken. The neighbours started enquiring about the ruckus they heard every night; they even exchanged meaningful glances among themselves. Jibon khura and Brinda khuri could not reply with conviction and bowed their heads in shame. When pieces of broken glasses, half-smoked cigarette butts were swept from the room, Brinda khuri despaired. She was surprised too. Her son did not even have betel nut or paan, which most people in Assam were in the habit of chewing. So from where did he learn to indulge in these habits? She started taking the garbage from the maid who swept the floor; bundling it all in a paper bag she got rid of it in the backyard without anyone seeing. She wanted to protect her husband from all this; he was already suffering from the turn of events and had high blood pressure. Brinda khuri felt cornered.

One day the maid confided in her that these items of addiction were not only used by her son but by her daughter-in-law too. Brinda khuri trembled like a leaf. She just prayed that the baby should be normal and healthy. She seemed to have aged suddenly in these few months. The house that once resonated with laughter and the conversation of guests had now become a ghost of its former self. Many of the regulars stopped visiting due to some reason or the other. They blamed Brinda khuri for bringing tea and meals to her daughter-in-law's bedside. They said it was her indulgence that spoiled her daughter-in-law. But what could Brinda khuri do? How could she keep the pregnant woman hungry?

She secretly hoped that things would be different once her daughter-in-law became a mother. Who hadn't seen a new mother's mind becoming like the soft yolk of an egg? She hoped it would happen to her daughter-in-law too. So, she counted down the days fervently.

~

God had heard her prayer; a healthy, beautiful child brightened the bleak house. It became busy with people and guests again as the functions to celebrate the baby's arrival ensued – a women-only bhajan in praise of Lord Krishna, the naming ceremony, the first rice-eating ceremony, and so on. People learnt to ignore her daughter-in-law's sullen behaviour and gave in to the toothless smile of the child that won over everybody.

Brinda khuri took up the responsibility of bringing up the baby readily. Perhaps that's why she failed to notice many things. The baby slept in their room. At night when the baby cried Siddhartha came to enquire and chose to sleep in the cot in their room. He hardly talked to his wife. She insisted that Siddhartha should leave his job, this house and this town. She even contacted her cousin brother in America and arranged for a job, but Siddhartha refused. He wouldn't leave his old parents behind.

Finally, one day, her daughter-in-law emerged from her room. Dressed in the kind of clothes they had never seen, and found smoking openly, people in the house looked at her as if she were someone from another planet. Brinda khuri did not recognize this woman. She could not understand how a new mother could be like the hard trunk of a tree where not even a woodpecker could make a dent. She could not fathom why she had this deep hatred for everything and everybody. She did not like the way people here liked to dress, she did not like the way they talked, she did not like her own people, even her own country. On the other hand, she liked everything about the 'other'. Their country, their lifestyle, their sense of fashion. Brinda khuri was clueless about her daughter-in-law's attitude and how to tackle it. What did she want? What made her so restless? She felt as if she was swimming in a sea where the coast was nowhere in sight. Her only solace was the baby, who brought some meaning to her shattered life. So she went around like a spindle working tirelessly in the house. Siddhartha's pets, the baby's care, looking after her husband's waist pain, high blood pressure, and caring for him after the cataract operation, the household chores – all these kept Brinda khuri busy from the morning till night. Meanwhile she observed, despite herself, the woman she could not recognize anymore.

One day, leaving behind her infant son she went away to Mumbai for ten days to attend her cousin's wedding. Next, she went to Delhi for another ten days to enrol herself in some course. Now she was ready to go to Goa for a friend's wedding. Brinda khuri knew that her son was spending a huge amount of money, without protest, to buy her flight tickets. These days she could not recognize her own son either. Slowly, he seemed to have become lifeless like a stone. Whom could she confide in? Who was there to lend her a shoulder to cry on? Her parents, uncles and aunts were all dead now.

That day the daughter-in-law was not at home; she had gone to Goa. Jibon khura was not at home either; he had gone to attend the shraddha, a funeral service, for an uncle.

Brinda khuri approached her son who was sitting alone in the verandah. She told him that if his wife was so keen to go abroad he should perhaps agree for everybody's peace of mind. She would look after the baby. At least if not permanently, they could go for a few years. At this, Siddhartha wailed so loudly, holding on to a post in the verandah, that the baby woke up with a start. Caught between the wailing son and the grandson, Brinda khuri did not know what to do. She finally suggested that something had to done; crying would not help. Whatever he did, the family would stand by him.

For Brinda khuri, this daughter-in-law was a riddle. However, she admitted, she had heard of other such women. Kushal Barua had celebrated his middle son's wedding with great pomp. During the post-wedding ceremony of *khuba-khubuni*, when a puja is held to propitiate the bad elements so that they would not affect the newlyweds, guests were ready to partake in the dinner arranged when they could not find the bride. After much searching, she was found under the bed in her room. She was thrashing her limbs and trembling and frothing at the mouth. The doctor came and said she was highly addicted to drugs. She was suffering from withdrawal symptoms. Then there was Kailash Sharma's daughter-in-law. He and his wife had told her that as a new bride she should not come to meet guests wearing short skirts as a matter of courtesy. She filed for divorce. Basanti Hazarika's son had asked his wife why she went out every night, and with whom; that marriage ended in divorce too. Brinda khuri had heard all this as gossip.

Her daughter-in-law returned from Goa. She brought cashew nuts for them and a rattle for the baby. The little smile on her face, and a few kind words made Brinda khuri happy beyond bounds. Thank God the clouds were receding.

~

But on the day when all the black clouds in the world gathered around Brinda khuri, Siddhartha was sleeping on the narrow cot in her room. The baby had pooped a few minutes ago. After cleaning him, Brinda khuri dozed off. She was tired after the day's labour. She started at the noise. The daughter-in-law had stormed into the room. Now she slapped Siddhartha, punched and kicked him. Jibon khura, the maid, Budhuwa, and Brinda khuri, all came running. Perhaps the neighbours had woken up too because one of the windows of Champa's house opened. She hurled the choicest abuses at him. She said she knew why he did not want to go away from this godforsaken place, despite getting such good breaks in his career. She screamed, saying she understood very well why he left his wife in the bedroom to sleep here; she had seen him sleeping in his mother's bed too. Jibon khura, the maids went out of the room with their heads bowed in shock. Brinda khuri entered the prayer room hugging the little baby to her chest and cried desolately. Her teeth bit into her lips and the blood that oozed from them stained the floor. She knew Jibon khura was standing at the doorstep. Siddhartha tried to stop his wife and bundling her hair in a knot he dragged her out of the room; he was trembling uncontrollably. Then leaning on a column, he told her, 'You don't have to stay here anymore. Please leave in the morning.'

In the morning she got ready to leave. Before departing, she lit three earthen lamps at the base of the sacred tulsi plant. The first one was meant to wish for Brinda khuri's death; the second one for the death of Siddhartha, and the third one for the death of Jibon khura. She warned Brinda khuri that she would fight legally to win custody of her son. Holding an earthen lamp in her palm, she cursed the household – let it be ruined, let wild bitter gourd creepers grow in its compound, let the ominous horned owl sit on its roof and eagles look for dead bodies in the house.

A big red car came to pick her up.

The story after that episode was quite short. She went away to Goa or Hong Kong to join some company. Before that she filed a case against the family. The baby had his first birthday. Brinda khuri was still at sea, unable to understand any of this. One day Siddhartha was found lying still on a mat spread under the bed. How could it happen? Siddhartha disappeared from the living world.

Some said, his friends mainly, that he had started taking such things that made his intestine rot with scabs. Some said he had taken lots of sleeping tablets. Others said he had been suffering from a brain disease for a long time; sometimes he saw everything turning dark and was about to buckle down, and only the strong medicines he took managed to keep him alive but, ultimately it killed him. Actually, his body had become like a termite hill, hollow from the inside. A little push, and it disintegrated.

~

Brinda khuri started suffering from a variety of pains. Jibon khura's health was also on the decline. The boy whose father left him when he was one was now three years old.

At times those three lit earthen lamps burned into Brinda khuri's brain. Her ears turned red with the poison of the words that woman had uttered. They pierced her diaphragm like molten lead. Her heart seemed to turn into a desolate desert. Before leaving their home with the lit lamp in her palm, her daughter-in-law had stood near the bakul tree and had lashed out, 'I know now why you labour like a maidservant, because you know you have sinned and are trying to make up for it.' Sometimes when Brinda khuri massaged her knees with oil after the day's work for relief from arthritis pain she wondered, had she spent all her life only doing chores at home, as that woman had said? She had uprooted the tulsi plant where her daughter-in-law had lit the lamps and thrown them in a corner of the backyard. One day when Brinda khuri went searching for something she found that the tulsi plant was growing luxuriously. She plucked it up forcefully; her face unnaturally red. She looked like a woman who had lost her mind.

~

I went to her house exactly at that hour that day. Khura told me that khuri was in the kitchen garden. I found her like that, uprooting the tulsi plant violently, like an insane woman. She came towards me and with her hands still muddy, grabbed both my hands forcefully. That silent noon she leaned on me and mumbled about those three earthen lamps. I could understand her anger at the tulsi plant, and why she did what she did. By now everybody in our family came to know about her daughter-in-law cursing the house when she left. I held khuri close to me for some time.

Her grandson called out to her. Slowly Brinda khuri went to the water tap in the garden and washed her hands and feet. She changed her sador and then entered the kitchen. I followed her too. I could see that a basket in the kitchen held a bottle gourd, a bunch of *khutura* greens, a ripe papaya, two lemons, a white gourd and two ribbed gourds – all produce from her garden. She brought me a cup of coffee in a mug etched with a sunflower. Half the mug was filled with froth. The milk was from the cow at home. Mixed with the roasted coffee, the aroma filled the kitchen.

'You haven't come for a long time, that's why I haven't made coffee for a long time too,' Brinda khuri said.

It was true. I hadn't visited Brinda khuri's house for quite some time. I had attended Siddhartha's shraddha, however. That day Brinda khuri had told me, 'It was he who should have performed my shraddha, but see, now I have to perform his.' There was not a drop of tear in her eyes; her face was dark like a burnt piece of coal. It was very difficult to watch that face. In fact, I had avoided visiting her because I was afraid of seeing that face again.

'How's the coffee? It has become a bit too thick. I know you don't take much sugar, so I have added only a little.' She ran her fingers through my hair. I could feel condensation forming on my glasses. My vision was becoming clouded.

'Aita, Aita,' the little boy called his grandmother. He drank the milk she gave him and now nagged her that she should finish the story. Brinda khuri told me as she sliced a papaya, 'Your uncle is not keeping well. He has to eat carefully, otherwise he gets ill.'

She washed her hands and held her grandson close to her chest. He hugged her and touching her cheeks with his own, repeated, 'You won't tell me the story?'

'Which story, my dear? I have forgotten.'

'That story, you know, about the huge tortoise living under the earth. We live on his back but if he shakes his limbs we get an earthquake.'

'Oh, the story I had told you on the day of the earthquake?'

'Yes, will you tell me, Aita?'

'I have lots of work now, my dear. I haven't cooked lunch yet. See, that aunty will tell you the story,' Brinda khuri pointed at me.

She started chopping the greens. The little boy came towards me. He clung to my neck with his soft hand and repeated, 'Will you tell me the story?'

'But I don't know that story.'

'Why not? You know, the story of the huge tortoise.'

'Where does it live?'

'You don't know even that? It lives under the earth. We all live on his back,' he seemed surprised at my ignorance, and spread his hands towards the trees and the sky.

'Is it true? Oh, I am scared.'

Brinda khuri smiled as she listened our conversation.

'Aunty, you know, that day the tortoise shook its back a little and everything trembled.'

'Were you scared?'

'Why should I be? I haven't done anything bad.'

'What do you mean by "anything bad"?' I lifted him up in my arms.

'Aita has said that if people do bad things the tortoise will be angry and will shake his back and everything will be destroyed. Isn't it, Aita?'

'Oh, he has started yapping too much,' Brinda khuri said indulgently as she took out the fish from the fridge.

'Khuri, why are you bothering so much about my lunch? Please keep it simple. Just make some mashed potato and a light dal; that will be enough with the rice,' I protested.

'Maybe we can manage but this little boy has to grow strong.'

'Are you going to tell me the story or not?' Brinda khuri's grandson was getting a little irritated.

'My dear, I am unable to tell that story. Only your Aita can tell that story,' I said.

The little boy looked at his grandmother. She was busy cooking fish curry with chopped gourd and khutura greens. When it simmered she squeezed some lemon juice into it. The aroma filled the room. In between she managed to make another cup of coffee for me. 'I had sent for a new packet. The earlier one was getting ...'

I held out my hands to take the cup from her. The aroma of the freshly made coffee once again filled the kitchen.

Stream

The woman could be five to six years over seventy, or could she be seventy-eight?

She looks as if all the moisture in her body has been squeezed out. This impression is aggravated by her long limbs and her height. But her voice is strong, and in her gait she is not at all slothful. However, when she walks, you can see that her right side is weaker. Perhaps that's why she drags her right foot a bit. Her hair is snow-white but it's still quite thick. On the two sides of her temple the hair even curls a bit. The hair on the eyebrows and her eyelashes have greyed too, but not completely. After a bath when she puts a red spot on her forehead and vermillion at the parting and goes to the garden to pluck flowers to offer at the prayer room, she does not look that old. In fact, she looks younger.

She now entered the house temple. They were Brahmins and the temple also held the holy *salogram shila*, the special stone worshipped as a symbol of Lord Vishnu. Hence there were lots of rituals to perform. This salogram was inherited from her husband's old family. So it needed to be given due respect and it took her some time to complete the puja.

Next, she went to the kitchen to make a breakfast of roti and fried vegetables. She brought down the gas stove from the slab in the kitchen. It was of an old make but it shone as if new. She used warm water to mix the wheat and then kneaded it for quite some time, leaving it on a wooden platter covering it with a soft towel. Sitting on the low stool, she chopped the vegetables for the curry. Depending on the season, the veggies varied. There was an artistic touch in the way she chopped them, as if embroidering flowers on a piece of cloth. When she cut the cabbage and placed it on a plate, the pieces looked like white skeins; when cut into rounds, the brinjal looked like round biscuits in a packet; the thinly sliced potatoes, ready to be fried in pure ghee, looked like finely sliced bamboo sticks people used as toothpicks; the evenly sliced rounds of *nol-koshu* soaked in a layer of gram flour to be fried later looked like a paper garland; the bottle gourd chopped in squares were like sugar cubes.

Once she finished chopping the vegetables to her satisfaction, she lit the two burners of the stove. By then she had finished rolling out the rotis as well. Putting the griddle on top of the smaller burner, she toasted the rotis with great precision. Puffed up, they turned into perfect rounds, like luchi fried in ghee. The rotis that looked almost like silk hankies were then folded and kept in the casserole, to keep them warm. After the roti and fried *bhaji*, she always made something sweet. It could be a tomato chutney, star fruit chutney or rice pudding.

That chore finished, she usually sat on a murha in the verandah. From the way she sat, you could make out that she was a bit tired, or perhaps she suffered from a nagging pain somewhere in her body. Her right foot especially gave her some trouble. She now tried to stretch it. Some time back she was quite ill. She had been on medication for high blood pressure for a long time, yet the stroke happened suddenly. The right foot had almost stopped moving. It was only recently that she was able to walk again, but she found that the leg pinched while she made breakfast. She could not remain standing for very long.

As soon as she heard her husband Janardhan Chakraborty blowing the conch shell and ringing the metal bell in the prayer room, she got up. She went to the kitchen to heat milk and water to make tea. She added a bay leaf and ground ginger into the mixture. When the aroma of the freshly made masala tea floated in the air, her husband sat down at the dining table. The old couple drank the tea silently. She continued to massage her right leg. Dr Chakraborty now opened the newspaper sitting on the verandah. By then Kamala's mother, the maid, arrived. She got busy supervising the housework. By the time her husband came from the bazaar, Kamala's mother had finished washing the utensils and clothes and sweeping the floor. Kamala's mother was never allowed to touch anything in the kitchen. She took the bag he gave her as if it were some revered offering meant for a puja. Then she spread the vegetables on a round *dala* made of woven cane strips. She washed each one of them well and dried them on a cane sieve. Then she segregated them into groups. She did not approve of only one variety of fish being brought from the bazaar. So Dr Chakraborty, from those long-gone days in the tea garden, always selected at least three varieties every time. He did not have to be told what vegetable to buy to accompany which fish; he knew the combinations by heart now. If it was *singora*, he would choose brinjal; if it was sol fish it would be radish; if rohu, then good quality potato; if it was hilsa or *kandhuli*, mustard and onion were a must. If he bought *moa*, he picked up brinjal of a different variety than what he bought for the singora. Dr Chakraborty knew the nitty-gritty very well indeed.

However, today he had brought only one variety of fish. The railway line on this side of the town was being widened. The construction had shut down railway traffic, cutting off the supply of fish. Hence the bazaar, usually overflowing with different varieties of fish, looked forlorn today and it was only hilsa he could get. His wife usually got upset if the fish weren't very big. So, though he could not manage his finances as well as he did during his tea garden days, he tried his best. Today too he brought quite a sizeable hilsa.

It was quarter to ten. She got ready to cook lunch and organized the fish, spices, rice and dal around her. She chewed on a paan at the same time. All signs of physical pain disappeared from her face. Dr Chakraborty got ready to go to his pharmacy. After he retired from his job at the tea garden, he had started attending the pharmacy at the chari-ali during the first half of the day. He did not go there in the afternoon after lunch. If some patient visited his house, he attended to them.

The old lady started cleaning and chopping the hilsa. There was roe inside. She cut the fish in such a way that each piece had a sliver of roe in it. She cut the head into four pieces. Then she started grinding the spices. The ground mustard seeds looked like sandalwood paste; with it she mixed chopped green chilli and a little mustard oil. As she rubbed the paste on the fish pieces, a strong enticing smell pervaded the room. She put everything in a steel bowl and covered it tightly. She then filled a wok halfway with water, put the bowl inside and placing the grinding stone on top, let the hilsa steam slowly. The water boiled with a reassuring *bok-bok-bok* sound, the grinding stone moved rhythmically, *thak-thak-thak*, and the bowl kept pace with its *khat-khat-khat*. The old lady listened intently for a few minutes to this orchestra. A smile ran through her lips. Now she ground cumin seeds on the grinding stone and lit the gas stove to cook the fish head with brinjal pieces. She removed the wok with the thick curry from the stove. Now she started roasting moong dal on a griddle. She did not use a ladle to roast the grains but a bunch of bamboo strips bound together by rope. Its *sarak-sarak* sound on the dry griddle and the sweet smell of the roasted dal filled the empty room. The dal, seasoned with dry red chilli and ground ginger, steamed hilsa, fish head cooked with brinjal and ground cumin seed – between all these preparations the old lady moved like a butterfly on flowers, going up and down. At these moments she remained self-absorbed in a world of aroma, taste and an unearthly pleasure. Now she forgot everything – her physical pain, her doctor son living in America with his American wife, the thousand and one problems and the complaints of her two married daughters. Also, though temporarily, she forgot about her husband weakened by diabetes. She even forgot about herself. A whole fish brought from the bazaar ended up in two aromatic curries, and now decorated two snow-white bowls placed on the dining table. They almost kept her longing to do more. She dipped the hilsa roe in a mix of gram dal powder and water, and fried them into crunchy rounds which she kept in a small bowl. The leftover ground mustard seed was mixed with finely chopped coriander leaves, a squeeze of lemon, finely chopped ginger and chopped green chilli. Ah, what a beautiful smell! The old lady lost herself in this fragrant world.

By a quarter past eleven or so, she finished her cooking. Her husband returned home only around one. Frankly, the dining table, festive with colour and aroma, did not attract either of them these days. They barely touched the food, but the festival of food happened nonetheless; that was the most important thing. The old lady's life revolved around it. The period between eleven and half-past one seemed like a heavy stone that sat on her chest. She sat on the wooden bench in the verandah for a few minutes, went inside, and emerged again to stand near the gate. Her right leg trembled with a shooting pain, it felt as if there were two burning coals on her head, and her body shook with restlessness. In these moments, her son moved around her, sometimes traipsing like a child or riding his new red cycle, sometimes ringing its bell impatiently at the gate. Often she saw her son going away somewhere. A huge airport, him disappearing beyond a glass wall with a backpack, not turning around once. Her daughters also appeared from time to time. They got down from a white Ambassador near the deep pink bougainvillea plant in the big compound of the house in the tea garden. The dining table was decorated like a festive Diwali spread in waiting. Sometimes a couple of their friends also came along. They too left one day. Each with a man in a flower-bedecked car, weeping. She always heard some voices resonating in her head – weeping, ululating, cars leaving amidst a lot of talk, announcements in a woman's voice at the airport she could not understand.

She listened intently to the sounds as she rubbed her right foot continuously. Then the sounds disappeared. There was silence all around, sometimes broken by the cooing of a dove, or the restless *sirik-sirik* cry of a pair of sparrows. Then they disappeared too, only a heavy silence swirled around her. Even her children could not enter through this wall of silence. She felt an intense desire to tear through the wall. Without knowing, almost in a trance, she would go back to the kitchen. She would take down the containers of *moori* or *akhoi*. She would melt some jaggery, churn it with finely chopped ginger and groundnut, and mix the puffed rice and stir everything vigorously. The enticing smell, the rich colour and the sound of the stirring ladle would fill her whole being. The silence she feared so much would disappear. The sound of weeping, ululating and a car driving through the noise, the echo of the announcement at the huge airport, would slowly melt into the jaggery mix. She would then pour the sticky mix on a plate lined with ghee and without any extra effort turn them into crunchy rounds of moori laddu. Wiping a big glass container meticulously, she would then fill it with the laddus. They filled up about a fourth of the container. Even then there would be another hour or so until lunchtime. She would then scrub everything in the kitchen though she had already done so earlier. She then went to the bathroom to wash her hands and feet, and perhaps change her sador too. She did not need to actually. The folds of the sador remained intact. What to do now? She would sit on the cane chair on the southern corner of the portico and stretch her right leg. Often, she dozed off a bit at this time. Her thin body bowed forward and she swayed a bit. Her forty winks would not last more than five minutes.

These days she hardly slept. But even then, with all her morning chores done and a quick nap enjoyed, another hour remained until the Fiat arrived at the gate. During this period she waited at the gate, trying to inspect every face passing by. Perhaps there would be a known face, who knew; someone might stop and ask, 'How are you?'

On the premises of their tea garden house, its roof covered by the pink bougainvillea creeper, there were two bakul trees near the gate. She had asked the gardener to plant them. She did not even have to stand waiting near the gate; just in a few minutes many greetings would welcome her, each emerging from the houses around, and each calling her in her own way. 'Dactoroni baidew', 'Amal's ma', 'Jutika's ma', 'Jethaidew', 'Sokhi', 'Mahidew', 'Pehi'.

All these names made her day, which was enhanced by the sweet smell of the bakul flowers that lay on the grass. The women sat on the portico or the green lawn. And then there would ensue a good session of adda, with many stories exchanged, filled with laughter and excited chit-chat. Then they would go to the drawing room. The tea pot would be ready on the round table and she would bring the big container with the freshly made moori laddus. Within a few minutes the glass container, filled to the brim, would be reduced to half. The women praised her cooking to the skies.

By the time her husband's car entered the compound, the adda was over. She then hurried to finish the lunch preparations. The potatoes had been peeled but they still had to be fried. Today the doctor also brought along a guest. The doctor loved the finely chopped fried potato crisps, as well as rounds of brinjal or pumpkin dipped in a gram-flour mix and fried brown. By the time the doctor finished his shower, all the items would be ready. He and the guest, a regular at their house, would then sit on the dining table. She would ladle out the hot rice and sprinkle a spoon of home-made ghee over it. Then would follow freshly fried potato strips, fried *bokphul* cutlets, pumpkin or brinjal sprinkled with *kaljeera*, onion seed. On one side of the plate she would pour moong dal, with scraped coconut. Next came fish dishes: a light curry of rohu with ground cumin seed paste, *bhangon* with mustard seed paste, banana flower cutlets mixed with ground rice. The last dish would be a tomato chutney with pieces of date and raisins. Her husband's silent appreciation, the guest's praise, the happy voices of her women friends biting into the moori laddu – all these brought a kind of satisfaction she could not describe.

Of late, something had been troubling the old lady. When she stood leaning on the gate, or dozed off sitting on the cane chair on the verandah or in the oppressive silence when even the pair of doves stopped calling to each other, she seemed to lose sense of time and place. The past – and the present – all their boundaries seemed to blur. She then started oscillating between light and shadow. Some scenes caught the light, others looked misty.

Look at this scene which is becoming clearer every moment. A house in Kolkata's Shyambazar. The girl comes from behind a curtain to the drawing room to face a roomful of unknown people. One among the group of women undid her pretty bun her aunt had fashioned and tied with a golden butterfly – to inspect the length of her hair. Another lifted the saree slightly to look at her feet. She felt more at ease when they asked her to sing a song. At that time, she was studying in Bethune College. Her expertise as a singer had by now moved beyond family gatherings and reached the halls of the college. The almirah with the glass door in the drawing room displayed the four awards she had received that year. Her father had pointed them out to the quiet, handsome man. He then walked up to the almirah. From the corner of her eyes she looked at the tall, wheat-complexioned man, his hair neatly brushed back. After the people left, the members of the family congratulated her for getting a groom who would be working in an 'English' tea garden as a doctor. It was from them that she first heard the name of Nahorjan Tea Estate in Assam.

Today, that young man with his brushed-back hair has retired. He had built this house in the nearby town and moved there with his wife. Now it was for him she was standing by the gate – waiting. She saw the white Fiat coming up the bridge. The car stopped at the gate but the back seat was empty. She lost her calmness suddenly. She remembered the uncouth men who came every month to collect money, weapon in hand. They had been pressurizing her husband to increase the amount they collected, almost like a tax, every month. Last week, they even addressed her, not the doctor, 'Hei old woman, if you want to stay in our state you better increase the amount, otherwise go back where you came from. If your old man doesn't increase the monthly payment, don't blame us if something happens to him!' Then they left. Now she felt as if they were looking at her. The driver Biren got down from the car with a bag in his hand.

'Your sir ...?' she could not finish the question. These days when she became anxious about something, her limbs started trembling.

'Sir has asked me to give you these vegetables. He will come home a little late; he has to attend to a patient whose condition is quite serious.'

Before he left, he added, 'Sir has asked if you need anything else.'

She shook her head and went inside. Opening the bag she spread out the vegetables on the floor of the kitchen. It was a special bazaar day and the produce were fresh from the village. She washed and dried the vegetables and put them in the fridge. Though the fridge was quite big it overflowed with all kinds of things, pots and jars. She pushed this and that and managed to fit everything in. Momentarily she thought: should she remove everything from the fridge and rearrange them? But she abandoned the idea.

If she sat for a long time at a stretch, her leg pained and she found it difficult to walk. She was also apprehensive that if she limped they would bring in that cook again. Her son had come to visit when she had the stroke. However, he came with his own agenda – not really to see her. He needed some old certificate from the medical college from where he had graduated. By the time he arrived, Dr Chakraborty had nursed her enough to have her up and about. As she was seeing her son after so long, the old lady tried to celebrate by preparing a festive table again. But when she was grinding mustard seeds for a curry her head spun. Her two daughters were also visiting at this time. So her son employed a trained cook promising to pay his salary himself and left a few days later. The cook was an expert, no doubt. Without using a drop of oil he could make a steamed but tasty bhaji. He could prepare a different kind of pudding every day of the month. But the condiments had to be purchased as per his needs and the recipes were also concocted by him. When the old lady recovered a little, she dismissed the cook. Her husband was not unhappy. Like her preoccupation with cooking, he had also developed an urge to buy the best of things at the bazaar. He was also tired of searching, as per the cook's requirement, cherries from some shop, aji-no-moto and vinegar, etc. from another. After his illness, he could not eat much but his tongue was yearning for the *shukto* cooked by his wife's expert hand. Neither of them thought it necessary to inform their son about the cook's departure. Afterwards, it was business as usual – her cooking indulgences and his bazaar.

With the chore of organizing the vegetables finished, she selected a raw papaya from the lot. Green, perfectly shaped. The white milk stuck like pearls on its stem, they had oozed when the fruit was plucked. She soaked the papaya in a bucket of water and went to the verandah to relieve her aching leg.

She smiled to herself. When she had arrived as a new bride in the house at the tea garden, she got irritated looking at the baskets of vegetables that grew in the backyard. She was particularly averse to the raw papayas. Her forehead almost always knotted with a frown at their sight. They got down from the train from Kolkata at the Amingaon railway station. From there they crossed to the southern bank of the Brahmaputra river by a ferry and from there they got into a train running on a narrow branch line to reach a small town. They spent the night there. The next day, they had to cross two small streams on elephant back. The tea garden's jeep waited on the other side. At last they arrived at the Nahorjan Tea Estate. Tea bushes and a thick jungle greeted her. Even before evening descended, the place became quiet. The silence was often broken by an elephant trumpeting, foxes howling or the call of nocturnal birds. Sometimes a leopard or a tiger passed by at close range. Baskets of vegetables, the pickings of the day, waited on the verandah daily. Also, there were the saucepans full of milk and baskets of eggs. Who would eat so much? What was to be done with all these supplies?

So the milk curdled, vegetables rotted, the eggs were sent back to the coops for hatching. Her only solace were the tanpura and a harmonium her husband had bought for her in the small town near their tea garden. She held on to these intruments possessively. Often in the evening, the doctor's house held musical soirees. By now she had become known for her melodious voice, not only in the tea gardens but even in the small township. She was even invited to perform at a few functions there.

At a time when she was collecting samples of local folk songs, her husband's parents visited to see how they were doing in this remote place. The doctor's father was a successful businessman. He manufactured leather bags for bicycles and made a lot of money. The day they arrived, quite a few people came to the house. The old couple liked the gesture thinking that it was the custom of the local people to welcome the newly arrived. The people sat on the carpet in the portico.

When their daughter-in-law came along with her tanpura and harmonium, they realized it was a *majlis* for which the visitors had come. That day her fingers ran on the harmonium reeds to the beats of a *jhumur* song the women tea labourers sang. Mini, a woman from the community, who came to help her with the chores, had taught her that song. It was a full-moon night. Moonlight filtered through the nets of the portico windows and created magic as it merged with a beautiful voice. Mini's song was about the Durga puja celebration in autumn, a girl wearing a blue saree and an expression of love. There were beats of *dhulki* and *madal* too.

Ashwin mashe Durga puja
Sabai pindhe neel saree
Salgo dada dekhte jabo
Dhaker kemon gurguri

(It's Durga puja in the month of Ashwin
Everybody is wearing a blue saree
Come, let's go together
To see, how the *dhak* beats)

Then she sang more songs woven around life in the tea garden which Mini had taught her. She did not notice when her in-laws had left the place. The passionate tone of the songs and the beat of the madal made her blood quicken. Perhaps she forgot the occasion, that her in-laws had been present. She lost herself in another world.

The next day, the doctor's bungalow resembled something like a battlefield in Lanka. The mother-in-law inspected the rotten vegetables, the curdled milk and the abandoned eggs, labelled her daughter-in-law a worthless housewife and abused her with stinging words. The doctor's father scolded him for exposing a Brahmin wife to public gaze and letting her sing like a courtesan. Her husband bowed his head at this onslaught and did not protest. The mother-in-law called the household help and made him carry the tanpura and the harmonium to the field outside. The father-in-law used an axe to smash the tanpura but for whatever reason, left the harmonium intact and put it on the wooden shelf on the verandah. Perhaps he remembered someone singing a kirtan in praise of Lord Krishna with a harmonium hanging from his neck. The whole house was cleaned scrupulously; the conservative, devout Brahmin parents sprinkled holy Ganga water on the floor. The milk was turned into thick kheer, and using it as stuffing, sweet *patichepta* rolls were prepared. The sour-sweet jujube and olives that lay on the ground in the backyard were turned into pickles and filled into glass jars. The vegetables were turned into various fries and curries. The chicken coop was cleaned. Even the soft chicken feathers were picked up from the lawn.

This huge makeover continued for a full month. Now the in-laws were ready to return home. Before that, a vegetarian feast with seven kinds of curries and other accompaniments was organized. And the woman – what was she doing? She seemed to become dumb. She walked like a person with chains on her feet, dragging them, trying to become a part of the huge *yagna*. When a kirtan-singing group was invited to perform, without knowing, she hummed with them. Her mother-in-law told her, not unkindly, that women should not sing bhajans – it was a sin. Four days after the kirtan and the feast were over, the old couple left. Before leaving, her mother-in-law gifted her a heavy *chandrahaar*, a gold choker, and blessed her, hoping she would soon become a mother.

After they left, she took to the bed. She did not speak a word, but kept staring unblinkingly at whatever drew her attention. She stopped eating, she did not sleep. She became weak. The doctor decided to give her saline injections. As he held the syringe in his hand, looking at her, he covered his face and cried desolately. How old was the couple? The husband not more than twenty-four and she, at the most, nineteen. The doctor bought a new tanpura and kept it close to her in the bedroom. She got up from the bed at last and wrapped the tanpura up in an old saree and placed it near the harmonium. That day she made kheer out of milk, and ground a basket full of rice grains to make *pithaguri*. She cut the stem of an aubergine with a circle of flesh stuck to it. The kitchen that her mother-in-law had organized nicely now filled with the smell of palm jaggery and kheer. She sat near the stove her mother-in-law used and put the flat iron griddle on it. She put small spoons of ghee on the griddle and a ladle of liquid pithaguri mixed with cardamom powder and milk; on it she spread the golden-coloured kheer; with the aubergine she spread the mix evenly. Her patichepta rolls were not thick and uneven like her mother-in-law's – they were perfect, thin and pretty like the orchids that bloomed in spring. Everybody who tasted the sweet went ga-ga over them. After a long time, her husband saw a half-smile hovering on her lips.

That tanpura still sat in a corner. Only the saree used to wrap it had been changed a couple of times. The old lady noticed that her leg was feeling better. She cut one-fourth of the raw papaya, ground a little ginger and made some *khar* in the typical Assamese style as a first course. She had learnt from tribal women how to make khar with just ginger and burnt banana stem. In fact, she picked up many recipes from different people. But she concocted her own recipes as well out of them. She gave them names and wrote them down in an exercise book. That book was still there in some corner. She did not need it anymore. Everything was now engraved in her brain.

The cell phone rang. Her son had bought it for her when he had come to visit. Usually at this time, her daughters called. She had guessed correctly – it was her elder daughter. She scolded her mother, asking if she was still cooking great varieties of food. She lamented once again that her father had so many illnesses because her mother made him eat this rich food. Her younger daughter also piped in. She was staying with her elder sister today. She also asked her mother not to feed her father so much. The mother responded briefly, as if agreeing with them. She knew very well why they were so concerned. They wanted their father to transfer the plot of land he had in Guwahati to their names, so that they both could build their houses in the city. She knew they were discussing this matter today. Her son on the other hand did not call much. When he did it was usually rather late at night. He often enquired if the cook was still there, whether she had stopped taking so much trouble cooking at this age, and she answered briefly without sharing too many details.

After these phone calls, she somehow felt very restless. Her chest constricted, perspiration lined her nose and forehead. Those sounds once again invaded her – the weeping and the ululating and the flower-bedecked car driving through it all, the announcements echoing at the airport. At these moments she opened the fridge and took a look at the vegetables again. She did this today as well. The banana flower looked very good. It must have come from the *athiya* variety. She wondered if she should pluck the flowers from the stem and keep it ready. Every flower had a white stem; unless you removed it, however well you cooked the flowers, they would taste bitter. This was a time-consuming task. As she got ready to do it, she heard the familiar horn at the gate. She went out. Yes, her husband had returned, and Biren was following him in with the doctor's bag.

She said, like always, 'Please have your bath.' At least Biren was there, and so the fridge could have some empty space. The doctor ate sparingly and she too, as always, ate like a bird.

Both of them sat at the dining table. The doctor was using a fork. That meant there had been a delivery case. She asked, 'Boy or girl?'

'Girl,' he answered, taking the covers off one bowl after another. He was about to say, 'Why do you cook so much?

Who will eat?' but did not. Instead he asked, 'What have you cooked today? Smells very nice.'

The old woman smiled a little. He looked at her for some time. He mixed some khar with rice and said, 'Today somebody from the garden had come. I have asked him to bring some jaoria fish. At this time of the year, the riverside churns this fish out in droves.'

The old woman saw, in her mind's eye, the hilly river and the fish with black scales. And the ground mustard seed, coconut milk, chopped coriander leaves, slit green chillies and ground cumin and coriander seeds. She entered a festive world of aroma, colour and taste. She forgot everything. Those sounds, those images – even the man sitting in front of her. Perhaps her own existence. Her world was awash with schools of silver-black fish, and what they brought to her – colour, smell, taste, touch – a festival of the senses.

The Loneliness of Hira Barua

I know when one is dead, and when one lives.
She's dead as earth. Lend me a looking-glass.
If that her breath will mist or stain the stone,
Why then, she lives.

– William Shakespeare,
King Lear (Act V, Scene III)

Hira Barua hurried more than usual to finish the chores in the house this morning. Not that she had too many things to do. In a corner of the compound, a couple lived with their son in a small cottage built for them. The woman got up early and helped her with the household chores, which were frankly not very heavy-duty, as Hira Barua lived alone. Sweeping the floor, mopping if necessary, and washing the utensils were all that needed to be done. Hira Barua liked to wash her own clothes. When she wanted some vegetables chopped, she left them in the kitchen for the woman to do it. On most occasions, this was not necessary either, as some leftover curry or a fried piece of fish remained in the fridge.

Hira Barua's sole preoccupation was looking after her tiny dog. Lobo, the maid's husband, had brought it from the weekly bazaar held at the foothills of Arunachal. The dog's face was almost fully covered by a mane of golden and white hair and its ears drooped. In size, he was no bigger than a rooster. Actually,

Lobo had brought the dog to sell to someone at a good price but Hira Barua fell in love with it at first sight and kept it. She named her Sonali, the golden one. She did not remember when she started calling her Sonamoni – my dearest one.

Hira Barua had been planning to give Sonali a bath for some time now. It was already getting warm and Sonali had to be bathed every day due to the heat. So she got ready for it this morning. Thankfully she was an obedient dog.

'Sonamoni, come, come, let's have the bath,' Hira Barua called, and Sonali came running, her collar bell tinkling.

'Oh, what a good girl, now come here, get up here!'

The dog jumped into the vessel of water which had been prepared for her.

'Now don't you sprinkle water on me! I have had my bath. Today we will have some guests over. Our Sonamoni is such a good girl,' Hira Barua cooed.

But Sonali did not listen to her keeper's words; she jumped down and shook herself dry, sprinkling the entire floor with water.

'You have become very naughty – didn't I tell you not to do this?' she scolded, wrapping Sonali in a towel and placing her on a mat outside under the sun.

'Sonamoni, I'll put you on a leash today. If I see you getting up from here and rubbing yourself in the dirt of the courtyard, I'll be very angry. I won't give you any meat.'

The Tibetan spaniel had been with Hira Barua for the last five years – or was it longer? – and stuck to her like her shadow. She understood every gesture of her owner. When Hira Barua said 'meat', she jumped up and stuck her tongue out, salivating hungrily.

'So you are already hungry? Wait for some time. Want to have a bikuti?' Almost unconsciously Hira Barua often fell into baby talk with Sonamoni. Today, too, she did the same, saying bikuti instead of biscuit. She brought her to the verandah, tied her to a post and went to have a bath again.

Yesterday, her next-door neighbour Mrs Sharma had told her that she and a few women in the locality would come to meet her around ten o'clock. Lobo's wife, Ramola, had kept ready a mix of gram flour, water, chopped chillies and onions to make fried savouries; there were already biscuits along with a comb of ripe bananas from the kitchen garden. So midday snacks for the guests would be no problem. Hira Barua changed into a new set of clothes and went to the drawing room to wait for her guests. By now Sonali's golden hair was becoming dry and smooth under the sun. Seeing her keeper, she started barking, wanting to sit near her under the fan and have a share of her biscuits. Ramola brought in the cane chair for Hira Barua, its handle broken, and fluffed up the cushion. Sonali sat on her own chair with utmost pride.

'Sonamoni, what do you want to have? Bikuti? My pretty little Sonamaoni took her bath so calmly today!' Hira Barua talked her baby talk with the dog as she ran her fingers through its smooth hair.

The dog wagged her tail, which looked like the white *kohua* flower that bloomed in autumn. At this time of the morning, Hira Barua had a cup of tea with two biscuits. The anticipation made Sonali restless. The conversation continued; one spoke and the other either shook her tail, barked, or stuck her tongue out. Today Sonali did not take part in the conversation; she was trying to hide something from her master. Hira Barua went to the kitchen to keep her saucer and cup. Sonali had hidden under her body a dry cowdung cake and now she started licking it. She had picked it up when she was made to sit under the sun after her bath. She was enjoying it to her heart's content when Hira Barua returned. Immediately Sonali sat over the cake and pretended to be asleep. Hira Barua laughed aloud and reprimanded her, 'Ah, that's why! You are eating something bad, is it? Let me see what it is!' Hira Barua frisked the cowdung cake out under Sonali's belly. She sat with her tail between her legs and looked at her keeper with her eyes, round as marbles, feigning innocence. Hira Barua could not stop laughing and pretended to scold her, 'Sonamoni is a naughty girl, she eats dirty things. No, no, don't do it, good girls won't do it.' But the dog knew she was speaking tenderly and became restless again. 'Now come, have a bikuti; good girls don't eat these things, you know.' Sonali started barking. Hira Barua looked out towards the gate. The women in the neighbourhood had arrived.

They had come to collect donations for the upcoming Narayan puja held by the community. They came to collect money at other times too, for Bihu and Durga puja. Today they enjoyed the savoury pakodas, biscuits and bananas offered to them and listened to the story of Sonali and her trick of hiding the cowdung cake. These days Hira Barua liked to regale people with stories of her little dog's shenanigans. Today, after a long time, she was talking freely and laughing too.

'You know, that was the day of the India-Pakistan cricket match. I had taken Sonamoni for a walk.'

As soon as she heard the word 'walk', Sonali jumped up and ran to the post where her chain was lying loose.

'We are not going for a walk now; come sit on the chair,' Hira Barua commanded Sonali, and she obeyed. Putting her face between her forelegs, she closed her eyes.

The dog's activities made everybody in the room burst out with laughter. Hira Barua started talking with renewed energy, 'So Sonamoni and I were walking on the road and had just reached Bharat's betel-nut stall. India had won the match and they started bursting crackers. Sonamoni's head started to spin and she fell down on the road unconscious.'

'Unconscious? Why?'

'Our Sonamoni can't stand loud sounds.' By now Sonali had jumped into Hira Barua's lap.

'What did you do then?'

'What else could I do? Bharat had this bucket of water to keep the betel leaves wet. I sprinkled some of that water on her.'

'Another day ...' Hira Barua stopped. The women were getting ready to go.

'We often wonder with whom baidew talks and laughs so much. Today we've come to know. Baidew talks with her dog!' the women said, amused.

Hira Barua got up from her chair to accompany the women to the gate, but she sat down again abruptly. Sonali too had jumped up to go with her but even she slunk back in her chair and went to sleep. Silence ruled the house. Lobo had left for work, his son was at school and Ramola had gone to the house where she worked as a part-time maid. In any case, their house was in the corner of the backyard and their day-to-day activities did not disturb her daily routine. Somewhere a cicada was calling incessantly. Why did she find everything so still today? Like every other day at noon, Sonali slept, Lobo and family locked up their house to go for work. Perhaps the women with their chats and laughter had broken the monotony and that's why the house seemed quieter now.

Hira Barua felt very tired. She lay on the armchair and closed her eyes. What did the women say? That she talked with the dog? But people could talk to dogs. Like she did with her Sonamoni. She heard the same thing from her maternal uncle but at that time she had found it very strange. People could talk with dogs? How could her uncle say something so atrocious? A light sleep washed over her. These days she often slipped off like this. Even at night, her sleep was getting lighter. It came and went at intervals. Often she could not fathom where she was, with whom, what she was doing; she lost her grip over many things. Then some images appeared. They, however, were always very clear; she could see the events as if they all had happened recently.

Like this picture of the house where Hira Barua had grown up. Her surname then was Chaliha. She was about ten or twelve years old. Her hair was short and a bit curly; she was wearing a pleated black skirt and a white blouse; the skirt reached down to her knees and a pair of gold earrings hung from her ears. Her complexion was pearly white and her eyes were black like a crow's wings. They shone with amusement as she said, 'Oh Mama, you are lying!'

'Why should I tell lies, Hira? It's true, one hundred per cent true.'

Her maternal uncle had arrived home after spending three years in England doing a specialized course in ophthalmology. His complexion was like Hira's, and now, after having lived in a cold country he looked even fairer. He actually looked like a foreigner. He was wearing a black suit and a red tie. After lunch, the people in the house sat around him, listening to his stories about the land beyond. At that time Hira's father was still working. He had bought a *bigha* of land and was getting ready to build a house. With a newly launched Mark 2 Ambassador in the garage, guests dropping in all the time, wearing nice clothes and eating good food, they led quite a comfortable life. When the new house had two rooms ready, the family moved in from the official quarters allotted to her father. The rooms were quite big, like two big halls, where even family functions like an engagement ceremony or a women's *sabah*, a congregation for singing bhajans in praise of Lord Krishna, could be easily held. The kitchen, bathroom, toilets all were ready. Four other rooms had their floors done. As soon as her father got transferred to this place he would finish up the place. Her uncle was sitting in one of these rooms now and regaling them with stories of the foreign land.

What was the woman's name? Hira Barua tried to recall. Mariam Austin – yes, Mrs Mariam Austin. She was the landlady of the rented quarters where her uncle used to live. They all listened as her uncle talked about the elderly Mariam Austin, who was almost ninety. Her husband had expired seven years ago. She had a son and a daughter holding high posts. But they lived far away. So the old lady was quite lonely. Once, when she was very ill with the flu, her uncle had given her a hot footbath which made her break down in unstoppable tears. The people in the family felt sad hearing about the old lady crying like that. Hira's uncle had said the old lady talked to her pet dog all the time.

It seemed like the eighth wonder of the world to the people in the room. Their eyes widened in astonishment. What kind of a dog talked to people?

Hira Chaliha was a good student. She remembered her uncle saying the dog's name was Robert and it was a Labrador. It was huge. Its colour was chocolate-brown. Hira Barua remembered clearly what her uncle had said, that the old lady talked to Robert day and night, sometimes laughed too, and even showed mock anger. She loved to talk about Robert if she could catch hold of anyone.

When she listened to the story of the old lady talking to the dog all the time, young Hira's face had clouded with sorrow. She asked her uncle, 'Mama, doesn't she have anyone else to talk to?'

'No, she doesn't. That's why she talks to the dog all the time.'

'Why don't her son and her daughter-in-law keep her with them?'

'In their country, they don't like to stay with their son and daughter-in-law. The children don't encourage it either but at least they keep in touch with her.'

'Doesn't she have grandchildren?'

'She does; they come during the Christmas holidays.'

'Who cooks?'

'The old lady herself.'

'Who looks after her when she is ill?'

'Luckily, the old lady is quite healthy. She takes care of her health pretty well, unlike our mothers and aunts here.'

'Who washes her clothes?'

'In their country, they have machines to do different chores.'

The conversation continued but the subject had changed. Hira's uncle returned home permanently in 1963. He often compared their kitchen and its firewood-lit stove with the one he saw in England. People listened to him as if he was telling fairy tales, about washing machines, gas stoves and ovens that ran on electricity.

Hira Barua started. She had put some clothes in the washing machine and forgotten about them. Now it was sounding a warning with a continuous *bip-bip*. It was drizzling outside. She put the clothes in the dryer and switched on the 'Strong' mode. The morning had been sunny, that's why she had decided to wash the bed sheets, pillowcases, and so on. Now she spread them on a clothesline in the verandah. She put rice and dal in two small bowls, put them in the pressure cooker and sat in the dining room. Somehow she felt tired quickly these days. She must visit the doctor, she thought to herself. Sonali was running around the room. Good that the electricity was working today; it made her day easier.

'Do you want to have rice?' Hira Barua smiled as she asked Sonali. Hearing her, the dog came running.

'You know, Sonamoni, today all these people asked me with whom I talk so much. I chat with my golden girl, isn't it so?'

The dog stared at her with eyes round like marbles. Hira Barua gave her a hard dog biscuit to chew on and then poured out the rice and dal from the pressure cooker.

She suddenly felt like going through her old album. She had asked her uncle for a photograph of Mariam Austin and stuck it on the corner of a page in the album. It was a colour photo. Somehow, today, Hira Barua felt like looking at the photo of the foreigner woman wearing a dress with blue and black patterns standing next to a huge dog, her lips painted with bright red lipstick.

Even after so many years the photograph was quite clear, with only a few white spots here and there. She looked at the photo for a long time. She had put the photograph in an envelope and taken it to her school. Her friends had looked at the old woman curiously. And at the dog too. So this was the dog that Mariam Austin talked to all the time? *Were there people like this?* the classmates had wondered aloud. Hira had also told them how she had cried when her uncle gave her a hot foot bath. She also told them about the day she fell down from the bed at night. She was unable to get up and then the dog brought the phone to her with his teeth. In that country there were centres which trained dogs to help people who lived alone in their old age. Robert was such a dog. There was even a door in the house which a dog could open. The police could enter the house through this door, so they could take the old woman to the hospital. After that incident the old woman had apparently started calling Robert 'my saviour'. When they heard these stories from Hira, her friends quieted down. They could not believe that this kind of thing happened in people's lives – as if it was a story from *The Arabian Nights*. They found Marian Austin's story stranger than a fairy tale.

Her drowsiness receded, and the images disappeared too. Hira Barua got up and went to the kitchen to have lunch. She arranged the rice and dal on her plate. She took out a piece of fried fish put in the fridge the previous day, mixed it with some rice, put it in a small bowl and called Sonali. Between the master and the dog, they needed just enough rice grains to fill a small bowl.

After lunch, as usual, she went outside to lock the grille door. Then she retired to bed. Sonali too put her head between her legs on the floor and went to sleep. On other days, Hira Barua had a nap but today she could not sleep. Perhaps because she had already taken a nap in the drawing room before lunch. She turned to the side of the bed and tickled Sonali's ears. Sonali had two long strands of hair that hung over her ears. Sometimes Hira tied them with two clips. Then she would tease the dog, 'Our Sonamoni has become Sharmila Tagore today. Look at her! Such long hair! So pretty! One day, I'll curl your hair like Sharmila Tagore's kiss curls, you will see how pretty you'd look.' Sonali would wag her tail lazily and go back to her slumber.

'What kind of dog are you? Do you want to listen to stories about the English lady's dog Robert?'

Sonali sat up and looked at her master with her marble-like eyes.

'Robert performed so many chores for the old lady. You know, he was the one who opened the door for the police to let them into the house. Will you be able to open the door? Oh, you are only interested in having a meal with meat.'

The mention of the word 'meat' made Sonali restless again. She stuck out her tongue and ran it over her lips.

'See what I mean? Can you ever be like Robert?'

Sonali went back to her nap. Hira Barua got down from the bed, put the dog in her lap and cooed, 'Okay, you don't have to be like Robert. He was huge, you are tiny. How can you do so much work? My Sonamoni is so pretty; is there anyone else as pretty?'

Nah, she couldn't manage to have a nap today. She went to the kitchen to make a cup of black tea. As she poured the tea it spilled on the gas burner. She wiped it with a cloth. Her cup was snow-white and on it was etched a sunflower motif. She touched the cup. It was exactly like this one but the flower was a rose. She had bought it when they went grocery-shopping. With her husband, Jibon Barua, father of her son, the person who brought her to this place called Hugrajuli. He was the eldest son of the family who lived in a house named Malati Kutir – a cottage surrounded by *malati* flowers, in the centre of Tezpur town. When he saw the cup he almost shouted, 'What's the point of buying these things for a rented house? This is a temporary house, you know that very well.'

Every Saturday Jibon Barua and Hira Barua went to visit Malati Kutir by the first bus that left at five in the morning. On the previous day, a Friday, Hugrajuli had a weekly haat where the farmers came to sell their produce. The couple bought the best variety of *joha* rice, duck eggs, fresh vegetables, bananas and oranges to take along to Tezpur. On that Saturday, Jibon Barua had also packed the white porcelain cup with the rose pattern with the other things.

Those were the days when the couple packed everything in their life, like the coffee mug, and carried it in the bus headed towards Malati Kutir. Jibon Barua's father Kanak Barua used to work as a clerk in the public works department. He had inherited the land where Malati Kutir stood from his father Krishna Chirostadar who worked in the government's land department. Most of the homeowners in the neighbourhood on the right flank of Shanti Path were relatives of the Barua family. Kanak Barua died early. Being his eldest son, Jibon Barua took over the responsibility of looking after his three brothers and two sisters right after graduating with honours in History. He came away to this off-track place known as Hugrajuli to work as a teacher in the high school. Though things were a little tight compared to the days when his father was alive, it was manageable. The visits of relatives had tapered off after his father died, but now, after Jibon Barua had got the job, they resumed. He had to give up his dream of going to university for a post-graduate degree. The brother next to him was enrolled at Silchar Medical College, the middle one was at Jorhat Engineering College, the youngest brother had gone to Mumbai, Bombay at the time, to do a course in dairy management. All the brothers had stayed in Jibon Barua's rented house and passed the matriculation exam from the Hugrajuli High School. He spent hours at night not sleeping, helping them with their studies. Then they went away to colleges for further studies. During the day he took up tuition classes for about five groups of students to augment his income, and on weekends went home to Malati Kutir, carrying the best of the things available in the local bazaar – rice, local molasses, fish, fruits, etc. In Tezpur, he had arranged with the local stores for payment of monthly purchases – from clothes for his mother and sisters to groceries. So everything was going on more or less well. He was happy that his three brothers did not neglect their studies – they were good students. They also did not have any other bad habits and soon established themselves well in their professions. The sisters were also married off.

But what about Jibon Barua himself? A throat problem and debilitating pain around his waist had left him bed-ridden. Malati Kutir disappeared from his diary. Their only son Aku, that is, Arnab Barua, went away flying to a distant land beyond their reach. The old Assam-style house of Malati Kutir, ensconced amid fruit and flower trees, was replaced by a huge multi-storeyed building. The building that came up in its place had at least seven to eight cars in the parking lot.

Hira Barua had entered this household when the old Malati Kutir still existed. At that time, Jibon Barua's brother was getting his M.D. in Delhi, the two younger brothers were midway through their chosen fields of study. Jibon Barua was pushing forty.

~

After having tea, Hira Barua switched on the TV. But the images on the screen became blurred. The sleep she had vainly tried to catch after lunch now seemed to overcome her. This was becoming rather common these days. When she opened a book or a newspaper or wanted to watch something on TV, drowsiness suddenly got the better of her. Then she left everything as it was and dragged herself to bed. But on the bed too, she could not sleep deeply and hung between wakefulness and slumber. She did not feel like getting up and doing something either. The midday merged into the afternoon and then into the evening. As night fell her drowsiness increased. Until Sonali came and started barking she would lie like this, sometimes opening her eyes, sometimes closing them. Like today. Sonali tried to wake her up as on the other days, but a great tiredness kept her confined to the bed. She tried to say something to the barking dog in a voice that was not clear, 'Sonamoni, can you open the door for the police?'

Automatically she spoke as if to a baby, 'You're a little doggie; the memsahib's dog was big, no? You have such little feet, you'll get hurt.' She took in her hand one little paw, soft and warm. The touch of the silky fur brought her out of a dark void. She got up. She saw that outside, evening had already descended. She opened the grille door. Sonali ran out immediately. She did not like to stay indoors at this time; she needed to use the bathroom, she liked to sniff at this and that in the compound and run around, and if other dogs passed by, bark at them from a safe distance from this side of the gate. Earlier, Hira Barua would also go out with her. But these days she had stopped. She was tired of answering the people who passed by. So many questions. She had lived in this neighbourhood for thirty years but she still remained a person who aroused curiosity in them. She wanted to breathe freely in the open air but instead felt choked. However, she was yet to get into this habit of lying in the dark at that time. The questions drove her inside and she tried desperately to find something to do.

Sometimes she opened the wardrobe to tidy the clothes which were already neatly stacked; sometimes she opened the meat-safe with the jars of rice, dal, and so on, and with a torch tried to inspect if there were cockroaches inside. She wiped the table and furniture all over again, folded the clothes one more time. Slowly, she stopped going out, leaving Sonali to go by herself. She was afraid of the questions. They were actually not too abrasive, just common questions asked as a matter of courtesy. But she was afraid of them.

'Masteroni! Masteroni baidew!' many of the older generation addressed her like this – wife of the master, the teacher. Most of the people knew Jibon Barua. He came to work here when he was quite young, worked until his retirement and then lived in this place for three years before he passed away. Hence she was their 'Masteroni' or 'Masteroni baidew'. The young people of the new generation, however, were not bothered to pay their respects. In the afternoon when they walked by the road in front of her house they were busy scanning their mobile phones. So Hira Barua had to deal with the middle-aged women who stood in front of their compound gates in the evening. They were nice people, simple and without any axes to grind. Their questions were easy and straightforward, their curiosity too involved simple enquiries. They did not know how to speak in double entendres. Yet, these questions confronted Hira Barua mercilessly. She found it difficult to breathe when she faced them.

Next to her house was the house of Sonaram Barman, who used to be her husband's colleague. He too had come to this out-of-the-way place in search of a living. *Who lived there these days?* Hira Barua wondered. Sometimes she saw the tribal couple who looked after their house. Barman 'master' had also retired; perhaps he had gone away to his original house in Nalbari. When she first came to this place, his wife was the first person she got to know.

As soon as she changed her clothes in the afternoon, Sonali started dancing with joy. She often wondered how the dog figured out that she had changed her clothes. Then Sonali would bring her chain with her teeth. Actually the chain was a thin one and was attached to a collar. Hira Barua had to search a lot for this light chain. The leather collar had worn out long ago; the present one had been fashioned by her. Sonali followed her like an obedient girl as Hira Barua walked on one side of the road holding the chain. Somehow she always stood out. Her looks, her manner of speaking, the way she wore even an ordinary mekhela sador set, made her look different from the usual lot. So, she and her dog out for a walk created quite a stir. Even the army jawans out on patrol duty passed some comment or the other at the little dog. This place with broken bridges, pot-holed roads and infested with terrorists was used to army patrols. Life went on despite the undercurrent of violence. Hira Barua took Sonali for the evening walks, the bazaar did business, schools and offices functioned as usual. As did the bomb blasts, murders, abductions.

When she went out for the walk, the first person she encountered was Barman's wife. 'Masteroni, how are you?' she would ask in her typical lower Assam accent. Sonali meanwhile would try to veer away in search of something to sniff. Pulling her by the chain Hira Barua would stop at Barman's doorway and answer, 'I am doing fine. How are you? How are Rinku and Sourav?'

In response, Barman's wife would launch into a long monologue, talking about her two children, her husband's recurring knee pain, the house they were building in Nalbari, Barman's retirement which was due in two years, and how after they left for Nalbari she would miss the two mango trees, the lychee tree, the three coconut trees, and so on. Then she would ask Hira Barua the main question, 'Masteroni, have you made any plans yet? How can you live alone among these people? They are not like us. Why don't you go to your in-laws' home?' Worry would line the simple woman's face as she advised Hira Barua.

Trying to avoid the query, Hira Barua would smile and instead ask her, 'People unlike us? You mean foreigners? Are they Germans or Americans? These people are our people, they speak our language too.'

'Don't joke!' the woman would say in a whisper. With all the hatred and fear she nursed against the local people of a particular tribe, she would start off on her diatribe, 'Masteroni, you can't trust these people. Haven't you seen how many people they have shot dead?' Her body actually shook as she uttered these words.

Her fearful tone would make inroads into Hira Barua's mind too. Hurriedly, she would drag Sonali away from the gate to the Barmans' house.

Once back in her own house, Barman's wife's simple question would make her sit in a corner and reminisce about Malati Kutir. Hira Chaliha had come to Tezpur to attend a wedding. She had met the man named Jibon Barua who was already on the wrong side of his thirties. Hira had by now completed her graduation. Her father had retired and his other children were now well settled. Only Hira, the youngest daughter, was to be married off. Jibon Barua too was thinking of settling down now. His brothers had decided on their careers; their future was secure. One of the sisters had been married off to a good family, the younger one was still in college but marriage proposals were pouring in. His mother reminded Jibon Barua from time to time that he should get married. But it was his colleagues who put pressure on him the most. Why, men of his age were already fathers, what was he doing? He must get married, they went on and on. Meeting Hira Barua at the wedding, Jibon Barua stopped short. He thought the name Hira absolutely suited her, as she sparkled like a diamond. More than that, the girl looked as if her heart nurtured a lot of love, her soft lips looked as if she could never utter a hard word. She seemed like a white dove, soft-natured, quiet, with whom living together would mean a peaceful, simple life without any problems.

So Jibon Barua and Hira Chaliha got married and she entered Malati Kutir as a new bride. Jibon Barua could not manage to refurbish the house or add an extra room on the occasion of the marriage. His three brothers were still studying in colleges far away from home. Thankfully, the sister was enrolled in the local college which meant they were spared any hostel fees. The other expenses of the household had to be met too. So Hira Barua had to use the toilets and bathroom her father-in-law had built. He could give her only the gold ring his mother had given him. The items comprising the bridal trousseau were placed in the room whose walls could do with a coat of paint. Hira Barua did not say anything. Jibon Barua did not let her take along any of these things when he brought her to this out-of-the-way, insurgency-prone place inhabited by a people different from her own.

It was a woebegone house she entered, comprising three rooms, without a verandah, and plonked in the middle of the half-bigha plot of land, surrounded by overgrown trees almost forming a jungle. She was greeted by a cheap, moth-eaten wooden cot, aluminium plates, that too with dents, a Janata stove, a firewood stove the centre of which had caved in, and an uneven floor. Moss, even a sapling trying to grow, and caterpillars showed up on the floor. The *satai* made of roughly hewn bamboo strips and strapped underneath the ceiling was drooping in the middle. Often something or the other fell down from the ceiling, straw or bird droppings. A flight of pigeons, salika birds and three pairs of doves had made their home between the ceiling and the satai.

Hira Barua had been brought up in quite a comfortable household, if not a rich one. When she entered this house she was taken aback. So she would have to live here? She was surprised. If Malati Kutir needed some repair, Jibon Barua immediately took care of it; if money ran short, he performed physical labour himself. But he seemed to be absolutely indifferent when it came to maintaining this house. The landlord was from Nagaon, on the south bank of the Brahmaputra. When he was posted here, he had bought this house from a local man, finding it extremely cheap. He rented it to Jibon Barua at a minimal amount and went back to his hometown – like the others. He was at least sure that with Jibon Barua living there, nobody was going to take it over. He had seen so many unattended houses taken over illegally in this area. Nobody dared to open their mouths in protest. Hira Barua's new life was to be launched in this house desperately crying for care. But when she mentioned the things that needed to be done in the house, her husband gave her a mouthful. Their real house was Malati Kutir; this was a temporary house where he had to stay only due to his job. He was not going to invest anything in this house. During this period Jibon Barua was also very busy with his private tuition classes and assiduously performing his duty towards Malati Kutir as the eldest son.

As soon as he left for school, the sparkling beauty called Hira brought out the broom, stick and dao to clean up the house. With the long bamboo pole she pierced the drooping satai to get rid of the bird droppings collected over the years. Above, on the ceiling, the bird droppings brought on a layer of white mites, quite difficult to see with naked eyes; they crawled all over the ceiling. Some of them were red too. Hira Barua almost screamed in fear when she saw these red mites, wondering if they were red because they had sucked on human blood. But who else was there at home? She checked her body intently – was there a mite sticking to her skin? The heaps of dry droppings fell down on the floor after her attack; she collected it all with a hoe, poured them into baskets to throw them outside and cleaned all the surfaces with phenyl and Dettol. Then she attacked the excuse of a bathroom, encircled by jute clothes stuck to a bamboo fence, and the urinal. She cleaned the bamboo strips of the fence covered with mud, put stone chips and sand on the ground to dry them and washed the place with antiseptic detergents. She scraped the floor of the room where fissures showed. She planted a cotton rose plant in the backyard. She fashioned an earthen platform to grow a tulsi plant. At the base she lit an earthen lamp every evening. The house that had fallen into disrepair and neglect for years seemed to breathe a little easier, smell a little fresher. Jibon Barua was not happy when he looked at the abrasions in her palms due to all the hard work and reprimanded her, 'Why are you labouring so much for somebody else's house?'

Hira Barua did not like the words 'somebody else's house'. She thought that the house you lived in, wherever it was, was your own house for the time being. But as was her nature, she did not say anything. Jibon Barua worked hard, to pay the college fees for his three brothers and his sister, the endless expenses at Malati Kutir to meet social obligations – somebody's wedding, someone else's birthday, a first rice-eating ceremony in some household. He also saved, though it was tough, to add a room to the old house. He even added an attached bathroom and toilet with twenty-four-hour water supply too. And he enjoyed doing it all. Hira Barua planted a *sewali* plant near the new room's window. The room was generally used as a guest room but Jibon Barua's mother made the rule that when her son and daughter-in-law came on visits, that was where they would stay, no matter which guest was staying in the house at the time.

The things that Hira Barua brought along as a bride, the new guest room, the house in the centre of Tezpur town, her hard-working sister-in-law and mother-in-law's care, all these things made Malati Kutir sparkle and seem inviting. Almost like a routine, Hira Barua arrived every week with her husband, carrying as many things as they could, fresh from the local bazaar. Every vacation – puja, summer holidays and even shorter holidays – saw them come running to Malati Kutir. For Jibon Barua 'house' meant Malati Kutir, 'own people' meant the relatives who lived next to their house, and 'own place' was Shanti Path – the road in front of their house. He did not feel any attachment to the place where he worked, it was 'somebody else's place'. In fact, he almost seemed to nurse a hatred towards Hugrajuli. He did not interact with the people who lived in the neighbourhood. As they set forth towards Malati Kutir in Tezpur whenever there was an opportunity, they could not accept invitations to lunch or dinner from the local people, neither did they make any efforts to. So slowly the invites thinned, and disappeared altogether after some time. When Hira Barua first arrived, the women in the neighourhood came forward to offer their friendship, bringing along a gourd or a bunch of greens like *tenga-saag* from their kitchen gardens. But her husband did not like it. 'Why are you mixing with these people?' he faulted her. So the bridge that could be built with local people broke down.

Once she got pregnant, Hira Barua stayed more frequently at her in-laws'. Later, her mother-in-law admitted her grandson in a school near their house in Tezpur. Hira Barua had protested: What was wrong with the school where his father taught? After all, his three brothers had done pretty well after graduating from that school; besides, Jibon Barua would be able to keep an eye on his son's studies too. Hira Barua continued to improve the living conditions of the house despite living amidst the people 'who are not like us'. But when she said she wanted to keep her son with herself in Hugrajuli, somehow her mother-in-law and even her sister-in-law protested vehemently. Hira Barua was shocked at this onslaught. So her son remained in Tezpur at Malati Kutir. Slowly, Hira Barua lost interest in beautifying the house she lived in. The sewali flower she had planted near her window in the Tezpur house had by now grown quite big. She missed the heady perfume of its flowers and the close touch of her son so much that she made trips to Tezpur as many times as possible.

Today, after a long time she remembered Malati Kutir. The nostalgia for the perfume of the sewali flower and the baby smell of her young son wafted in from somewhere. Where had they gone beyond her grasp and melted into the mist? She started talking to the dog who was sitting near her feet. As usual, her voice took on the tone of baby talk.

'Sonamoni, you haven't seen Malati Kutir. How can you? You were not even born then. You know, it's there no more. Malati Kutir has disappeared.'

Yes, it was true. The room that filled with the sweet smell of the sewali flowers had disappeared. The house that waited for Jibon Barua to arrive every weekend with rice pudding made with the aromatic joha rice, cakes baked with duck eggs, pitha made with *bora* rice, had somehow ceased to exist. And its people too. Hira Barua ran her fingers through Sonali's thick hair and mumbled, 'Nothing, there is nothing, you know, Sonamoni. All gone!'

It was about three years before Jibon Barua's retirement that it happened. And quite suddenly too. In the place where the Assam-style house stood came up a huge three-storeyed building. The three brothers built their own modern flats on the three floors and allotted the top floor to their elder brother. 'After all he is the eldest – he should be on top of us,' was the argument. Very politely they informed their elder brother that he did not have to contribute anything to the construction cost; he just had to build his own living quarters. The next brother offered to stand as guarantor for the housing loan he could arrange for his brother; the middle brother informed them that the architect could organize the mason, carpenters, and so on. The youngest brother suggested that if Jibon Barua found it difficult, he could suggest a good contactor. In reply, Jibon Barua smiled like an idiot. Hira Barua was standing next to him on the hard, uneven surface of the open space where the top floor was supposed to be built, covered with leftover construction material. She could smell something rotten. Perhaps a rat or a bird had died nearby. The smell came from the heap of wood piled in a corner. Jibon Barua's mother said, 'Your brothers have done a lot, now you build your part of the house.' In reply, Jibon Barua once again smiled like an idiot. That day he did something he had never done before. They had arrived in the morning but he hurried Hira Barua to get ready to leave for the place which he thought belonged to 'other people'. Usually when he visited Malati Kutir he stayed a couple of days more because everybody in the family insisted. That day Jibon Barua boarded the evening train with Hira Barua and their son Anku to return to Hugrajuli. At night, he lit the torch to check the nooks and corners of the house. There was no way to call it a home; it seemed like a guest room for a couple to rest on a pilgrimage, providing the barest of necessities. He went to check the kitchen garden in the backyard. It was green with a variety of vegetables. He had seen the woman, quiet like a dove, going about this patch. He could hear laughter from inside the house. Their son, who was now in the tenth standard, was sharing a joke with his mother. Under the moonlit sky the greens in the garden took on different hues. The echo of the mother and son's laughter and the green of the lush growth seemed to meld together.

He stood there and made two decisions right away. He would bring his son here, admit him in his school, and let him appear for the matric exam from this school itself. His brothers had kept aside one room for their mother in the three-storeyed house where Anku had to stay and found the space too crowded for his studies; when his married aunts visited, even they stayed in this room. He also decided that he would buy this house. The landlord was getting old, and his sons were least bothered about this ramshackle house in this odd place. They did not even feel like coming to collect the rent; until the landlord grew too old, he used to come himself. These days Jibon Barua sent the money on his own. He did not even receive an acknowledgement that the money had been received. He decided to go meet the landlord next day.

The old man was too sick to walk and was confined to bed; he somehow signed the papers with a trembling hand and sold the house to Jibon Barua at a very nominal price. The old man's sons sighed with relief: 'Good, the job is done.' Though the money he had to shell out was not much, Jibon Barua still had to request Hira Barua if she could sell the jewellery to fill in the gap. Hira Barua gave him her jewellery without a question. She did not regret it at all. Mother, son and father joined hands to refurbish the house as economically as possible. The people at the old Malati Kutir never once stepped into the house ensconced among fruit trees full of mangoes and jackfruits with the excuse that the road was too bad and the bridges were dangerously fragile. For the housewarming, Jibon Barua and Hira Barua invited their neighbours for a meal. When Hira Barua wanted to inform her in-laws' family in Tezpur, her husband lost his temper. Still Hira Barua went. Only her doctor brother-in-law was at his place. The others had transferable jobs. They had rented out their flats for a good amount of money. At the entrance to the house, Hira Barua stopped. Why, even the two *nahar* trees and the flower garden had disappeared. Jibon Barua had planted the flowering trees with his own hands. In the place of the green patch there was a two-storeyed shopping complex. It was full of commercial outlets, doctors' clinics, a pharmacy and an X-ray centre. Behind it was the three-storeyed building. In one of these rooms sat her mother-in-law. Anku and Hira Barua were shocked to see her body so bloated. Where was that woman who always ran around with a broom and a bucket, mopping the floor? She almost begged them to take her to Hugrajuli. Hira Barua was surprised. How was it that the woman who never ever stepped into their house was now eager to go there? She seemed caught in a puzzle without an answer. There was a time when the old lady was opposed to sending her grandson to the place inhabited by 'uncivilized' people, but when Jibon Barua wanted to take him away to Hugrajuli that fateful day – and he was in his final year of school too – she did not object at all. When she heard that her son was building a house in the trouble-torn area she only said, 'Good, you can live in peace at least.'

Everything had changed. When Anku and Hira Barua went upstairs they found the place unkempt and full of junk. The doctor's wife served them tea, and with it sweets and samosas purchased from the shop nearby. The sweets smelled rancid. The tea came in two paper cups, as they do in railway stations, and even the snacks were served in paper plates. The doctor's wife made a face, her lips painted a deep chocolate, as she said, 'Tell me how many times I should wash the crockery after serving tea to my guests? That's why I am giving you tea like this. It means less work.' The paper cups were perhaps bought some time ago; now that there was hot tea in them, a musty smell assailed their noses. For some reason, in that foul odour Hira Barua found a similarity with the rotten rat or bird whose odour had emanated from the pile of woods on the terrace allocated to her husband once.

~

Today something overcame Hira Barua as she remembered the old lady in England that her uncle had described. She kept sitting there with Sonali in her lap. In between she soaked some *chira* mixed it with a little sugar and that was all she ate. She often did that these days. As long as she had a piece of fried or dried fish for Sonali, she did not bother to cook lunch for herself.

'My little one, do you know the people in uniform took away your brother Anku dada? We were watching the planes going up and down. Anku dada's uniform too had a picture of a plane stitched on it. He was very young. Do you remember him?'

Hira Barua recalled that scene. Anku had joined the Air Force after passing the Higher Secondary exam. He had obtained very good marks. He was eighteen then. Jibon Barua retired from his school that year. After the result, he called up all his brothers to inform them about the good news. They expressed their happiness but did not ask the main question: what career he was thinking of taking up. With that kind of result, Anku could go for anything. The problem was elsewhere. Could a retired teacher manage to meet the expenditure of higher studies? Jibon Barua always thought that there would be never any problem on this front with three well-established uncles whom he himself had nurtured. He had almost zero savings. Whatever he had, he spent on the house to make it livable at least. Before retiring to bed at night, every day his wife had to fill the water filter with buckets of water. These days she could not even lift a small bucket; the veins in her right hand stood out and the joints creaked. So having running water was an urgent need, but it also cost a lot. Jibon Barua could not conduct tuition classes any more; he had a throat infection. The doctor advised him against over-exerting himself, which could lead to something more serious.

Though Anku could get into all the good institutes he had aimed for, his father was apprehensive about his son doing those courses on a school teacher's pension. Jibon Barua had dutifully informed his brothers about Anku's good chances in prestigious institutes too, but their congratulations were just meaningless words with no real intention of helping out, or even an enquiry about how he was going to manage the expenses. So Jibon Barua had his son admitted to a college not far away, where he could commute from home by train. This information too was passed on to the uncles. They said it was a good decision, that it was better the boy stayed at home. There were so many stories they heard these days about young boys going astray while living away from home. Also that these days a general course of study was a better choice, as there were many careers one could later opt for.

Jibon Barua and Hira Barua were completely in the dark about whom their son had contacted, how he managed to get into the Air Force and how he then went away to Jammu & Kashmir. He informed them only when everything was finalized. Hira Barua often remembered how he left with the bag on his shoulders. And she remembered her husband's face. It had turned crimson and he was shaking a little.

~

Hira Barua started dozing even as she sat. Soon, getting up with a start, she went to her bedroom. As she lay on the bed, she felt that her head was spinning a bit. Two images often got juxtaposed in her mind when she lay like this. A young boy, the logo of a plane stitched on his shirt pocket, going away with a group of unknown men. He was looking back; his eyes were clouded by the same shadow that she had often observed when he started his daily college commute from home by train. From then on, his bright eyes lost their sparkle, a shadow fell over them. He stopped talking to them. That talkative boy disappeared somewhere. She saw the floating image of those dark, accusing eyes. When he encountered that look in his son's eyes, Jibon Barua could not meet them; he looked at the floor instead. Hira Barua often looked as if mesmerized, at those eyes where the sadness and accusations of a world gathered. Not once did he tell his parents or ask their opinion; he just left. And he never tried to have a conversation again. By then Jibon Barua had left this world to have a heart-to-heart talk with his son.

Now another image floated in. It was dawn. Her husband complained of chest pain; a wheezing sound came from deep in his chest and then everything was over. Hira Barua floated as if lifeless in that pool of images. When she felt breathless, she sought out her dog, but these days she disappeared like this from time to time. She felt her chest constrict if she found Sonali missing. During these moments, she shouted from the verandah, 'Sonamoni, Sonamoni! Come, come, have your rice, have your bikuti!' Sonali would come running from somewhere with her tongue hanging out. Often her paws had mud sticking to them, thistles would be caught in the fur on her face; sometimes there might even be a leech on his body. She smelled something odd. Hira Barua brought out a brush and dog powder. Cleaning Sonali up and sprinkling the powder on her thick hair, Hira Barua began speaking to her dog, but this time she didn't use baby talk and spoke in a clear voice instead.

'You know, Sonamoni, after Anku-da went away, my husband seemed to retreat into a cocoon. Not even three months had passed since Anku-da's departure when he too went away. You were not born at that time – how would you know?'

The dog seemed restless again, so Hira Barua began scolding, 'Where do you want to go? Sit down! Look at your face – what is that smudge?'

But she quickly switched to baby talk, 'No, no, you shouldn't be a dirty dog. I'll clean you up again, wait!'

She chained Sonali to the post in the verandah and went to cook lunch for both of them. For herself a bit of rice and a curry with salt and mustard oil, for Sonali roasted fish mixed with rice. Sitting down to have her spare meal, she spoke to the dog again, 'I had stopped halfway. So listen, Anku-da was in Kashmir. There was a lot of trouble there at that time. They were not allowed to step out of the barrack –' but before she could complete the sentence, Sonali ran away again, having finished her meal. Yet Hira Barua continued, alone, 'He couldn't come ...'

It was true. The recruits of the Air Force were not allowed to come out of their quarters. Anku could visit only one week after his father's death. Her brother-in-law who was also posted a little distance away could not arrive in time for the cremation. Everything was taken care of by the neighbours. Hira Barua could not remember who did what – his past students, colleagues. One thing she remembered, however, was that his brothers had organized a big shraddha ceremony in Tezpur. Anku could not be persuaded to go there to join the occasion. One of his uncles accused him, 'You're very adamant.' Saying nothing in reply, Anku had just left. The brothers had asked Hira Barua about other things, their elder brother's savings, life insurance policy, and other such matters, before discussing amongst themselves. 'How can anyone be so stupid these days?' They had asked Hira Barua to leave this godforsaken place now that she was a widow. But when Anku was about to leave for his posting, he assured her, 'Don't worry. I'll send you money every month.' She had also assured him, 'I'll manage with your father's pension, don't worry about me.' She could not look at her son's eyes shadowed by a dark something.

When she went out in the afternoon for a walk with Sonali, people asked, 'Masteroni, why are you living alone like this? Why don't you go live in your son's house?'

How could she explain to these simple tribal people about her son's 'house', where temperatures often fell below zero degrees? And that her arthritic pain increased in the cold? So in reply she only smiled. Eventually she stopped going out. Anku sent money every month; Jibon Barua's pension also came in, and was enough for her simple needs. Her husband had built two small rooms in the compound where the tribal family lived, and most importantly, Sonali had come into her life. Her brothers-in-law, her own sisters and brothers avoided coming to this remote place by car, so they wouldn't have to negotiate half-broken bridges and roads full of craters. They could not even think of coming by the ancient metre-gauge train or the overcrowded buses used by the locals. Secondly, they were not really bothered about the woman who did not expect anything from life anymore.

Anku got his B.Sc. while still working, then an MBA, did very well in the departmental exams and got promoted to higher posts. People were now trying to contact Hira Barua, searching for a prospective groom for their daughter or some unmarried girl in the in-laws' family. The mobile phone Anku had bought for her rang from time to time, but after Anku married a Punjabi girl from Chandigarh, the calls stopped. Anku had brought her – tall, fair and healthy – to meet his mother and did not hold back on the expenses for a party he threw for the neighbours. Amarjit – that was her name – made Anku rent a van so they could travel almost 200 kilometres to buy a washing machine. A couple of times Anku and her daughter-in-law took her to the place where they lived. But after some time, Hira Barua became impatient to come back to the house Jibon Barua had refurbished, ensconced among fruit trees and flowering *kamini-kanchan*, *gulach* and *madhoi-malati* trees. She missed Sonali terribly, who was being looked after by Lobo and his family.

She sometimes could not recognize her son, who conversed with his wife in Punjabi. He seemed to be someone else. She felt somehow that within a week after she died, he would go back to his normal life, go watch movies and plays, dance at the parties that were a common part of their lives. Sometimes she felt when her son and daughter-in-law spoke in a language she did not understand, they were talking about her; she felt if she stayed too long, they would find it inconvenient. If she left they could again go back to their regular lives. When she looked at her son, in his eyes she saw a reflection of that darkness she feared. In that shadow she had lost the son who had clung to her neck saying, 'Today I'll sleep next to Ma,' when she visited Malati Kutir. She tried to find him by walking down that shadowed path. When she heard him quarrelling with his wife, his voice rising, she felt as if that darkness intensified to give way a pitch-dark abyss.

Today the women visitors in the morning took her back to her innocent schoolgirl days when her mind was yet to be serrated by sorrow, a mind that was deeply affected by the story of the lonely white woman about whom her uncle had told her. She could see that woman across the seas in her imagination; the image was etched in her mind. At night she could not sleep. Mariam Austin invaded her thoughts again and again. Towards dawn when she went to the bathroom, she did not notice that Sonali had left the room. She talked to her incessantly.

'You know, my dear Sonamoni, I am very afraid of your Anku-da. I am on tenterhooks, afraid that he will scold me anytime. He went away, with that bag on his shoulders; we couldn't say anything, we couldn't do anything to stop him. He doesn't like us; he's very angry with us.'

Hira Barua got up. She realized that Sonali had been absent from the room all this time and started calling out to her, 'My dear, dear Sonamoni, you are a good girl, come, come, I'll give you bikuti.'

But Sonali was nowhere to be seen. Hira Barua seemed to lose her mind. She went to the small cottage that belonged to the tribal family. All of them started looking for the dog. At last Sonali appeared; her mouth had nettles, her hair was full of dirt, and emanating a particular smell which her master found difficult to identify. Hira Barua busied herself with water, brush and dog shampoo. She mixed some rice with roasted dry fish and gave Sonali a meal. For her own meal she poured some water over cooked rice and chopped an onion to make *poita-bhaat*. She had been eating this meal for quite a few days but now found her tongue somewhat thickened and unable to taste anything. She had not gone to the bazaar for a long time.

As she thought of the bazaar, the word jolted her out of her stupor. She thought of Mariam Austin again. She brought out the old album but did not look at any of the pictures. The album was full of pictures of Anku at a young age. Most of them were taken by his uncle in Tezpur. When she looked at the pictures of her son, Hira Barua felt her chest tighten with pain. He snapped the connection himself, he had cut the umbilical cord ruthlessly on his own. He did not want to keep in touch with the life he had left behind. Was this true of his relationship with his mother too? Would he come after a week of her death? Or not at all? It would not be unprecedented if he did not. This house was not dear to him. What kind of attraction did it have for him? Nothing. And that girl, her daughter-in-law? Who was she to Hira Barua? Even after learning of her death, he would go to his workplace as usual, perhaps the next day itself. He could not afford to keep his work pending. He had to put aside the thought of his dead mother. After all, when his father died, he came only after a week; she had fainted several times from crying her heart out; even then he did not come, or could not, immediately. Jibon

Barua's body was kept under the bakul tree. Hira looked at that patch in the courtyard. She walked slowly to the spot; she felt herself turning into a corpse as she saw in her mind the bier with her body lifted by some unknown people. The body was bloated and the smell of death hung over it. The people were discussing in whispers, 'The woman was lying dead for two days, nobody knew about it. How could they, she was like a living dead. Being alive or dead was the same for this woman.' Would her body have scabs, like her old grandmother from her father's side? Or would her feet be swollen like eggs? Like her mother-in-law's in Malati Kutir?

Hira Barua felt her head spin while standing under the bakul tree; her limbs trembled. Will she die now? At this very moment? She held on to a branch of the tree and somehow dragged herself to her room. This happened quite often these days. Was it the same with Mariam Austin too? She took out Mariam Austin's photograph from the album and looked at the old woman in a dress with black and blue flowers. Her lips were painted blood red; next to her was sitting a huge dog.

She was not sure where Sonali had disappeared again. These days this happened often but Hira Barua kept on talking to her as if she was talking to a baby: 'You are a hopeless dog. The one with the memsahib granny was a real dog. Do you know what she used to call him? "My Saviour". If I lie dead would you be able to open the door? No, you won't. You slink under the bed at the slightest rumble of a cloud and lightning. And then how you shake!' Hira Barua laughed aloud. 'Do you remember, my little one, how I had taken you to the veterinary hospital to cut your nails? The way you trembled made people around me ask if you were suffering from malaria.' She laughed so loud that someone from the next house came out and tried to find out what was going on.

~

Mariam Austin had died long ago. Her uncle had died a few years ago too. Even then, the memories seemed to cling to Hira Barua as if they had happened yesterday. Listening to her uncle, the young Hira Barua ... no – it was Hira Chaliha – found her eyes moisten as she asked her uncle, 'Why doesn't the white granny go to the bazaar?' Everybody in the room had laughed at her innocent query. Her uncle had laughed too and said, 'Yes, she does, she goes to the supermarket.' He had described the supermarket and malls in that land. She was astounded. How could a bazaar be like that? No dirt, no hullabaloo, no talking nineteen to the dozen and haggling, not even a salesperson to man a shop? One could not call this a bazaar. If you wanted to understand a proper bazaar, you would have to go to the Dakshin Hengera haat, Rangamati bazaar and the Tipai Tea Garden haat. People all around, quarrels over prices, noise, a variety of things on sale, and amidst all this, songs blaring from a radio, a magician performing tricks, an astrologer sitting with his parrot assistant. One could call this a bazaar. Nobody could stay silent in that bazaar.

That eleven-year-old girl, Hira Chaliha, why was she so keen to send that grand old lady to a bazaar like this? Why was she thinking of obliterating all that woman's loneliness by making her roam around in a bazaar? At that time, going to the bazaar with her father was an exceptionally pleasurable experience for Hira. So many people, so many things on display, laughter, merriment, all rolled into one. Her father had installed a small seat in front of his own cycle for her; she also had a special pair of shoes to go to the bazaar. Every Sunday or Wednesday if her father said, 'My dear, let's go!' she was ready in a jiffy. After that she entered a different world. Everybody knew her and addressed her fondly, vendors gave her something or the other from their stall. In the winter she wore a sweater but once in the bazaar she took it off as she felt too warm. From where did that warmth emanate? From the people around her?

These days Hira Barua felt a coldness gripping her all the time, so she wrapped a shawl around her, whether in winter or summer. Today she felt greedy for the warmth she had once felt in the bazaar. Could it be possible? Would she feel the same warmth today too in the midst of the people? Would the cold that troubled her dissipate if there were people around her?

Hira Barua got up suddenly and opened her suitcase. Her clothes were sitting there without a crease. When did she last unfold her neatly arranged mekhela sador? She picked out a plain white mekhela, a sador with a narrow violet border and a white blouse. She wrapped a light shawl around her and pulled out a small bag from among bags of various sizes that Jibon Barua had collected. He had them specially stitched to carry things when he would go to Malati Kutir; the big one was for *aijong* rice, the smaller ones for joha and bora, a special one to fit in combs of ripe bananas and another for duck eggs. Hira Barua felt the bags, running her fingers across them. They shopped in the bazaar so many times, for so many things, but now she could not remember where – the bazaar disappeared for her. She looked at the calendar to check the day. The page had not been turned for some time. In the past, Jibon Barua used to do this. The dates on each page had notes scribbled next to them. How much was borrowed from whom, how much interest to give to whom, how much of the EMI was left to pay, everything was clearly noted down. This calendar too across which she now ran her fingers, contained similar notes. She looked at the mobile phone. This one had been bought by her son at the same time he got the washing machine for her. It had mostly been left unused. Earlier, she would sometimes call her son. Often he did not take her call and even if he did, he excused himself with a 'Very busy now, will call back later.' For a long time Hira Barua waited for the call to come 'later'. Eventually she realized that the wait was useless. And that girl who could not utter a word in Assamese, how could she accept this house in a remote area as her own? Impossible. How could she form a bond with this woman who hardly spoke and could not communicate with her? So it was natural that she forgot to call Hira Barua even once in 365 days. But Hira Barua charged her phone regularly. Sometimes a song played on the phone; she would listen to it intently. These days she stopped doing even that. She charged it to use as a torch at night. She checked the day on the phone – Saturday. This meant it was the day of the weekly haat.

She folded the bag and stepped out of the house. The road was uneven with stone chips and potholes. But people, rickshaws, cycles and a few cars tackled it anyway. All of them were on their way to the haat. Hira Barua took a rickshaw and joined the procession. The rickshaw-puller started chatting with her.

'Are you new here?'

'Why, I've lived here for ages.'

'Where is your house?'

'Near the bridge, you know. On its front there are two bakul trees.'

She had planted them when she had arrived here as a new bride. Now the trees had grown to resemble the top of a temple, reaching the sky. The grass beneath was always covered with its white flowers.

'Oh, you mean the house of Jibon mastor? Why, I was there when he was taken to the cremation ground. I even went to your house to have chira and curd as per custom.'

Hira Barua kept quiet. She was in shock; she did not know who had done what, who had taken care of the rituals, the customary meal after a death. Had this man been there? She could not remember at all.

'Sir was a very nice man. Many a time he hired my rickshaw to go to the bazaar. He was very fond of people,' he said.

She asked him how much she should pay.

He said, 'Give me whatever you like. You are from Sir's house after all.'

Hira Barua gave the middle-aged man a ten-rupee note. He returned five rupees to her.

'If you ever need a rickshaw, send Lobo to get me. I am usually by the peepul tree,' the rickshaw-puller said.

Hira Barua got swept up in the stream of people.

'Baidew, take this gourd, it's from my own house,' a woman said. She was wearing a blue mekhela tied to her chest like the tribal women of the area; the betel nut she was chewing had reddened her lips and her face was crimson under the sun.

'How much is it?'

'Ten rupees.'

Hira Barua took out the money and gave the woman her bag. The woman opened her own packet of betel nuts and added one to the gourd Hira Barua had bought.

'You will enjoy the gourd curry, just see,' the woman said as if she knew Hira Barua well.

'Yes, of course!' After a long time, a smile lit up Hira Barua's face.

She then went towards the lane selling fish. She saw a man sitting with his stock of white *pava* fish. Jibon Barua had loved pava fish and bought it whenever it was available; he bought them for Malati Kutir too and while having a meal of fish curry with their son, Anku, told him funny stories. She remembered the laughter father and son had shared.

She bought half a kilo of the fish. Then she bought tomato, mustard seeds, potato and onion. When she saw a cane basket with silver-coloured *puthi* fish, she bought a few of those too. She came across a man sitting with a basket of guava the colour of the cream of milk. Hira Barua could not help going closer. It was exactly this kind of fruit that a tree at Malati Kutir would bear. Jibon Barua brought it from Guwahati once. The leaves were dark purple. Hira Barua had planted the sapling herself. Eventually it was laden with guavas just like this. Hira Barua, with the help of her sisters-in-law, had prepared guava jelly. She saw in her mind that orange-coloured home-made jelly.

Anku used to love the guava jelly. Jibon Barua liked to have it with fried luchi. Some days if she wanted to fry luchis for him in Hugrajuli, he objected, 'Let's go have some at Malati Kutir.' She sighed – he was a man who could not even enjoy a luchi while away from his home.

The fruit-seller was now shouting, '*Goya, goya, misti goya!*' He rubbed the guava with the cotton towel on his shoulder. A man came with his bicycle, stood in front of him and asked, 'Why are you shouting, "goya, goya"?' Hira Barua could make out from his tone that he belonged to her hometown in upper Assam. A man sitting next to the fruit-seller was selling bamboo fans. He now shouted, 'Oh, you don't know? It is *sofri aam*.'

'What kind of aam is that?' Hira Barua asked, unable to resist. A woman sitting next to them was selling silkworm. She corrected him as she smoked a *bidi*, 'Oh, he is joking. It's *madhuri* aam.' Within a short time, the goya, or sofri aam, or madhuri aam, whatever you liked to call it, was sold off, leaving the basket empty.

Coming out of the bazaar, Hira Barua saw that the rickshaw-puller was still waiting. She climbed onto the rickshaw. She was feeling warm, perhaps because she had been under the sun for so long. She folded the shawl and kept it in the bag.

'Baidew, why did you have to go to the bazaar?'

'He would have brought whatever you wanted.'

Lobo and his wife went into a tizzy seeing her getting down from the rickshaw. Their eight-year-old son came forward to carry her bag lying on the rickshaw.

As they were about to go inside, they saw a Mrityunjoy ambulance coming to a stop in front of the house across the road. Most of the people in the neighbourhood were gathering there. They too stood by the road. The daughter-in-law of the house was pregnant. She had now gone into labour and her family members had dialled 108 in preparation for her to the hospital. Even as the expecting mother moaned in pain, she smiled at Hira Barua. Hira Barua waved.

Lobo's wife had cleaned and cut the fish by now. Hira Barua asked her to grind some mustard seeds. She changed her clothes and lit the stove. She took great care to cook the fish curry with ground mustard and coriander leaves. The aroma filled the kitchen. She put three pieces of fish in a bowl and went to Lobo's house. His wife was hesitant to accept the curry. She lifted the curtain and keeping the curry on the bamboo stool, told them, 'Please have this. What will I do with so much food?' She ran her eyes around the room. The few inexpensive things were arranged very neatly. She admired the scene.

Hira Barua kept the guavas aside. After a long time, she felt like making some jelly. Her son used to like it so much. Would he remember today the orange colour of the jelly? Suddenly it occurred to her that the money Anku sent from time to time had not been arriving for a while now. The pension that Jibon Barua left behind was enough for her simple needs, but she liked signing and receiving the money because she felt that her son still remembered her. She wondered if Lobo's son would also love the colour of the jelly. She washed and rubbed the guavas dry, and put them in the basket. She thought of the pregnant woman going away in the ambulance and how she had smiled despite the pain. What will it be? Boy or girl? She must visit the house after the woman came back home. She could also take along a bottle of jelly. Surely the woman would like it?

Hira Barua had had taken her bath before going to the bazaar, but now she had a second one. She was ready to have lunch when she realized that Sonali was nowhere to be seen. She called out to the dog and went to the backyard garden looking for her. But there was no sign of her. Where could she be? She had been thinking how Sonali would enjoy a meal of rice with pava fish and how she would dance with joy at her good fortune. Then she spotted Sonali under the mango tree in a corner. She was busy having sex with another dog, not exactly her breed, but similar. So this was the mystery behind Sonali's frequent disappearances of late? Hira Barua grinned.

After lunch, her eyes drooped with slumber. She was feeling rather tired. Perhaps because she had walked too much, trying to make her way through the jostling crowd. She went to her room and lay down on the bed. Instantly, she fell into a deep sleep.